# THE THIRD PLACE

# THE THIRD PLACE

A Viennese Mystery

## J. Sydney Jones

This first world edition published 2015
in Great Britain and the USA by
SEVERN HOUSE PUBLISHERS LTD of
19 Cedar Road, Sutton, Surrey, England, SM2 5DA.
Trade paperback edition first published 2015
in Great Britain and the USA by
SEVERN HOUSE PUBLISHERS LTD.

British Library Cataloguing in Publication Data

Jones, J. Sydney author.
  The third place. – (A Viennese mysteries novel)
  1. Werthen, Karl (Fictitious character)–Fiction.
  2. Lawyers–Austria–Vienna–Fiction. 3. Murder–
  Investigation–Fiction. 4. Franz Joseph I, Emperor of
  Austria, 1830-1916–Fiction. 5. Vienna (Austria)–
  History–19th century–Fiction. 6. Detective and mystery
  stories.
  I. Title II. Series
  813.6-dc23

ISBN-13: 978-0-7278-8526-5 (cased)
ISBN-13: 978-1-84751-626-8 (trade paper)
ISBN-13: 978-1-78010-679-3 (e-book)

*All Severn House titles are printed on acid-free paper.*

Severn House Publishers support the Forest Stewardship Council™ [FSC™],
the leading international forest certification organisation. All our titles that
are printed on FSC certified paper carry the FSC logo.

Typeset by Palimpsest Book Production Ltd.,
Falkirk, Stirlingshire, Scotland.
Printed and bound in Great Britain by
TJ International, Padstow, Cornwall.

*Once again, for Kelly, my partner in crime*

*The Viennese call it the 'third place': first is home, next comes work, and then there is the coffeehouse.*

# PROLOGUE

I t was his place. All 148 seats, 37 tables and three stations – Austerlitz, Wagram, Königgrätz.

Herr Karl was an Austrian patriot; it was not his fault his favorite tactical battles resulted in crushing defeats for Austrian forces.

He deployed his lesser waiters Napoleon-like to these stations, caring for every whim of their prized clientele.

Yes, *his* place. Even though Herr Regierungsrat Wolfgang Mintz owned the Café Burg, Herr Karl was its lifeblood.

He had spent his career here, beginning as a youth. While men like the customers he now served were busily studying calculus, Latin and romance languages in their adolescence, Herr Karl had left school early and toiled as a scrub in the vast kitchen of the café.

But he had progressed over the years, venturing into the main hall when he was thirteen, clearing and wiping tables, straightening chairs, even being allowed to replace newspapers on the giant rosewood display rack by the front entrance. Then at sixteen he exchanged the full apron for a half one, a cutaway black suit and the white shirt and tie of an under-waiter. That was the life, he thought. Never mind that at that time the Herr Ober, the head waiter and majordomo of the Café Burg, Herr Siegfried, was a tyrannical ogre.

Herr Karl liked that description; it was muttered by a steady customer the day Herr Siegfried gave him an *Ohrfeige* – a slap – for dropping cutlery and disturbing the clientele.

'An ogre,' Herr Bergstrom had said under his breath, yet loud enough for Herr Siegfried to hear and for his face to redden.

That had been a wonderful day for Herr Karl. The beginning of his real profession, truth be told. And the beginning of the end for Herr Siegfried.

Herr Karl had nothing against the man, to be sure. Herr Obers were meant to be autocratic, to command the respect of those under them. He learned a good deal from Herr Siegfried, particularly in regard to his physical bearing.

'One must look the part of Herr Ober to *be* Herr Ober.'

That was Herr Siegfried's motto. Herr Karl had taken it to heart and also taken to doing a routine of vigorous calisthenics each night after work: sit-ups, trunk twists, pull ups on the door frame. By the time he was eighteen he could do several hundred sit-ups at a time, and he could feel it in his body, sense it in his movement – cat-like, yet assured. Quiet authority began to ooze from him, he felt.

Herr Karl was just twenty-six when Herr Siegfried died of apoplexy; the man had the good manners to do so at his home and not at the café. Despite his relative youth, Herr Karl was catapulted to the exalted position of head waiter. No longer simply addressed by his surname, Andric, but as Herr Karl.

And thus he had been addressed for the past thirty-two years.

Ach, where has the time gone? he wondered.

Flown away, as have the customers for the day, he told himself.

Time to close. The under-waiters had done their tallies; the night crew was on the premises, ready for the cleaning, preparing the café for the morning. Time for Herr Karl to leave as well.

He looked at the standard clock above one of the hat racks. Not quite ten yet. If he hurried, he could get home with enough time to finish painting the last of the French troops in their royal-blue uniforms and black tricorn hats.

Herr Karl, like many men who had never served in the army, who had never fired a shot in anger at another, was fascinated by all things military.

Perhaps Frau Polnay would serve him some warm milk upon his arrival on this bitterly cold March evening. A very thoughtful landlady was the frau. They shared a kinship of sorts; a kinship of service to others.

Other Herr Obers, on their monthly get-togethers at the Waiters' Association, would voice surprise when they learned that Herr Karl was still in rooms and did not have his own place. But Herr Karl was pleased with the arrangement; a perennial bachelor, he had no use for more than a pair of rooms.

He tipped his hat to Kleinman, the supervisor of the cleaning crew, bidding him good night. He turned up his collar of his heavy coat against the chill wind off the Danube Canal. The sidewalk was treacherous, for the local merchants were forgetting their duty: they had not salted their patch of sidewalk in front of their shops as Herr Karl had in front of the Café Burg.

Well, as he had *directed* the young under-waiter Falk, it should be done this afternoon when the temperature began plummeting. There was a boy who would never make Herr Ober, he thought. Can't even learn to brush his hair properly, leaving a dusting of dandruff on the shoulders of his black cutaway as if he lived in perpetual winter. He'd had to give the youth a dressing down just the other day for forgetting a cloud burst – the extra glasses of water – to Herr Bergstrom, their oldest regular, still with them after all these years.

Herr Karl hurried out of the Inner City, reaching the broad expanse of the Ringstrasse, virtually empty at this time of night.

Once away from the café, he allowed his mind to dwell on the matter at hand.

What a most unpleasant man, he thought. And what a fund of information he had. It gave Herr Karl a slight shiver to think that the man had tracked him so thoroughly and was so conversant with all his little schemes with the café suppliers and his workers. Very unpleasant. The fellow had calmly sat there across from him this afternoon in the café with his strange hands occasionally appearing on the table; the little fingers of each poked straight out while the hands were clenched.

The man had given no name and it finally dawned on Herr Karl that he was actually performing a bit of extortion on him, demanding that he convince his friend to add a name to his list. Even had the name scrawled on a slip of paper he passed to Herr Karl.

Failing that, Herr Karl's employer would be informed of his little schemes, the man warned in his odd little accent.

Nothing for it. He had called Johann at his office and set up a meeting for tomorrow. Johann was none too happy about it, either, but the meeting was arranged.

The stranger was a horrible man with a face as devoid of emotion as a corpse.

Herr Karl took his usual shortcut through the green space separating the twin museums, passing under the watchful eye of Maria Theresa mounted atop her bronze memorial. He could remember the unveiling of that monument only fourteen years earlier. Herr Karl had taken a special day off for the occasion:

Maria Theresa was a personal favorite of his. If only Franz Josef would reinstate her Chastity Commission, they would not have to shoo away the ladies of a certain profession every day who gathered about the entrance to the Café Burg, hoping for a well-appointed customer on his way home from afternoon coffee and cards.

There was a place for such women, he thought, and it was not in front of his café.

From above, Maria Theresa's outstretched hand always seemed to offer a personal benediction and salutation to Herr Karl. He saluted her on high as he passed.

His arm did not finish the salute, however, for a blinding light and searing pain exploded in his head, the back of his skull shattered by a blow so extreme, so well placed, that he could not even let out a moan as he crumpled to the frozen ground.

The assailant quickly lifted the body, slamming the back of the head against one of concrete pillars surrounding the monument and through which an ornamental metal chain was looped.

There was a hollow plonking sound as of a pumpkin being split open.

The killer left Herr Karl sprawled half on the icy path and half at the base of the monument. Those who later discovered the body would surmise that the unfortunate man had slipped on the unsalted ice and cracked his head.

# PART ONE

PART ONE

# ONE

Werthen kept a keen eye on the judge, Dr Felix Landauer. It was after lunch, and Landauer, dubbed 'lounging Landauer' for good reason, was suppressing a monumental yawn following his intestinally challenging meal of *gulyasch* soup followed by four sausages, red cabbage and parsley potatoes, topped off with a cheese plate and *palatschinken* with chocolate sauce, and all washed down with a liter of the finest Gumpoldskirchen white wine.

It gave Werthen indigestion just to recall the litany of food-stuffs he had witnessed the judge ingest at Kulauer's Restaurant and Weinhaus, favorite of the legal elite of Vienna.

It was just as Dr Landauer lifted an insouciant hand over his mouth to cover a yawn that Werthen made his announcement.

'I think we can all agree that it was too dark for Herr Karlsen to recognize the defendant. Too dark for him to identify even his own mother.'

He gave the seven men of the jury his meaningful glance, to let them know he understood they were not fools to be led by the nose by Advokat Pinkop, the prosecutor.

Pinkop, of course, chafed at this, interrupting in a chirrupy voice that brought Landauer out of his near somnolence, sputtering and blowing and jiggling his jowls like a whale breeching.

'I must protest, Advokat Werthen,' Pinkop said in a voice that sounded like he was in training for the Vienna Choir Boys. 'That is supposition on your part. Darkness has not been established in evidence.'

Pinkop looked to Landauer for assistance, and the judge, not knowing where legality lay but not much liking Werthen on principle for his activities as a private inquiries agent in addition to his lawyerly duties, agreed with the prosecutor.

'My apologies to the court,' Werthen said, and once again shot a meaningful look toward the jurors.

In the event, said jurors had no need to leave the august precinct of the courtroom to reach their verdict. Five to two for acquittal.

'By damn, that was well done.' Werthen's client, Herr Vogelsang, clapped him on the back, as well he should. If convicted of breaking the arm of his arch-rival on the tennis courts, Vogelsang could have gotten four years.

'Nothing to thank me for, Herr Vogelsang,' Werthen said, gathering his papers. 'Perspicacious jurors. They could see you were innocent.'

'Clever of you about the lighting. Never occurred to me.'

Werthen smiled, not responding and not wishing to continue the conversation. Truth be told, he did not care for Vogelsang, not in the courtroom and not on the tennis court. The man tended to be full of bombast in both spheres. The type to puff out his chest after hitting a forehand winner on the line.

'You were absolutely right, though, Advokat. Karlsen couldn't have seen me that night. Not plainly, anyway. Hah, what a genius you are.'

The comment chilled Werthen to the bone and he shivered uncontrollably. He dropped his file, papers floating down around him like autumn leaves.

Vogelsang bent to help him retrieve them, and it took all of Werthen's will power to keep his hands off the man.

'I'll see to that,' he murmured, gesturing Vogelsang away.

Now he remembered why he had given up criminal law for so many years.

And he wished he could rid the system of the prohibition against double indemnity.

He had just managed to get a guilty man off.

At the office later that afternoon, he was still fuming. Familiar with the symptoms of such disappointment and utter disgust, he could also recognize them clearly in the face of their young office boy, Franzl Hruda, who brought him the afternoon papers.

'Why so glum, young man?'

Franzl shrugged, puffing his lips. 'Don't know.'

'I'll bet you do. You're usually the sunny one around here. Not feeling well?'

He shook his head vigorously. 'It's not that, Herr Advokat.'

'Werthen,' the lawyer corrected. 'Herr Werthen will do.'

'It's just . . . well, just that my aunt can't afford them, you see, says they're silly and not something a young man like me needs, birthday or no birthday.'

'Perhaps we can slow down and take it point by point,' Werthen said. 'By birthday, I assume you mean it is your birthday?'

A sullen nod.

'Well congratulations, Franzl. How old are you then?'

'Eleven, Herr Ad— Herr Werthen.'

'Wonderful age, eleven,' Werthen said. Though recalling now his eleventh birthday at Hohelände, his family estate in Upper Austria, he could sympathize with the youth.

'And what is it your aunt cannot afford?'

Franzl chewed his lower lip for a moment. 'She's right, I guess. It is silly. I mean, I'll never be an artist.'

'You would make a difficult witness to question in court, Franzl.'

'Oh, right. Sorry. I just had my eye on a box of charcoals for sketching. Lovely to work with, they are.'

Werthen nodded at this admission. 'Your aunt sounds like a practical sort of woman, Franzl.'

'You're right about that,' the boy said sullenly.

Werthen caught himself from making further excuses for the boy's guardian. No need for further explanation. He put himself into the shoes of this eleven-year-old and remembered his own disappointment at that same age when, in love with words and writing, he had desperately wanted the 1872 revised edition of the complete works of Shakespeare translated by Schlegel and Tieck; instead, he had gotten a Purdey twelve-gauge shotgun.

*It'll make a man of you*, his father had said. *Books are fine when you have a grand library to put them in. But a gun, now that will teach you about life, about the hard facts.*

'So how about taking a walk?' Werthen said, catching Franzl off guard.

'I've got the afternoon rounds coming up, sir.'

'I'm sure we can put them off for an hour or so. After all, it's not every day a chap turns eleven.'

Outside, the afternoon had turned chill – it was still several days until the first of spring. Franzl had almost to run in order to keep up with Werthen as the lawyer strode purposefully toward the Graben. Once there, they went to mid-block and Franzl followed him through the doors to Pichler's, an art supply store that had been, as the engraving on its windows announced, in service to the crown for over a century. Werthen could not imagine any of the Habsburgs delighting in a fine set of charcoals or expertly mixed oils, but such products had been available at Pichler's, one assumed, if anyone from the court should desire them.

Franzl's face lit up like a Christmas tree as he surveyed the myriad of mahogany racks containing art supplies, from sketching pencils to canvases.

Werthen came to an abrupt stop in the middle of the shop. 'So, birthday boy, what will it be?'

'Sir?' Franzl was confused.

'It's your day, so your choice. A set of charcoals if you please, or—'

'Oh, no, sir. I couldn't. It wouldn't feel right. Like I was tricking you or something. Complaining just to make you feel sorry for me.'

Werthen was about to reply that as a lawyer, he was seldom tricked. Then he remembered how Vogelsang had bamboozled him this very day. Yet there was another realization: the tension from that trial was beginning to dissipate. He smiled at the boy.

'Franzl, I do appreciate your sentiment, and even more so the depth of thought and self-reflection that prompts such a statement. However, I assure you I do not feel manipulated. So, no more arguments. I am your employer and as such I order you to find yourself a fine set of charcoals.'

'Sir—' Franzl began, but a mock-stern expression from Werthen stilled him.

Werthen pulled the pocket watch out from his vest pocket. 'You have ten minutes, young man. Look lively.'

Franzl was off like a rabbit, a broad smile on his face.

Meanwhile, Werthen focused his mind, trying to keep evil thoughts regarding Vogelsang at bay. So concentrated was he in this effort that he did not even notice that Franzl had already returned clutching a small wooden box of charcoals.

'Is that what you want, then?'

'It's a wonderful one.'

'Not very many charcoals.'

'I'm just a beginner, sir.'

'That's not what your teacher tells me.'

'Frau Blau is just being polite.'

'Even the archduke complimented your horse drawings at the Christmas exhibition.'

Franzl blushed at this, but nodded as well. 'He did like them, didn't he?'

Werthen paid for the charcoals.

As they made their way along the windy streets, Werthen suddenly said, 'I think it is high time I get another case.'

'Another legal brief, sir?'

'No. I mean a real case. An investigative case.'

'I think that's a wonderful idea, sir.'

'And you know what else I feel like now?' Werthen asked.

But he did not wait for a reply.

'A fine mélange for me and a large cup of chocolate smothered in *schlagobers* are in order for you, I believe.'

Franzl's eyes grew as large as half-crown pieces as Werthen led their way to the Café Frauenhuber.

# TWO

No Herr Otto today, Werthen noticed as they entered the soothing, serene precincts of the Frauenhuber, his own personal 'third place,' as the Viennese liked to refer to their café. Home, work, café. In that order. But Fritz, another waiter, recognized him and led him and Franzl to a window table. Werthen ordered for them.

Franzl was looking about him in amazement, taking in the sight of all the affluent customers seated in Thonet chairs at their marble-topped tables, at the bustle of servers holding silver-plated trays full of cups and water glasses over their heads; experiencing the hum of low conversation going on all around them, the slap of Tarock cards at one table, the sizzle and snap of newspaper pages being turned.

'I've never been in one of these places,' Franzl said, as if he were forbidden the very use of the word 'café.' 'They usually shoo me away from the doors if I get close.'

'Well, no shooing here. You're gainfully employed, now, Franzl.

A regular citizen. Now tell me. What fine drawing are you going to do with your new charcoals?'

The boy brightened. 'Frau Blau wants me to do more figure work. There's this old fellow with a long beard and deep-sunk eyes who she pays to model for us. That'll be a treat. Did you ever want any art stuff when you were my age?'

'Books were more my thing,' Werthen said as Fritz arrived with the coffee and hot chocolate.

They were sipping their respective brews when the jingling of the bell over the main door caught Werthen's attention. Herr Otto, attired all in black, entered, his cheeks red from the cold. It was odd to see the head waiter entering the front of the café. But Herr Otto seemed preoccupied, in some sort of distress.

The man quickly made his way through the main hall, nodding at familiar customers. When he saw Werthen he made special eye contact, lifted a fisted hand with forefinger an inch from the outstretched thumb to indicate 'just a moment,' and then disappeared behind swinging kitchen doors. In a moment, as promised, he reappeared, top coat and hat removed, now dressed in the full tuxedoed regalia of the Herr Ober. He made his way quickly to Werthen's table.

'I am so pleased to see you, Advokat Werthen.'

'I missed you when we first arrived,' Werthen replied. He and Herr Otto had a long history, beginning with Werthen aiding him in a false accusation of theft from his former position as head waiter at the Café Landtmann. Since that time, they had been allies, and Herr Otto had always managed to find Werthen a quiet table at the Frauenhuber when needed, always made sure to save a fresh edition of *Neue Freie Presse* for his perusal.

'If it is not a disturbance, Herr Advokat, might I request an appointment with you?'

'Legal matters, Herr Otto? A will perhaps?' Werthen smiled at him.

'In your other capacity, Herr Advokat.'

Werthen's heart quickened. A case. As he had told Franzl, he was badly in need of one.

He nodded at the black armband Herr Otto was wearing. 'Does *that* have anything to do with it?'

Herr Otto sighed. 'I have just returned from the funeral. A colleague. From the Café Burg.'

'Herr Karl?' Werthen had read about the unfortunate death of the man, slipping on an icy patch between the twin museums and cracking his head on a cement pillar at the base of the Maria Theresa monument. Herr Karl was something of a legend, known even to Werthen, who seldom visited the Café Burg. The 'little general,' his regulars had dubbed him, both for the man's love of military lore and for the way in which he ran things at the Burg.

'It was an accident. What is there to investigate?' Werthen asked.

'If I could talk to you at your office . . .'

'Of course you can.'

'Perhaps later this afternoon, then, Herr Advokat. I have only come in to check on the books. Say in an hour, then?'

'I look forward to it,' Werthen said. 'And I am sorry for your loss.'

Herr Otto smiled at this, nodded to Franzl and was on his way.

Werthen looked at his young companion. 'Don't let it get cold. Better drink up.'

'You think somebody killed this Herr Karl fellow?' His eyes once again grew large at this possibility. 'You were hoping for a case. Maybe this is it, Herr Werthen.'

'Maybe,' Werthen allowed. 'Maybe.'

An hour later Werthen was seated in his office on the Habsburgergasse trying to concentrate on the file in front of him – a draft for the will of one Herr Schminkel, who could not decide to whom he wished to leave his most prized possession, his stamp collection. Werthen had created his own nickname for this client, the Flatulent Philatelist. Of an advanced age, Herr Schminkel did not seem to be fully in control of his bodily discharges. Werthen always made sure to apply a bit of 4711 *Kölnisch Wasser* to his pocket handkerchief in advance of any meeting with the man.

A gentle rap at his door and his secretary, Fräulein Metzinger, poked her head in. 'Herr Swoboda and Herr Falk to see you, Herr Werthen.'

This took him aback; he was eager to speak with Herr Otto and now two new clients had arrived to interrupt that interview.

'Are they scheduled?' he asked, irritation in his voice.

'Herr Swoboda said that a meeting had been arranged,' the

secretary explained, keeping her voice low so the visitors would not overhear.

Werthen was at a loss to remember any such arrangement, but finally relented.

'Send them in, then. The other gentleman I mentioned should be coming shortly.'

Fräulein Metzinger nodded curtly and withdrew, presently followed by Herr Otto and another younger man in tow.

Werthen felt an idiot. He had always known the waiter by the soubriquet Herr Otto, never even wondering about the man's surname. Now the problem is, Werthen decided, which one was he, Swoboda or Falk?

He rose from his desk. 'Come in, come in. Please be seated,' he said effusively, waving his hand at a pair of leather armchairs on their side of the desk.

Fräulein Metzinger had already relieved them of their hats and coats in the other office; Herr Otto sat with prim dignity, perching almost on the front of the cushion, hands in his lap, while his younger companion let himself fall back into his chair, legs akimbo and hands gripping the arms of the chair. There was a frosting of dandruff on the shoulders of the young man's dark suit.

'So, Herr Otto. How may I be of service to you?'

Herr Otto glanced momentarily at the young man next to him before speaking. 'Well, as you earlier learned, it is in regard to the death of Karl Andric. You see, Herr Advokat, his death was not an accident. It was murder.'

Werthen allowed the word to soak in for an instant before proceeding.

'You suspect this because . . .?'

Herr Otto shook his head adamantly. 'Not a suspicion. A fact.' He looked at the young man next to him.

The young man's hands gripped the arms of his chair even more tightly now, white showing at his knuckles. Herr Otto broke the silence. 'This is my wife's nephew, Herr Werthen. Rudolph Falk. I was instrumental in getting him a position at the Café Burg. He has something to share with you.'

The young man seemed at a loss for words.

'Tell him, Rudi,' Herr Otto prompted.

Finally the young man sighed. 'I saw it all,' he said. 'That night, I saw it.'

'Saw what?' Werthen asked.

'Herr Karl, he was walking home. It was late and cold and he went off the Ring and into the park between the museums.'

'And you just happened to be there at this same time?' Werthen said.

To which comment Rudi Falk reddened violently.

'Tell him all of it,' Herr Otto said.

'It was like this,' the young man said. 'Herr Karl and me, we had words that day, last Monday. He was always at me how to serve and how to look. Never a kind word; always carping at me.'

'He was only trying to make a better waiter out of you, Rudi,' Herr Otto said.

'It didn't feel like that to me, did it? Felt like persecution, like he had it out for me for some reason.'

'And so you were following him that night,' Werthen said, 'to talk to him or threaten him?'

Rudi Falk sat bolt upright in his chair. 'See?' he said to Herr Otto. 'I told you they would start accusing me. That's why I didn't go to the police.'

'Relax, Herr Falk,' Werthen said. 'I was only trying to get to the bottom of this more quickly. So you followed Herr Karl from the café after he closed that night. Correct?'

Falk nodded sullenly.

'And he went into the small park between the museums. Then what?'

'Well, he was walking by that big monument with the woman up there—'

'The Empress Maria Theresa,' Herr Otto told him with the voice of a disappointed school master.

'Right, some famous woman, and Herr Karl – this was sort of funny – he made to salute her like he was a loyal soldier, but he never got closer to the army than his collection of toy soldiers, they say.'

'And then what happened?' Werthen prodded.

'Then suddenly this other figure appeared from behind one of the stone pillars right in back of Herr Karl. He wore a long coat and hat and Herr Karl never even knew what hit him. The man swung something a few feet long and round like a pipe and crushed the back of Herr Karl's head. He folded like a dead weight. Then the man, he pulls Herr Karl's body close to one of the pillars and cracks the back of his head against it. Made a sickening sound. He left the body there by the pillar, slipped the pipe up the sleeve of his coat and off he went.'

'And where were you all this time?' Werthen asked.

'When Herr Karl stopped to salute, I jumped behind a bush. Almost came out though, figuring this was as good a place as any to talk with him. And then this figure suddenly appeared and I stayed put. There was no time to warn him – it all happened so fast.'

'And when the assailant left the scene?'

'I went to Herr Karl, naturally. I could see right off that he was dead. And then I panicked. I mean, if I went to the police, I figured they'd suspect me. Like you asked, what was I doing following my boss? And everybody at the Burg knew we didn't get along.'

'But you did finally tell your uncle.'

'It was just too much for me today at the funeral,' Falk said. 'I had to tell somebody.'

'Did you see the assailant clearly?'

He shook his head. 'It was dark. Too dark.'

Werthen pictured the scene; the nearest street lamp was on the Ring. The young man was right. Too dark for identification.

'You said it was a "he." Could you actually tell if it was a man or woman that attacked Herr Karl?'

Falk shrugged. 'What woman's going to kill him?'

Werthen ignored this. 'Man or woman?'

'I don't know. I just figured it was a man who would kill like that.'

'A large figure or small figure?'

Another confused shake of the head. 'Medium. About the size of Herr Karl, but he was not a big man, either.'

'Can you help us, Herr Werthen?' Herr Otto finally asked.

'I assume you mean can I investigate and not involve the police?'

'It could put an end to Rudi's career. We can pay. I have spoken with the head of our Waiters' Association. We have a fund. Herr Karl was one of ours.'

Werthen held his head in his hand and tapped a reflective forefinger against his cheek. It would mean withholding evidence from the police, but it was not as if he had not done so before.

'I'll need a list of names of associates, friends – anyone connected with Herr Karl,' Werthen said by way of answer.

# THREE

'I think it's wonderful,' Berthe said as they stood in front of a woodcut by Emil Orlik at the Galerie Pisko later that evening. They were having a rare evening out with Frau Blatschky taking care of their young daughter, Frieda.

'It will take your mind off the Vogelsang affair,' she added. 'Though I really do believe you should get that man hanged before you attempt any other cases. I never could abide his arrogant, preening rooster attitude on the court.'

Werthen said nothing for a moment. He understood his wife's flippancy. She was attempting to be charmingly insouciant but he knew she was put off by the Herr Karl commission. It would involve investigating a bloody, violent murder committed by someone who – having so carefully staged the killing as an accident – would not take kindly to Werthen digging and prying into the death. Added to that, Werthen would be doing it behind the back, as it were, of the police.

'It's very Japanese,' he said, eager to change the subject.

'Not at all,' Berthe insisted, misunderstanding his referent. 'From what I have read of the Japanese, they are a most humble people. Quite modest, especially in public.'

'The woodcut, not Vogelsang. It's got a Japanese feel to it. Like a Hiroshige woodblock print.'

Orlik, he knew, had only recently returned from a prolonged sojourn in Japan.

'It is quite lovely,' she allowed, turning to him and suddenly taking his hand in hers.

They ended the evening at the Café Imperial, near the Galerie Pisko. It was not Werthen's sort of place, but the evening had turned wet and proximity was more important than atmosphere.

Entering the low-lit room, they were surprised to find Karl Kraus occupying a window table. He brightened when he saw them and gestured for them to join him.

Kraus was the uncrowned king and champion of rectitude in the written word and the avenger and scourge of hypocrisy in his journal, *The Torch*. Tidy, gnome-like, misshapen and bespectacled, Kraus dressed like a banker and thought like an anarchist. Best of all, he had his ear to the ground, was privy to the secrets of Vienna and occasionally shared these with Werthen.

It was, however, a surprise to see him here at the somewhat stodgy Café Imperial, home to musicians perhaps, but not known for its writers. The Café Central was his usual haunt.

'Good to see you, Kraus,' Werthen said, pumping the small man's delicate hand with eagerness. Kraus winced – not so much at the pressure but at the physical contact. 'What draws you out of the hallowed halls of the Central?'

They sat at his table and Kraus nodded politely at Berthe, then said to Werthen, 'The noise. The infernal, eternal chattering, clacking of chess pieces, slapping of newspaper pages being turned. I ask you, how can one read a newspaper so aggressively?'

'It *is* quieter here,' Berthe allowed, scanning the spacious coffeehouse located in the elegant Hotel Imperial, former palace of the Duke of Württemberg. There was a hushed mumble of voices from the well-dressed and middle-aged clientele; none of the sudden outbursts of laughter or argument as could be heard at the Central. The waiter arrived at their table and Werthen ordered a cup of gold each for him and his wife, a melange with added milk – it was too late at night for full-strength coffee.

'Indeed it is,' Kraus replied. 'I am contemplating moving here altogether. Herr Viktor indicates a regular's table could be made available for me.' Saying this, Kraus nodded a greeting to the head waiter standing tall and proud near the front door. 'He has hopes I will attract the literary crowd once I am settled in.'

Werthen was dubious of that, knowing the herd instinct of writers. But he did not want to disabuse Kraus of the level of his magnetism. They spoke for a time of new stories that Kraus was covering for his magazine, and of Werthen's disillusionment in court this morning. Soon Kraus had also learned the nature of his most recent case.

'Ah, Herr Karl. A most robust Herr Ober, I do admit. But the poor man fell, no?'

Werthen was honor-bound not to divulge the particulars of Herr Falk's eyewitness account. He merely smiled knowingly at Kraus.

'Ah, I see. Murder most foul but you cannot share the details.'

'Something like that,' Werthen said.

'It sounds like you knew the man, Herr Kraus,' Berthe said, suddenly taking an interest in the case and putting concerns for safety aside. 'Did he have any enemies?'

Kraus snorted at this. 'Does the despot spawn usurpers?'

Werthen ignored this seeming non sequitur. 'Which means he did have enemies?'

'Don't we all? But a Herr Ober has a special set of possible foes. Customers, for one. Of the disgruntled variety.'

'Enough to kill him?' Berthe asked skeptically.

'A man's café is his home away from home,' Kraus pronounced. 'We must never forget that. Deny him such comfort, and a man may take desperate measures. I recall hearing of one such instance. A Herr Bachman, I believe, who was forbidden service after it was discovered his Tarock games were played for high stakes and with a deck of cards not altogether as it should have been.'

Werthen pulled out his leather notebook and pencil from his breast pocket and began taking notes. 'Bachman, you say. Profession?'

'Café habitué, what else? I am sure someone at the Café Burg could enlighten you further as to the man's full name. And there is also the question of spite or ambition. I am not old enough to recall personally that Herr Karl was preceded by the imperious Herr Siegfried, but I have heard the tale from other café historians.'

'There is such a profession?' Bertha asked.

'Of the amateur variety. But there are several here in Vienna who would enjoy the chance of contributing to a *Kaffeeklatsch* column in my journal were I to institute one. They do have tales to tell.'

'Herr Karl's predecessor?' Werthen nudged.

'Yes,' Kraus said, picking up the thread of his former conversation. 'When Herr Siegfried died, Herr Karl was promoted to

Herr Ober and made a clean sweep of any remnants of his predecessor, getting rid of any reminders of the man. Are there relatives, perhaps, who took unkindly to such a posthumous slighting? After all, the position of Herr Ober is a keenly sought one. Which brings me to the converse of this proposition—'

'Who stands to benefit from Herr Karl's death?' Berthe said.

Kraus nodded at her, for him a startling sign of approval. 'Yes. Who might be promoted to new Herr Ober at the Café Burg now that Herr Karl is no longer with us?'

Werthen scratched a penciled name next to Bachman: 'Herr Falk?'

But then why would the young man come forward with a tale that could possibly incriminate him? Or was he being clever? Werthen wondered, assuming people would think exactly that way.

'It could also be a matter of professional jealousy,' Kraus said. 'Jockeying for power in their Waiters' Association. Seeking pride of place in the Viennese folklore enshrining notables in the trade . . . No, nothing to smile at, Frau Meisner. This is all quite serious. It's a man's career, after all. Who knows what lengths he will go to in order to secure prominence? The list grows long  and we have yet to examine Herr Karl's heritage or his promotion of the arts.'

Werthen and Berthe both looked blankly at Kraus, waiting for an explanation. None was forthcoming.

Finally Berthe all but pleaded, 'Not so sibylline, please, Herr Kraus.'

'Yes.' He held up a forefinger dramatically. 'There is also the modern sibyl to discuss. The psychic, Hélène Smith, is in town and offering a seance at Princess Dumbroski's salon this weekend. To be a fly on the wall at that performance!'

Neither Werthen nor Berthe responded to this, waiting for Kraus to wander back to his original point.

'Sorry.' He tapped a forefinger to his right temple. 'It's filled with information of all sorts. Sometimes it's as if I pull out the wrong file drawer. I was adding further to your list, Advokat. Do you know Herr Karl's last name?'

Werthen had to shake his head at this.

'I thought not. Though supreme in his leadership at the café, the Herr Ober has no surname. He is simply Herr Karl or Herr

Viktor.' Kraus made a dramatic pause, then, 'Andric. His name was Karl Jakov Andric.'

'Sounds Serbian,' Berthe said.

'And it is, dear lady. Bosnian Serb, actually. Herr Karl's family arrived in Vienna not long after Franz Josef became emperor, escaping Ottoman rule. They were Christians, and only too happy to finally make it to a Christian land. Ironic, however, Herr Karl's choice of trade, don't you think?'

'You mean the Turkish connection?' Werthen said.

'Exactly,' Kraus said, looking at Werthen as a pleased head-master might gaze at a bright pupil. 'The family flees Turkish Ottoman rule only to have the son take up a trade created by the Turks. It is a pleasing story for schoolchildren. The loyal Polish trader Kolschitzky rewarded for his spying services during the Turkish siege of Vienna by making off with bags of coffee beans found in the camp of the vanquished Turks. Beans which only he knew what to do with. And like most children's tales, it is mostly myth. The Armenians preceded Kolschitzky, but then who cares for the truth when fable is so much more alluring?'

'But what could Herr Karl's ancestry have to do with his death?' Berthe said, growing exasperated at Kraus's asides.

'This is hearsay, Advokat,' Kraus said, directing conversation at Werthen in silent rebuke to Berthe – a woman daring to continually badger the greatest intellect of Vienna. 'So do not quote me, but from my unofficial café historians I have heard that Herr Karl's father was something of a revolutionary while in Bosnia; eager, though a Serb, to keep that region independent of greater Serbia. It is said that perhaps his emigration was not stirred so much by dislike for the Ottomans but by fear of retri-bution from Serbian nationalists. Perhaps they took out revenge on his son at long last. There are rumors, after all, of a secret organization formed by the Serbian military last year. The Black Hand. Quite dramatic, don't you think? The purpose of said secret society is assassination.'

Werthen did not bother to write down anything more than Herr Karl's full name. This avenue of investigation seemed too incredible to warrant exploration.

'And now we come to your comment about Herr Karl's promo-tion of the arts being a possible motive,' Werthen said.

'This is rather more clear cut,' Kraus said. 'Herr Karl helped to turn the Café Burg into one of the more hospitable cafés for literary gentlemen. Not the Jung Wien crowd, of course, but feuilletonists for the newspapers, minor journalists, a playwright here and there, even a novelist – who shall go unnamed – overly in thrall to symbolism. Well, whatever one's taste in words, this seems a noble enough effort. I mean, those fellows should have some place to gather. That was not the thinking of Herr Moritz Fender, however. He wrote a scathing critique of café literati a year or two ago, swearing it was the death of Austrian literature, that it made for sheep mentality and for seditious ideas because of all the international newspapers available at such cafés. He made special mention of the Café Burg, as I recall. And of its Herr Ober, whose doing it was to turn the place into a minor literary haven.'

'Perhaps we should warn Herr Viktor before he puts himself in harm's way,' Berthe quipped.

'Interesting,' Werthen said, closing his notebook and placing it back in his breast pocket. 'As always, Herr Kraus, you have proved to be a fountain of information.'

'And I do hope to hear from you with any results. My little write ups of your investigations have proven to be quite popular.'

'We really should be going,' Werthen said, looking at Berthe. 'Our cook is sitting with Frieda. Mustn't be too late.'

'Ah, yes, the pleasures of domesticity. I fear I have only articles to proofread waiting for me at my humble abode.'

They made farewell pleasantries, and as they were leaving Kraus smiled at both Werthen and Berthe. 'This has been fun. You know, I might think of taking up detective work myself. Seems quite easy.'

# FOUR

Frau Polnay had left the room as it was when Herr Karl was renting it.

'Strange he never mentioned relations,' she said again as Werthen entered the spacious cupola room overlooking a small park.

'Well, he wouldn't have, would he?' Werthen continued to improvise. 'His cousins are in Bosnia. I gather he had no direct contact. Still, relations. They are curious to know of any legacies.'

'Pahh. Legacies? Herr Karl? He spent every spare coin on these toy soldiers.' She gestured to an immense table set right under the main windows. It displayed a miniature battlefield with brightly uniformed troops deployed over a vast created landscape of green rolling hills and woods, a river of glass cutting through it.

'And Bosnian,' the landlady said disparagingly in back of him. 'Herr Karl?'

With a name like Polnay, the woman must surely also stem from some far distant corner of the empire, but she was Viennese to the core – even in her prejudices.

'I believe I can deal with things from here,' Werthen said. 'If you'll just give me a bit of time to detail the belongings . . .'

She shrugged at this, not taking the hint and not budging an inch, arms clasped over her massive bosom, her red nose a clarion call to arms. The lady clearly enjoyed her evening tipple.

So be it, he decided. He pulled out his leather notebook and pencil, pretending to note down various possessions. Herr Karl *had* died intestate, as Werthen had already ascertained, but there were no relatives – Bosnian or otherwise – seeking inheritance rights.

He first examined a small writing desk tucked into one corner of the room, hoping to find personal papers, a note, anything to provide a motive for the man's death. The top of the desk was covered in a large, clean blotter; pen and ink stood next to this.

'He liked to keep things tidy, did Herr Karl.'

'So I see,' Werthen said ruefully. The drawers displayed the same extreme order and tidiness. Two of them were filled with neatly filed, year-by-year records of his purchases of lead soldiers, numerous colors of paint for the uniforms and materials for designing and constructing various landscapes. Two other drawers contained well-worn volumes on war, from Herodotus on the Persian Wars to von Clausewitz.

'Maybe you could push on then and get to the bottom of this list of possessions. I need to clean the room. New tenant coming in the first of the month.'

Werthen did a quick survey of the large wardrobe in another corner of the room. A row of waiters' uniforms to one side and casual clothes to the left. Casual for Herr Karl Andric meant three-piece worsted suits in various shades of brown.

Frau Polnay moved to the table by the window and Werthen took the opportunity to feel the exterior of each suit for any contents in the pockets.

Nothing there.

'I hope they have children,' she said.

Feeling her eyes on him, he slipped the paper in his own pocket, unread, and turned to her. 'I beg your pardon?'

'The relatives in Moldova—'

'Bosnia,' he corrected.

'Well, wherever. I hope they have children, so they can enjoy these.' She gestured at the miniature clash of armies laid out on the table. 'Never could understand a grown man being so involved in such things.'

Werthen made no comment, moving on to the small alcove sleeping area off this main room: a single cot-like bed with a bedpan underneath. A night stand was placed at the head of the cot and atop it was a water bottle capped by a cloudy drinking glass turned upside down. There were bubbles in the stale water.

Werthen was amazed and somewhat depressed by the sheer scarcity of the man's life. Almost sixty, Herr Andric had made little more of a dent into the fabric of material life than a newborn. But there were his soldiers.

'The undertaker did send this over,' Frau Polnay said from the main room.

Werthen returned to that room and saw her holding a small linen box.

'What he had in the suit he was wearing when he . . . when he passed on.'

She handed it to Werthen and he took a moment to go through the items. There was a small leather coin purse with two crowns and twenty heller in it; a handkerchief, still crisply pressed and a small pen knife with the initials K.A. engraved on it. A pocket-sized cardboard-covered notebook held lists of needed materials for the café: coffee, toilet paper, cream, cleaning liquid. These were written in a fine hand.

Frau Polnay was looking over his shoulder. 'Such wonderful penmanship he had.' She sighed. 'Quit school as a youngster, but he believed in self-improvement. Always reading. Always learning new words. He would try them out on me some evenings. Made me feel a right fool.'

Under the notebook lay a slip of paper with a name written on it: Hermann Postling.

'Do you know this man?' he asked the frau, who was still peering into the box.

'Can't say as I do. Not Herr Karl's writing, that's for sure.'

She was right: the half-printed, half-cursive letters had none of the flair of Herr Karl's hand on the shopping list.

The name meant nothing to Werthen, either, but it was a piece of detritus from a life that seemed to accumulate very little of it, and when Frau Polnay looked away he slipped it in the back flap of his leather notebook.

Werthen handed the box of belongings back to Frau Polnay and moved to the table by the window. Here there was a world of material activity. As he stood over the table, he suddenly saw the world as Herr Andric had, in miniature and in the controlled chaos that is war.

He looked at the hundreds of tiny infantrymen and cavalry, noting first that there appeared to be three different armies. One – he was certain by the blue jackets, white trousers, black leggings and black bicorn hats – had to be French. They were accompanied by cavalry troops wearing the tall bearskin hat and cloak, also of the French of Napoleon's army. There were other infantrymen dressed in white coats and pants with black leggings and some with dun-colored coats. All of these wore tall visored helmets ornamented in brass with a brush of quills on top. Every Viennese schoolboy could recognize these as Austrian troops from the Napoleonic wars. He made a guess that the third army, dressed in white trousers and white leggings with dark blue jackets, white bandoliers and tall shako hats must be Russian.

What he was looking at was a re-enactment of the 1805 Battle of Austerlitz, in which wily Napoleon destroyed the Third Coalition, taking Austria out of the war and effectively putting an end to the Holy Roman Empire.

Werthen smiled at himself, surprised that his schoolboy history lessons had stuck this long.

'Herr Karl seems to have had a singular focus,' Werthen said.
'Yes, he did enjoy his little hobby. Spent hours with his

"comrades" as he called his toy soldiers. If he were setting up a new order of battle, I might not see him for days.'

'Did friends ever come to visit?'

'Herr Andric had his clients at the café. He always said that was enough socializing for him. He would go to Association meetings, occasional dinners with the other head waiters. And there was the Oberstabelmeister, of course.'

She dropped this bomb with smug aplomb.

'The Master of the Staff,' Werthen said, incredulously, 'for the emperor?'

She nodded importantly. 'Yes, Oberstabelmeister Johann Czerny. The very one. He and Herr Andric were school chums, it turns out. Both went out in the world as young boys and made something of themselves. Well, one more than the other, but still . . .'

'And there were no other friends? I mean, someone who might feel they have a claim in the estate?'

She shook her head at this as if it were a fantastical proposition. 'We would sit sometimes together of an evening. He was a sly one, Herr Andric. Seemed solemn as a corpse, but he could tell a tale or two of things his customers got up to. Made me laugh till my sides hurt sometimes. There was this one fellow he caught cheating at cards, if you can believe it. Made his living at Tarock. Had to ban the man from the café. Made quite a scene, Herr Andric said.'

Werthen perked up at this mention, remembering Kraus's list of possible suspects.

'Did Herr Andric mention him again? Was the man causing any problems for him?'

She shrugged. 'Not that he mentioned.' She tilted her head and squinted an eye at him. 'Curious type, aren't you?'

'It's the curse of being a lawyer. Always wanting to get to the bottom of things.'

Werthen quickly checked his notes from last night and found the name of the card sharp, Herr Bachman. He made a note, pushing him to the top of the list.

How one could have a 'soiree' in the middle of the afternoon was a mystery to Berthe, but that was what Princess Dumbroski chose to call this little gathering. Granted, with the brocade curtains closed in the drawing room of her Ringstrasse apartment, it did seem like nighttime. The medium needed the darkness; it was explained to the assembled guests.

Among these was Rosa Mayreder, who invited Berthe to accompany her at the last moment. And with Karl's parents in town and eager to spend time with Frieda, Berthe felt no compunctions about accepting. The room was quite full of other guests, as well, several of whom Berthe recognized and others whom Frau Mayreder needed to identify for her. In the former category was the journalist, Herr Sonnenthal, suitor of Karl's secretary, Erika Metzinger. He was in earnest conversation with the artist whose work they'd viewed last night, Emile Orlik, and he in turn was accompanied by the artist Gustav Klimt, who had once been a client of theirs. Dressed in a long, flowing caftan, he winked a hello to Berthe. At his side, and fairly towering over the stumpy, burly artist, was his mistress and muse, the designer, Emilie Flöge, also attired in one of her caftan creations, in bold, flowing patterns. The two of them were like exotic flowers amid the somberly attired remaining guests.

Among the other assorted people gathered at Princess Dumbroski's was a young and rather handsome man in proper frock coat, whose rosy cheeks made him look as though he were still studying at the gymnasium.

'Baron Anton Kiss,' Frau Mayreder informed her when Berthe pointed him out. 'Son of the *gnädige Frau.*'

The 'dear lady' in question was, as all Vienna knew, Katharina Schratt, Burgtheater actress and special friend of the emperor for over twenty years.

Guests helped themselves to a sideboard with sherry and Madeira in cut-glass carafes and canapés from Demel's. Princess Dumbroski fashioned herself a cosmopolitan, flitting from one property to the next in London, Paris and Vienna, where she had made her home for the past year. No one knew the definitive story of the mysterious princess who had so suddenly appeared on the international social scene. Some said that she was of Ruthenian aristocracy; others that she was heiress to a rail fortune, and still others that she had been the most highly paid courtesan in Petersburg. The one thing that was clear was that Princess Dumbroski was very wealthy and could well afford such extravagance.

Truth be told, Berthe decided to attend the soiree not for the promised seance but to see the notorious dueling princess up close. She had scandalized all of Vienna upon her arrival, fighting a duel with a minor countess over the flower arrangements for a musical event. The two women had fought topless with swords, it was reported, and all the seconds as well as medical attendants had been women. Needless to say, Princess Dumbroski had won the duel, injuring the countess in the arm after having herself sustaining a cut to her face, a scar she proudly bore now as a badge of honor.

Just then, the princess swept into the room, accompanied by a tall, handsome woman with a placid expression on her face.

'*Mes cher amis*,' the princess began, her voice carrying to every corner of the room. The buzz of conversation abruptly ended; eyes turned toward the hostess.

'I am so pleased you could all come today, for we are in for a treat, I promise. I am sure our illustrious guest, Madame Hélène Smith, needs no introduction. She has channeled messages from Mars, allowed us to communicate with Victor Hugo and other greats on the other side. And today she has agreed to channel a voice from beyond for one of us. So, without further ceremony, I give you Madame Hélène Smith.'

There was a polite but subdued round of applause. Berthe wondered if the guests had been aware that they might become more than curious observers to this performance. The medium nodded her head slightly at this applause, but said nothing. She sat at a small table placed in front of a wall of books in leather bindings and began taking deep breaths. A servant turned down the gas lamps in the room until the medium was barely visible. A nervous cough as though at a musical performance, then those gathered also became quiet. All eyes fixed on Hélène Smith, who continued to take deep breaths.

Suddenly her head slumped forward as if she had been violently struck. Someone let out a gasp. Her head lolled like that for a moment, then began to move in small circles. A thumping sound startled Berthe. Smith must have kicked one of the table legs, but it was too dark to see clearly.

A hoarse, gruff male voice emitted from the woman's mouth: '*Ki vagy te?*'

Frau Mayreder and Berthe exchanged glances. 'Hungarian?' Frau Mayreder whispered.

'*Ki vagy te?*' Said more imploringly this time. '*Honnan való vagy?*'

Guests standing nearby stirred nervously at the otherworldly sound of this voice.

Then it was as if Smith split in two, for her somnolent self straightened, turning her head to the right, eyes closed. 'I am a friend,' she said in heavily accented German. '*Barát vagyok.*' After a moment's pause: '*Beszélsz német?*'

Berthe, from a trip to Budapest, knew this phrase. It meant, '*Do you speak German?*'

Smith turned her head to the left as if replying to her own question: '*Igen*,' the raspy voice replied. 'Yes. Why have you awoken me?'

The medium turned her head to the right. 'There is someone in this room who wants to communicate with you. I feel the energy, I sense the need.'

'*Bosszú*,' the angry voice said. 'Revenge me. They may take my life for fighting for my country, but not the family estates. Revenge me.'

And then, out of the gloom a glowing presence appeared, seemingly from nowhere. There was a startled intake of breath from more than one guest as the apparition came close to Princess Dumbroski, who appeared to take no notice of it. Berthe could discern that the figure appeared to be that of a stooped elderly man, wearing a felt Magyar hat and boots.

'Fraud!' It was a strangled shout from someone among the guests. A man brushed past Berthe, still cursing under his breath. It was the young baron that Frau Mayreder had earlier identified for her. He stomped out of the room, slamming the double doors in back of him.

Everyone's attention had been drawn to the dramatic departure of the young man, and when they looked back to where the apparition had been, it too was gone.

The medium appeared to slowly awaken from her trance.

'All is well?' she asked meekly.

Princess Dumbroski rushed to her side, patting her shoulder. 'Yes, my dear. Everything is fine.' Then to her servant: 'Turn the lights up, please.'

Speaking to the guests, Princess Dumbroski said, 'It would appear to be an unwelcome ancestor. One of those fusty gents you try to avoid at family reunions.'

There was a round of relieved laughter at this followed by an instant hum of excited conversation. Herr Sonnenthal came to join Berthe and Frau Mayreder. As usual, he seemed to know all, a trait that made him an excellent journalist.

'I didn't know you were a fan of the metaphysical arts, Herr Sonnenthal,' Berthe said.

'Nor I of you,' he replied with a smile. 'It should make an interesting column for the *Arbeiter Zeitung*: what the first society gets up to of a Saturday afternoon.'

'So, we're first society now,' Frau Mayreder said. 'How nice to hear.'

'What was that all about?' Berthe asked.

Sonnenthal raised his eyebrows at her. 'Baron Anton Kiss de Ittebe et Elemér, to give him his full name, is the great grandson of a Hungarian general who fought for Hungarian independence in the 1848 uprising. He was executed for his efforts and his property confiscated by the emperor. I believe the execution order came from Franz Josef personally – one of his first orders as the young emperor.'

'Rather an awkward seance, then, for the young man,' Frau Mayreder said. 'His mother the mistress of the man who gave the order.'

Sonnenthal raised his eyes at this and nodded. 'Good copy, though.'

Berthe felt sorry for the young man. He had looked pained as he left the room. A man aggrieved. 'And the glowing figure was supposed to be this great grandfather, one assumes. It gave me a fright.'

'Staged, of course,' Sonnenthal added. 'Clothes impregnated with phosphorus obviously. Perhaps he's still hiding under the table.'

Glancing at the table, there was no cloth on it for concealment. But Sonnenthal was unconcerned. 'Sleight of hand, surely. Perhaps even a secret door in that wall of books. And it was easy enough for the princess to slip our friendly medium the guest list. Time enough for her to do some research on the ancestors of those present. Baron Kiss was prominent on the list, one imagines.'

'But she spoke Hungarian,' Berthe said.

'Madame Smith is actually Catherine-Elise Müller. She may

have been born in France, but her father was a Hungarian merchant. That is probably the reason she picked on the poor young fellow.'

'Seems cruel,' Frau Mayreder added.

'What do you expect from a duelist?'

'You think the princess put her up to it?' Berthe looked over to where Princess Dumbroski was guiding Smith to various guests, landing now at Klimt and Flöge, who seemed to be full of questions.

'Really, Berthe,' Frau Mayreder patted her hand. 'You are a sweet innocent.'

'But why?'

Frau Mayreder shrugged. 'Because she can. Because she feels in competition with Frau Schratt as the most renowned hostess in Vienna. Perhaps it was a broadside shot, a declaration of war between them. So many possibilities.'

Berthe looked again at their hostess. There was a cruel hardness to the woman's features, a calculating look to her eyes. And suddenly she understood why people like Frau Mayreder, Herr Sonnenthal and even Klimt had been invited. These were the sort of people that would make the incident known, in print and in the rounds of gossip.

Berthe decided she would not want Princess Dumbroski for an enemy.

# FIVE

Werthen arrived at the Rathaus punctually at eight in the morning the following Monday and made his way to the Viennese City and Provincial Archive on the third floor. The attendant at the front desk, in white duster, was the punctilious sort, and Werthen had to display his legal credentials in order to search the files. Herr Bachman, he told the attendant, had come into a legacy and it was his task to contact the man.

'With one "n?"' the man asked with a sigh.

Why are civil servants never civil? Werthen asked himself for the hundredth time.

'Yes. One "n." Wolfram is the first name.'

At least there was something to make the search easier: how many Wolfram Bachmans with one 'n' could there be in the city? Werthen had spoken with Herr Otto on Sunday and managed to discover Bachman's full name. When blackballing the man from all respectable cafés in Vienna, Herr Karl had presented the Waiters' Association with the full name, and Herr Otto had made a note of it.

Ten minutes later the attendant returned with a bulky file box of *Meldezettl* – registration forms. Each time a person changed residences in Vienna, a new registration form must be filed; one deregistered from the former address and registered the new one, providing date, address, name, occupation, birthplace, religion and marital and family status. Some overly conscientious Viennese even went through this process when going on holiday.

The attendant nodded at a table in the corner of the office. Werthen took the file and began the search, hoping that whoever organized the forms had a proper sense of alphabetization. Opening the file, he was greeted with a cloud of dust that set him sneezing violently. Glancing toward the main desk, Werthen saw the attendant making no effort to suppress a smile.

Looking at the top form, he saw that it began with 'Bachman,' first name, 'Berthold.' He pulled out the bottom registration form, and saw it was already to 'Bachman, Arnuf.' He fanned through the mass of files until he got to first names beginning with a 'T.' From there he thumbed through the Ulrichs and Viktors until he finally came to 'W.' There was a Werner, Willibald, even a Wojtek. Finally he had it: Wolfram Bachman. He scanned down the information: an address on Florianigasse, only a few blocks from Werthen's apartment building on Josefstädterstrasse. It seemed Herr Bachman was prolific in one respect: he was married with five children. Not exactly the profile one expected from a card sharp. Even more perplexing was his listed occupation: pastor.

Werthen stared at the paper a moment longer, then flipped to the next form. Yes, he told himself. More like it. A second Wolfram Bachman. He turned to the next form: Xavier Bachman. He went back to the previous one. At least he now knew how many Wolfram Bachmans there could be in Vienna. This one lived in the Second District, on Asperngasse, just off the Praterstrasse. By the date of the form it appeared he had taken up

residence there just a month earlier, moving from a more pres-
tigious address in the First District. The date tallied with when
Herr Karl had caught the man cheating at cards and banned him,
thus depriving him of a livelihood. Bachman listed his profession
as entertainment artist.

Well, Werthen would soon see how entertaining the man was.

It was a fair day, though blustery, and Werthen decided to
walk, making his way through the First District and crossing
over the Danube Canal at Ferdinandsbrücke to reach the Second
District. Putting the investigation of Herr Karl's death out of his
mind for the time being, Werthen instead focused on the past
pleasant weekend. Not that long ago, Werthen would hardly have
used the word 'pleasant' to describe his parents' visits, but the
birth of Frieda had made a real difference, turning often interfering parents into doting grandparents. On Saturday evening
Berthe had entertained the table with her description of the seance
she'd attended. And then yesterday they had made a trip to the
woods to see the progress of his parents' new home. With winter
all but passed, construction had begun again at the site, and it
was beginning to take shape. It was less than a mile from
Werthen's own country house in Laab im Walde. At first this had
rankled, but even that feeling of annoyance at being hemmed in
had disappeared, and he was happy for their proximity.

I must be getting old, he thought as he proceeded down the
busy Praterstrasse to the first street on the right. He consulted
the address he had written down at the archive: Asperngasse 12/3.
It almost took him back to the canal.

The street door was unlocked, so he did not bother to ring
for the portier. It was an old and shabby baroque building, three
stories high, but there were no stairs for him to climb, as apartment three was at the back of the ground floor, little more than
a tram-sized slice of the building by the looks of it, with a grimy
window on the gloomy courtyard. Werthen turned the mechanical
bell on the door several times but no one responded. He went
out to the courtyard and peered in the window.

'He'll be at the Wurstelprater,' said a squeak of a voice from
behind him.

Turning, he saw a thin little woman wearing the long white
canvas housecoat of the Viennese portier. She stared at him with
rheumy eyes.

'Is this Herr Bachman's apartment?'

She snorted at this. 'Glorified clothespress, more like. But it's all he can afford. So if you are another one of those debt collectors, I advise you to look for better pickings.'

'No,' Werthen said. 'Actually, I have come with good news for Herr Bachman. He is the recipient of a legacy from a recently deceased uncle.'

This made her sallow face light up. 'My. Herr Bachman an heir. Who would've thought? Maybe he can pay last month's rent now.'

'So he still lives here?'

She nodded but said nothing.

'You mentioned the Prater,' he said.

'No. The Wurstelprater. But how do I know you aren't a bill collector? He has to pay me first, you know.'

Werthen handed her his business card with 'Wills and Trusts' displayed more prominently than 'Criminal Law and Private Inquiries', and that did the trick.

'He's at the old Hanswurst puppet theater next to the Kino Lux. Unless he's taking time out for a game or two in the taverns.'

She made a wiggling motion with her hand around an imaginary glass to indicate Herr Bachman enjoyed his wine.

Werthen returned to Praterstrasse and made his way along the street past the Carl theater and the Admiral Tegethoff monument to the Praterstern, the star-like confluence of six main avenues and the entrance to the former hunting grounds of the Prater. To his right was the Haupt Allee, leading to the noble Prater, where the first society liked to drive their equipages of an afternoon to see and be seen. Straight ahead was the entrance to the people's Prater, or Wurstelprater, named after the Hanswurst puppet shows once so popular. Werthen's first case as a private inquiries agent came to a climax in this precinct; he still remembered the shame and terror he'd felt for having put Berthe, then his fiancée, into the gravest danger. He passed the giant Ferris wheel, built for the 1898 Jubilee celebrations of Franz Josef's fiftieth year on the throne. Just beyond that was the amusement park of Venice in Vienna – Werthen felt a special twinge at remembering the events of his earlier case – and then came the Kino Lux. Beyond that began a scattering of smaller wooden booths offering everything from pretzels to off-tune singers warbling about the Vienna Woods. ·

Werthen quickly found the small puppet theater amid these. Bachman – he assumed the man behind the makeshift stage was the person he sought – was in the midst of shuffling cards with a good deal of artistry, making them flow as a waterfall from one hand to the next. A nursemaid with her charge asleep in a pram was staring wide-eyed at the cards and the dexterity with which Bachman maneuvered them. She had the fresh looks of a country girl. Werthen doubted that her employers – most likely residents of the more fashionable Praterstrasse – intended her to take their child on a stroll in the rowdy Wurstelprater. She was on a lark and meant to enjoy herself.

Bachman suddenly stopped shuffling, slapping the cards onto the small waist-high stage, making a staccato beat as he spoke. 'Aces,' he said. 'Where are you my charming aces, the noblest of cards? I shall find you, I know.'

With the pack almost dealt out, he finished the trick dramatically by suddenly calling out, 'Here you are, my lovelies!'

Then, with his eyes closed and the cards face down in his hands, he slapped down four in a row – all aces.

The nursemaid's eyes grew even wider at the bit of legerdemain; she could not help but clap her hands in glee, at which the baby in the pram awoke, crying. She suddenly remembered her duty and hurried the child off toward the less carnival-like regions of the Prater.

'That was very fine of you to leave a bit of *trinkgeld*,' Bachman shouted sarcastically at her. Then, noticing Werthen watching him at a distance, he said, 'I won't bite, you know. You can come closer. I enjoy performing for free.'

Werthen tipped his homburg at the card sharp and approached. 'Herr Bachman?'

This made the man look up from the deck he was again shuffling. 'Never heard of the man.'

'Don't worry. I haven't come to collect a debt.'

Bachman eyed him closely. 'No, I suppose you haven't. By the looks of you, you've come about other quasi-legal matters, though. The hat, the coat, the way you carry yourself. Let me guess. A mortician.' He laughed at his little joke, and the laughter turned into a deep, wracking cough that brought tears to the man's eyes.

Recovering, Bachman said, 'A lawyer, to be sure. I can't afford lawyers.'

'I haven't come to offer my services. I've come to ask you about Herr Karl.'

'Does he have a last name?'

'I think you know who I mean.'

Bachman set the cards down. 'You really don't remember me, do you, Advokat Werthen?'

This took Werthen aback. 'Do I know you?'

'It was a number of years ago, now, but there you have it. Story of my life. I remember people, but I'm not the sort people remember.'

Except for his red, pitted, bulbous nose, Bachman was right: he was nondescript. For the life of him, Werthen could not place the man.

'Graz,' Bachman hinted. 'The criminal justice system, to be specific.'

Had he been a client? Werthen would surely remember . . . And then he had it.

'Bachman. Advokat Bachman.'

'The very one,' Bachman said. 'Though they did take my license away, if you remember. I'm not a lawyer any longer.'

'Yes,' Werthen said, now remembering that Bachman had been caught improperly influencing a witness in an attempt to get a wealthy client off. He had been lucky to escape with expulsion from the Lawyers' Chamber and not a prison term himself.

'And so you have turned to . . .'

Bachman raised his hands in a monumental shrug. 'What's a man to do? At university I used to make a bit of cash on the side with friendly card games, even a bit of magic. So, once I lost my license, I went back to what I knew. Couldn't stay in Graz, of course.'

'Of course,' Werthen agreed.

'And yes, I was only too familiar with Herr Karl, damn his eyes. I even went to his funeral, hoping to get a chance to urinate on his grave, but the people lingered and it was getting cold.'

Werthen marveled at the man's candor. 'So you admit you had a grievance with the Herr Ober?'

'Grievance? Call it what it is, man. He cheated me. Should

have been drummed out of his Waiters' Association as I was from the Lawyers' Chamber.'

Werthen shook his head. 'I don't understand what you're getting at.'

'What I am getting at . . .'

Bachman's attention was diverted for a moment by a street urchin who came up to the booth hoping for free entertainment.

'Hop it out of here, you,' Bachman growled at the youth, who wisely moved off, but thumbed his nose once he was a safe distance away.

Bachman noticed the gesture. 'Makes a man happy he never married, never fathered such a brat.' Then, turning back to Werthen, he said, 'Anyway, as I was saying, Herr Karl swindled me out of a full month's payment. One of the customer's complained to him that I was cheating. Well, of course I was cheating. How do you think I make a living? That's what I paid the jumped-up waiter for. A bit of protection.'

'You mean you were paying Herr Karl to play cards at his café?'

'You always were a bright one, Advokat Werthen. Yes. Five crowns a month so that if a customer complained he would say no, no, no, Herr Bachman is a most trusted client. And so forth. But this customer was a bit more important than the others. I should have figured that out, the way the fool tossed his money around. He threatened to go to the Waiters' Association, and so Herr Karl suddenly found his ethics and banished me. Got the whole Association to do so. Bastard.'

This turn of events left Werthen speechless for a moment.

Bachman suddenly smiled broadly. 'Now, hold on. If you've come to me with questions about Herr Karl, I doubt very much it has to do with my card playing. So I ask myself, what would a criminal lawyer be doing making noises about the accidental death of a crooked head waiter? And I tell myself, Bachman, Advokat Werthen would not waste his valuable time unless, yes, unless Herr Karl's death was not so accidental after all. Hah! Wonderful. You mean some hero saved me the trouble and killed the little sneak?'

'That is about the size of it,' Werthen allowed. 'It would appear to be murder.'

Bachman pressed hands together as if in prayer, looking heavenward in thanks. Then to Werthen: 'And you suspect me?'

Werthen nodded, beginning to feel something of a fool.
Attempting to salvage some bit of dignity out of this meeting,
he said, 'But by the way you are so broadly smiling, I assume
that you have some proof that you were not involved.'

'That's the Advokat Werthen I remember. Too true. I seem to
remember from the newspaper accounts that the fellow slipped
on icy paths last Monday night. Is that so?'

'Yes. His body was not discovered until the next day.'

'Monday night.' Bachman's face squinched up in a mock
display of attempting to remember something. 'I seem to recall
that Monday. That would be the tenth of March, right?'

Werthen nodded again. 'Out with it, Bachman. Enough with
the silly games.'

'As you wish, though games seem to be all I have left. At any
rate, I have the lawyer's dream come true – an ironclad alibi.
After closing up my booth that day – miserable weather it was
with frozen walkways. The cold plays havoc with the fingers,
you know. Slows down the shuffle something awful—'

'Bachman!'

'All right. I closed up early and stopped off at my favorite
tavern just down the row here.' He gestured to his left. 'Well, it
seems I imbibed a bit too much on an empty stomach. A fellow
customer made a disparaging comment about my ability at card
tricks – I am not a violent man by nature, you understand, but
this remark just caught me at the wrong moment. So I smashed
my mug of wine over his head. Next thing I knew, one of Vienna's
finest constabulary had me by the collar and I spent the night in
jail. Happy days, though. The other fellow did not press charges.'
He tapped his nose, a secret to share. 'Couldn't really, as he's
got his own strange business in "imported" linens he wouldn't
want the police to become curious about.'

'When did this occur?'

'Well, as I said, I started at the wine earlier than usual. I
believe I had found my way to my cell by nine o'clock. Check
with the local station on Taborstrasse – I'm sure they'll remember
me. Managed to take a few coins off the duty sergeant in a
friendly game before they released me the next day.' Bachman
smiled at him, displaying browning teeth. 'Sorry I couldn't be
more obliging. Now, if you'll forgive me, I have a dishonest
living to make.'

# SIX

F alk was at his position at the Café Burg when Werthen arrived. Today, however, he was dressed in the cutaway of a Herr Ober. He directed Werthen to a table in the far corner.

'That was fast,' Werthen said, nodding to the man's new attire.

'Temporary only, sir,' Falk replied as he pulled out a chair for Werthen. Their nearest fellow customers were several tables away. 'It is rumored they will hire from outside.'

Werthen sat, raising his eyebrows at this comment. 'Not the usual practice, is it?'

Falk shook his head, clearly disappointed.

'And why do you think that would be, Falk?'

'I couldn't tell, sir. One would have to inquire of Herr Regierungsrat Mintz. After all, he is the owner.'

Werthen made no reply to this.

After a moment, Falk inquired: 'What would sir like today?'

'Some honesty, for starters. You haven't really been straight with me, have you, Falk?'

'I don't understand.' He looked around as if fearful someone might be eavesdropping.

'About Herr Karl and his little improper payments, shall we call them. Were you a part of it?'

'Only in so far that I had to pay into his phony retirement fund.'

'Slowly, Falk. What fund is that?'

'Like I say, a non-existent one. It was a monthly contribution. All the staff had to pay into a retirement fund, supposedly with the Waiters' Association. In reality, it was Herr Karl's retirement fund. We paid and the account never seemed to grow. Bad investments, he would tell us. A shortfall at the Borse. What do any of us know about stock exchanges? But I did a little investigating. It's been fine days at the stock market these past years.'

'Did you know that certain customers were paying him? A card shark, for one.'

Falk shook his head. 'I didn't know, but that's not a surprise.

Herr Karl was an inventive one. Every supplier to the café, from toilet paper to coffee beans, had to pay Herr Karl a little gratuity, a percentage off the top of the bill or risk losing his account.'

'And no one thought to tell the owner?'

'And then what? Herr Mintz would have simply replaced Herr Karl with someone who would only do the same, maybe even worse. It comes with the job, you know. Nobody becomes a Herr Ober because of the honor attached to the position.'

Werthen marveled at his own naiveté: that was exactly what he *had* thought. But reflecting on it now, it made perfect sense. A Herr Ober held power at a café, and power meant nothing if it was not used.

'Is there anything else I should know about Herr Karl before I go? Any other reason someone might want to kill him?'

'You think somebody did him in because of his little money schemes? Half the Herr Obers in Vienna would be dead if that were the case.'

'How about the rest of the staff? Were they as resigned to Herr Karl's extortion as you were? Nobody harboring a grudge.'

'We're talking about a few crowns here and there. Hardly enough to kill for.'

'Then something else. Anything odd transpire with Herr Karl lately?'

'Well, I was thinking after I talked with you the other day. There was a man came in here about a week ago. It might have even been the day Herr Karl died. He had a talk with Herr Karl, like we are doing now. Private. Out of the way. It was a busy day, though, and a valued customer was asking for Herr Karl. So I came back here to see if I could get his attention. Before I did, the man said something like, "Be sure you do." That idea, anyway, like he was giving the orders. And Herr Karl's face was as pale white as one of our tablecloths. The man noticed my presence then and put on a broad smile, and Herr Karl went to the customer and nothing more was said of it. But it seemed strange at the time.'

'This man. Can you describe him?' Werthen asked.

Karl chewed his lip for a moment. 'He was one of those fellows that don't stand out very much, if you know what I mean. Slight build, medium height, so far as I could tell with him sitting down. Clean-shaven, close-cropped hair. Nothing about him to make him memorable. It was just the way he made his face change once he saw me approach that makes me remember. It was like he put on a mask in an instant. There was something almost scary about that change.'

'Could he have been the assailant you witnessed killing Herr Karl?'

'That is what I have been mulling over since seeing you. I just don't know. Maybe they were both about the same size, that's all I could say. But there's something else I've been trying to remember. Something peculiar. Something about the awkward way he held his cup. But it won't come.'

Werthen knew the feeling. 'Don't focus on it too much – sometimes that helps. And when you remember, get in touch, no matter how trivial it seems.'

Falk sighed and nodded. 'And you haven't gone to the police.'

Werthen shook his head. 'I told you that I would protect you as much as I could, but you have to be completely honest with me.'

'I am. I swear I am. So, can I get you something, Herr Werthen?'

'A small mocha would be good, Falk. No need for you to serve it. We don't want the others getting suspicious.'

As Werthen sat over his coffee, he made notes in his pocket notebook and then read where things stood thus far. 'Herr Karl Andric, head waiter at the Café Burg, died the night of Monday, March the tenth after leaving the café. Apparent accidental death by slipping on ice between twin museums and cracking his head on a concrete pillar. Not so, says waiter Rudolph Falk, nephew of Herr Otto's wife – Otto is to be trusted. He got his nephew the job at Burg. Falk, put upon by Herr Karl, followed him that night to talk with him and witnessed his brutal slaying by a man or woman of medium height but with enough strength to cave the back of Karl's head in. According to Falk, this had to be planned, for the killer brought what appeared to be a length of pipe along tucked up the sleeve of his overcoat. Do I believe Falk? Is he using me to help make himself look innocent? Falk had a motive – he wanted to be head waiter, though in the event it did not work out that way. Also, Herr Karl was basically extorting the young waiter, along with the other staff and commercial suppliers.

'Falk later informs me that there was a man who seemed to

upset Herr Karl a couple of weeks before. A nondescript man of
medium height with nothing remarkable other than something
odd or awkward about the way he held his coffee cup. Falk
cannot remember exactly – check back in later about that? What
to make of that? Could be anything. "Be sure you do," Falk
overheard the man ordering Karl. More interesting. Still, where
does that lead? Could it be about Herr Karl's little money-making
scheme that he was running at the Café Burg? And what is the
"something peculiar" that Falk is trying to remember about this
mysterious stranger?

'From Kraus, off the top of his head, I received a small list
of others who might stand to gain from Herr Karl's death: the
disgruntled customer, Herr Bachman, who in fact turned out to
be a former colleague in the legal profession from Graz. Bachman
opens up the new angle with news of Herr Karl's kickbacks. But
he also has a perfect alibi for the night of the murder: he was in
jail.

'There was also the suggestion of descendants of the previous
head waiter at the Café Burg whose legacy was expunged when
Herr Karl took over. Possible retribution? Unlikely, but worth
tracking down. And then there are other ambitious waiters, not
only at the Burg, but at other establishments who might actually
kill for the position of head waiter. Or perhaps even professional
jealousy vis-à-vis other head waiters in the Waiters' Association.
I need to follow up on that as well.

'Less likely was Kraus's theory about Herr Karl's Bosnian
Serb roots, of his father's revolutionary activities somehow
coming to impact on the son, and of the ominous-sounding Black
Hand. Kraus the dramatist? Put to the bottom of the list.

'A "maybe" is Herr Moritz Fender, the literary critic who
scolded cafés such as the Burg for fostering lightweight literary
circles. Not urgent, but must talk to him eventually.

'And finally, from a visit to the landlady, Frau Polnay, I learned
that Herr Karl had one friend, and he a mightily influential one
at that: Oberstabelmeister Johann Czerny, Master of the Staff at
the Hofburg. Would Czerny know anything of Kerr Karl's illicit
dealings? Would he have more information about his friend's
state of mind just before his death? Any word of threats or the
like? Yes – follow up with Czerny.'

Werthen stared at the page for a moment, then noticed a slip of paper just protruding from the top of the notebook behind the final sheets. He opened the notebook to these sheets and saw the piece of crumpled paper he had taken from one of Herr Karl's suits at his rooms. Written on it was the name 'Hermann Postling.' He had quite forgotten about that, but now inserted it in the notebook as a bookmark for his notes on Herr Karl. A piece of detritus, but he had earlier thought it worth keeping. Perhaps he should check the handwriting to see if it was Herr Karl's or not.

He looked at the clock near the entrance. Four-fifteen. Where had the time gone? Tomorrow would be another day, and Czerny would be at the top of the list.

# PART TWO

PART TWO

# SEVEN

T hree days to spring, Werthen thought with irony the next morning as he trod through the half foot of snow that had fallen during the night. Buds on the lime trees in the Volksgarten looked like they might reconsider their early unfurling. The roses were still tied down and mulched: gardeners at the city's park never erred on the side of optimism.

He didn't mind the snow; in fact, he was enjoying it as Vienna had strangely little of it this winter. It was mild enough to overturn rational faculties and make one wonder what odd forces had been released with the new century.

He made his way through the Volksgarten on his usual route to the office on Habsburgergasse, stopping off at the House Master's Bureau in the Albertina wing of the vast urban palace cum castle of the Hofburg. It was stifling warm inside the front office; a bell over the door announced his arrival and a grey-faced man in his forties, bundled in muffler and white housecoat, looked his way with an expression bespeaking either irritation with the public in general or distress at an attack of gastritis. His pinched nostrils flared as he spoke.

'How may I help you, sir?' It was an art form to be able to turn what should be a courteous question into a threat.

'I would like to see Oberstabelmeister Czerny.'

The clerk, whose name by the tag on his coat was called Plauder, seemed to have trouble understanding him.

'Czerny,' Werthen said again, louder this time. 'I would like to schedule an appointment.'

'I heard you the first time,' Herr Plauder said, squinting at Werthen. 'In regards to what? This is a rather busy time of the year for the Herr Oberstabelmeister with Easter approaching.'

Werthen felt the hairs at the back of his head bristle at the man's imperiousness.

'In regards to a private inquiry,' he said, setting down one of his business cards on the counter separating him from the clerk.

The man stared at it incredulously. Werthen gazed around the sterile and lifeless-looking office. In apartments all around him in the Hofburg was opulence and luxury: Gobelin tapestries, star parquet floors, crystal chandeliers. Not a trace of it here, however. He could be in the provincial offices of a postmaster. A photograph of Franz Joseph in the regalia of office and striding at the head of a procession was the one ornament in the room.

Plauder looked up at Werthen. 'Herr Oberstabelmeister Czerny has no availability until after Easter.'

'You might tell him it is in regards to his old friend, Herr Karl Andric.'

'I do not tell the Oberstabelmeister anything. *He* is in command.'

'Relay a message, then,' Werthen insisted. 'It is rather urgent.'

The man sniffed once, turned the card over and then back to its face, slipping it across the counter to Werthen. 'Write the message on the back. I will put it in his box.'

Werthen did so then handed the card back to the clerk, who made no move to pick it up.

As he left the office, Werthen decided that he perhaps might need to consult an old ally with a bit of influence with the Hofburg, Archduke Franz Ferdinand, for whom he and his wife Berthe had already accepted a number of commissions.

At the office, Fräulein Metzinger was at her desk already and young Franzl was bundled up, a packet of letters in his hand ready to be delivered.

'There is someone waiting for you,' she said, looking a bit flustered. Fräulein Metzinger was not the flustered type.

'Who is it?'

'He wouldn't give his name, only his rank. A lieutenant major.'

'He looks grand in his uniform,' Franzl piped in.

'I am sure he does,' Werthen said, taking a stock of correspondence his secretary had placed in his in-tray.

Werthen opened the door to his office, a knot of expectation in his stomach. He knew from long experience that it is only the criminal class who do not feel such expectation when meeting with authorities; this knowledge, however, did little to calm him.

The officer was seated in the chair facing Werthen's desk, a black helmet fitted with a gilt double-eagle insignia held in his lap. He wore a smart-looking red tunic with shiny brass buttons, white buckskin breeches, high black boots and a long sword at his side, all of which bespoke a member of the Trabant Life Guards, the bodyguards of the emperor. The uniform bore the high stiff collar that covered most of the neck – another sign of the personal staff, for such a collar had become regulation attire after it had deflected an assassin's knife half a century before when a Hungarian nationalist had attacked the young emperor.

The man immediately stood, ramrod stiff, the helmet – its four-inch pike on top – tucked automatically under his arm now. He nodded briskly at Werthen.

'Herr Advokat, my apologies for coming unannounced like this. It is, however, a matter of some urgency.'

Werthen motioned toward the chair. 'Please, sit and tell me what it is, Lieutenant Major . . .'

'Simmreich, sir. Lieutenant Major Bernhard Simmreich. And if it is all the same to you, I would rather we discussed the matter once we are underway.'

'Underway? Where to?'

'Schönbrunn.'

Simmreich said nothing else – that one word let Werthen know this was an imperial summons. He controlled a sudden urge to laugh, something he often did when nervous. Probably not something this young and earnest officer would understand, however.

'Well, then, shall we be on our way?'

Fräulein Metzinger cast him a concerned look as he told her he had an urgent meeting and would be back later. Once on the street, the officer steered him to a coach and pair of horses waiting nearby. There was nothing ostentatious about the carriage; Werthen had not even noticed it when arriving just moments before. The driver was not dressed in uniform, but rather looked like a fiaker driver. When they were settled on the leather benches inside, the carriage rattled out of the warren of cobbled streets of the First District to the Ringstrasse and thence south to Babenburgerstrasse, turning off the Ring and reaching Mariahilferstrasse, which would lead to the country palace of the Habsburgs – Schönbrunn.

Simmreich sat stiffly and said nothing.

'Are you going to tell me what this is about now?' Werthen finally asked.

'I have been instructed to tell you that Prince Montenuovo will receive you at the palace.'

Werthen tipped his head in appreciation of this bit of information. Montenuovo was one of the most powerful men in the
empire, though his rank as second to the master of the court did
not reflect that. He had his hand in everything that had to do
with court matters or the life of Emperor Franz Josef. Werthen
had had dealings with Montenuovo before, and knew him to be
as wily as a fox. That he was an arch enemy of Franz Ferdinand,
nephew to the emperor and heir apparent to the Austrian throne,
and a man with whom Werthen had also had dealings, sometimes
complicated matters for Werthen.

'I hope to find the prince in good health,' Werthen said.

'I am sure you will,' the lieutenant major replied.

They were the last words spoken for the duration of the trip.

Finally arriving at the summer palace, Werthen could see that
the snowfall was heavier here near the outskirts of town; crews
in leather aprons were out in the immense central court in front
of the palace scraping snow off the pebbled approach road.
Liveried servants breathing vapor bubbles awaited the carriage,
and soon Werthen found himself escorted down a long back
hallway to the private apartments of this vast palace complex of
fourteen hundred separate rooms. He was led into a room whose
walls were covered in the red brocade of the imperial apartments,
furnished with the white and gold of *Blondel* chairs and desk the
emperor personally prescribed. Werthen's trips to Archduke Franz
Ferdinand's headquarters at the Belvedere let him know that the
archduke's accommodations were paltry in comparison. Here was
the seat of power. Real power.

Simmreich, still without further explanation, took Werthen's
hat and coat, though he would rather have kept the coat in
the glacial climes of this room. A fire burned in a baroque fire-
place, but as its heat rose to the twenty-foot molded ceilings, the
fire did little to take the chill off the air. The lieutenant major
motioned him to be seated, and he did so as Simmreich slipped
out of the room. Werthen took a deep breath, wondering what
Prince Montenuovo – and by implication, the Emperor Franz
Josef – could want with him. The door by which Simmreich had
taken his leave opened once again and into the room came a
familiar figure.

'By Jesus, it is you, Werthen! They've got us both.'

Werthen could not help but smile at the unexpected arrival of his colleague and sometimes partner in detection, the eminent criminologist, Dr Hanns Gross.

Werthen stood and put out his hand as the two approached. 'It seems they do, Gross. It must be something very urgent to call you away from your professorship in Prague.'

Shaking hands, they both took the measure of the other.

'You're looking fit—'

They spoke at the same time and smiled at this. It helped Werthen soothe his nerves to have Gross on hand, as well.

The door opened again and in walked Prince Montenuovo, a punctilious little man dressed in the eighteenth-century livery of a court councilor.

'So, you have been reunited,' he said. 'It is good to see you both again.'

'Save the pleasantries for later, Prince,' Gross blurted out. 'What's this all about?'

Werthen all but winced at the abruptness of Gross's query. The famed criminologist was not one for decorum.

'As you wish, gentlemen.' Montenuovo smiled with his mouth, not his eyes, and sat in a chair behind a large expanse of gilt desk. He made no offer of a seat to them, but Gross was not waiting for an invitation, dropping into a chair like a man exhausted from a long march. Werthen remained standing for a moment.

'Sit down, Werthen,' Gross commanded, as if *he* were master of the court.

'Yes,' Prince Montenuovo intoned, unruffled by Gross's brusqueness. 'Do take a seat, Herr Advokat.' He placed his delicate hands on the desk in front of him, interlocking the long fingers. 'Now, to the matter at hand. You have been summoned on a matter of the utmost urgency and secrecy.'

The prince paused dramatically to see what effect this pronouncement would have.

'One assumes so,' Gross said with a degree of irritation. 'Otherwise why would I be whisked away from pressing duties in Prague, or my esteemed friend here summoned like some common lackey?'

This comment seemed to sail over the prince's head like an evil wind to which he paid scant attention.

'I must first confirm your willingness to aid the empire in this matter. And that you will do so with the utmost discretion.'

Werthen made to speak, but once again Gross took charge. 'Well, of course we are, my good man. We're both loyal subjects.'

'Advokat Werthen?' Prince Montenuovo nodded at him.

'Doktor Gross in this case speaks for me, as well.'

'There. You see?' Gross thundered. 'Now, let's get on with it. What matter of state is there to deal with? Missing documents at the General Staff? A spy in the Ministry of War? Something we can get our teeth into, I hope.'

Prince Montenuovo again smiled with his mouth only, an expression that looked much like a grimace. 'Nothing quite so melodramatic, I am afraid, though nonetheless important to the empire. It is a matter of a missing letter.'

'Ah, a missive from one head of state to another,' Gross said. 'Information that could tip the balance of power.'

This time Montenuovo actually did grimace, Werthen noticed.

'Not quite,' he said. His hands were still interlocked on the desk in front of him, but now the knuckles were turning quite white.

'Perhaps you could apprise us of the situation without further surmises on our part,' Werthen said diplomatically, earning another scowl from Gross.

'Indeed. Yes. I assume you both know of Frau Katharina Schratt?'

'Wonderful actress,' Gross said, not offering to make it easier for Prince Montenuovo.

'Yes, of course. The star of the Burgtheater. But I also assume you know of her . . . friendship with the emperor.'

Gross continued his little game. 'I rather thought she was the favorite of our beloved empress, may she rest in peace.'

'Yes, there was that . . .' Montenuovo began.

Werthen finally came to his aid. 'We, like most of Vienna, know about the emperor's friendship with the good lady for over two decades. And of rumors that such friendship may extend beyond the platonic.'

'This missing letter, then,' Gross said, 'is from one to the other, I assume.'

'From the emperor to Frau Schratt,' Montenuovo explained.

'And it contains some evidence to indicate the non-platonic nature of their friendship?'

'There you have it, Doktor Gross. A missive of a delicate

nature that should not fall into the wrong hands. The newspapers, for example. We have press censorship here, of course, but were the letter to be sold to a foreign newspaper . . .'

'But the emperor must surely be forgiven a dalliance following the tragic assassination of his wife,' Werthen said.

The other two were silent and he slowly realized what a naïf he was.

'Oh,' he said. 'It was written while Empress Elisabeth was still alive. Is that it?'

Montenuovo nodded. 'A keepsake. A memento that Frau Schratt kept locked in her desk drawer for these many years with the waxing and waning of the special friendship. She was quite put out, you know, following the empress's death, that she was no longer protected from intrigue and calumny. Others in the royal family did not really care to see her involvement in public affairs nor her influence over the emperor.'

Montenuovo made another dramatic pause. 'It was a difficult time for the emperor, but lately they have made up. And now she has discovered this missing document. Were it to fall into the wrong hands it could prove more than a mere embarrassment.'

'What's in it, for God sake?' Gross said.

'The emperor does not say, merely that it must be found.'

'And you expect us to retrieve it?' Gross asked. 'When did it go missing?'

The prince shrugged. 'Frau Schratt is rather vague about the timing. It appears she last saw it about a week ago. Then, having cause yesterday to examine files in the locked drawer where the prized letter was kept, she discovered it had disappeared.'

'Not merely mislaid?' Werthen asked.

Montenuovo shook his head. 'She is sure of that. Apparently she went through the documents several times. It is missing. Purloined, one assumes.'

Werthen was a realist; there seemed little chance of finding the letter after several days had transpired, let alone a week.

'Why us?' Gross inquired, interrupting Werthen's thoughts.

Prince Montenuovo looked surprised. 'Well, because you have proven yourself in the past to be of service to the royal house.'

'Why not the emperor's own security detail. Or the police?'

'The emperor is fearful that such a delicate matter will get out. The more who know of the missing letter, the greater the likelihood that it will become known. Loose lips.'

Werthen was about to say that there was a greater likelihood of the letter being made public by whomever stole it, but Prince Montenuovo explained further.

'Also, quite frankly, I believe that he does not want to lose face with his inner circle. He is their father figure, the old emperor. He has no desire to display to them feet of clay.'

Gross nodded at this, but seemed unconvinced.

'And there has been no letter to the court to extort money for the return of the letter?' Werthen asked.

'None. Truth be told, we would be willing to pay far more than any newspaper. Thus . . .'

'The supposition is,' Gross said, finishing the prince's thought, 'that whoever stole the letter is not after money, but mischief. He or she wishes to inflict pain and embarrassment on the emperor.'

'Exactly.'

'Was there any sign of a break-in at Frau Schratt's residence?' Werthen asked.

'*That* we leave for you gentlemen to discover,' Montenuovo responded. 'The good frau is expecting you at her Gloriettegasse residence this very morning. You can ascertain such information as you require. You will accept the commission?'

'Do we have a choice?' Gross asked sarcastically.

'Of course we will, Prince Montenuovo,' Werthen said for them both.

'That is well. As I have said, it is a matter of the utmost urgency. The emperor will see to your university leave, Doktor Gross. And you will be recompensed for any case work you must leave for the time being, Advokat Werthen.'

Which meant, Werthen told himself, that the matter of Herr Karl's death would be placed on the back burner for now. But there was nothing for it; the emperor, perforce, came first, even if it seemed a paltry domestic matter. After all, it was the twentieth century. Who cared? Everyone knew men had affairs; most certainly powerful men. What damning information could the letter contain? he wondered.

'Well, it seems you have things all arranged, Prince,' Gross said, rising without waiting to be dismissed. 'I suppose we will be on our way.'

Montenuovo remained seated. 'We will expect daily briefings, beginning this afternoon. You may use my private telephone for messages.'

He handed across an embossed card with the double eagle prominent on it.

'You take it, Werthen,' Gross said. 'You know how I am with bits of paper.'

The prince blanched at this comment, but Gross was oblivious to the offense he gave.

'You will also each need an authorizing letter from me as proof of your royal commission.'

He handed each such a letter now, and this time Gross said nothing, merely tucking it into his coat pocket.

The lieutenant major again saw them out. There was a private fiaker now awaiting them at the front of the palace.

'At least the good frau had the decency to find a home in close proximity to the summer palace,' Gross said with heavy irony as he heaved his bulk into the carriage. It was well known that the emperor had purchased the villa for Frau Schratt exactly because of this proximity. He had a special door cut in the walls around his grounds so that he could easily visit the actress for a breakfast tête-à-tête.

# EIGHT

They made small talk as the fiaker left the palace grounds, turning right on Hietzinger Hauptstrasse and over the bridge into the cottage district beyond, and past the famed Dommayer's Casino where Johann Strauss debuted. Gross was elaborating on his latest article on the use of fingerprints in a Prague murder case as the fiaker turned right onto Gloriettegasse, a quiet, tree-lined lane full of green-shuttered baroque villas. Frau Schratt's was at number nine, painted in Habsburg yellow, as were most of the other villas on the street.

There were definite benefits to being the special friend of the emperor, Werthen thought, as he and Gross descended the carriage and approached the front door of the villa. The actress could hardly afford such a place on her ten thousand gulden per year pension from the Burgtheater.

The door opened just as Werthen was about to rap on it. They were confronted by a squat, scowling woman in a blue linen shirtwaist who had about her the appearance of a matron at a women's penitentiary. One rather long hair sprouted from a mole on her left cheek. She squinted disapprovingly at Werthen as she noticed his eyes focusing on the mole. Undoubtedly the legendary Netty, long-time housekeeper to Frau Schratt, Werthen assumed, a woman so fiercely loyal that – as gossip had it – she had kept the First Lord Chamberlain himself waiting at the doorstep in the rain while King Ferdinand I of Bulgaria, an ardent admirer of Frau Schratt, was hustled out the back entrance.

'I believe Frau Schratt is expecting us,' Gross said. 'We have come from Schönbrunn.'

The woman merely grunted at this introduction, opening the door wide enough for them to enter past her.

'You'll find my lady in the conservatory.' She set off down the entryway which led into a long interior hall. They passed a music room, a dining room, a small sitting room and finally there was quite literally light at the end of the tunnel, for they eventually entered a large glassed-in veranda and conservatory from which there were pleasant views of the snow-covered gardens to the rear of the villa. Werthen noted a number of cast-iron radiators along the walls of the vast conservatory; it was as warm as a hothouse in summer. Large potted palms dotted the expanse of tiled floor.

The housekeeper led them through a virtual jungle of palms and ferns to a far corner of the conservatory where table and chairs were gathered in a neat Biedermeier ensemble. In one of these chairs sat a woman of middle age, somewhat portly yet stately in appearance, with a magnificent head of golden hair and piercing, intelligent blue eyes. A handsome woman for almost fifty, Werthen thought. As handsome off the stage as on, for Werthen had last seen her several years earlier in the Ferdinand Raimund play, *The Spendthrift*. She had retired a couple of years ago when her friendship with the emperor was at a low ebb, and she had traveled a good deal. Now back in Vienna, she had gone back to the stage intermittently.

Frau Schratt nodded her head merely to note their arrival, sweeping a hand to two empty chairs.

'It is an honor to meet you,' Gross said, taking the lead.

'And I you,' Frau Schratt said. 'The renowned criminologist.' Then to Werthen: 'And our local legal lion.' Her smile made these meaningless puffs of flattery seem sincere. She had obviously done her homework, learning her lines like the consummate actress she was.

'Yes, quite,' Gross said, obviously feeling that he had come out the loser in these comments. 'We have spoken with Prince Montenuovo.'

She reacted to the name as if it were the scratch of a fork against a porcelain plate. 'Yes, the prince would have been appraised. I was hoping the emperor would look after this himself, however.'

It was public knowledge that Montenuovo and Frau Schratt were on less than friendly terms. The prince, like many at court, did not approve of the emperor's intimacy with the actress, not for reasons of false morality but simply because she wielded power with Franz Joseph. Some called her the uncrowned empress, and she did have his ear on matters, not only pertaining to the Burgtheater but also to matters of state.

'The missing letter,' Gross prompted. 'We have heard that it is of a rather personal nature, but is there anything else in its contents we should be concerned about?'

She cast her eyes to the domed roof of the conservatory and took a deep breath. Then, fixing her gaze on Gross, she said, 'If you mean that someone mentioned in the letter might benefit from possessing it, then no. That is not the case. There are matters of a rather personal nature in it, as you indicated. I kept it because it is the dearest love letter I have ever received.'

'But?' Gross said, sensing that something else was on offer.

'Well, if you must know, there are also references to a personage that were better kept from the public eye.'

Werthen and Gross said nothing, waiting for Frau Schratt to complete the thought.

She sighed – a dramatic gesture Werthen had witnessed her perform on the stage, a gesture filled with both longing and regret.

'The emperor makes a rather critical comment of the German Kaiser in the letter. Humorous, but if made public it could badly damage relations between our countries.'

'We understand that you noticed only yesterday that the letter was missing,' Werthen said.

'That is correct.'

'Was there any sign that the drawer where it was kept was interfered with?'

'No.' Another monumental sigh from Frau Schratt. She knew where this was headed.

'We need to examine all the outer doors,' Werthen said.

'Please do,' she said. 'But I doubt you will find anything. My son, Toni, examined the exterior doors closely yesterday and could find no sign of the locks being tampered with.'

'Still . . .' Werthen said.

'Be my guest. I fear, however, that what we have is, as the Americans so charmingly say, an "inside job," which pains me greatly. It means that someone on my staff is responsible for the theft. Someone I trust and treat almost as family.'

'Let us examine things first before coming to that conclusion,' Gross pronounced.

They did so for the next hour, closely examining all outer doors and locks for any telltale signs of forced entry or the use of picks. The same was true for ground-floor windows, all inspected for any suspicious scratches at hinges or latches. They also paid close attention to the inlaid Louis XVI escritoire in question, a fine specimen, Werthen thought, in oak with a pear wood veneer and inlays in the drawers below. Not something the one buys on the stipend from the Burgtheater. They examined the bottom right-hand drawer where the letter had been kept, careful to use a piece of silk cloth Gross always carried with him.

'We'll need to brush this down, Werthen, for fingerprints. I must confess I was in such a hurry this morning that I left my traveling kit back at the hotel.' He pulled out a small magnifying glass from an interior pocket, eyeballed the outside of the drawer and made an explosive sound of disgust. 'Though I doubt we will come up with any discrete set of prints. One wonders about the general condition of the Villa Schratt if this drawer is any indication. It looks as if it has not been wiped down in months.'

Later, examining the rest of the study where the escritoire was located, Gross quipped, 'There is not even a chimney for the chap to drop down in.'

A bad sign, Werthen thought, for it was neither funny nor practical. It indicated the criminologist had come to the same conclusion as Frau Schratt.

'We need to talk to the staff individually,' Gross quickly added.

This took another three hours, twenty minutes of which were wasted in convincing Frau Schratt that her housekeeper, Netty, should be included in the list.

'She will not be treated as a suspect,' Gross finally argued, 'but she is a most valuable witness with regards to the rest of the staff. She surely knows their little habits and quirks. Their weak points and strengths.'

In the event, Netty proved less cooperative than hoped, bristling at their questions, insulted that she be included along with the other staff. They were finally able to ascertain that she, along with Frau Schratt, possessed a set of keys to the bureau in question, but that she had not used the set in months. Indeed, the house had been closed up until recently, when Frau Schratt returned to Vienna.

'Then the staff is quite new,' Werthen said.

'No. Frau Schratt kept them all on retainer during her travels. Not what I advised, of course. Idle hands and all that. But she is a good and loyal employer. She hardly deserves such treachery.'

Gross quickly pounced on this comment. 'Then you believe it is one of the staff?'

'I'm sure I could not say. You're the famous detective. I leave it up to you.'

'Do you always keep your keys on your person?' Werthen asked.

Netty cast him a look as if he had just proposed an immoral act. 'I most certainly do not. When not needed, they hang from the hook by the cupboard.'

She pointed in back of them. Seated around the pine table in the kitchen, both Gross and Werthen turned to see the large ring of house keys hanging just where Netty indicated.

Available to anyone who might want to use them.

They proceeded to speak with the gardener, who did not live on the premises – one Herr Johann Pinkl, whose gnarled hands and lumbering demeanor was at odds with the image of someone rifling through papers in a bureau drawer. Gross handed him a recipe that was lying on the kitchen table for today's dinner.

'Looks like fine fare tonight,' Gross said with bonhomie.

Johann fiddled with the paper, turning it this way and then that, reddening as he did so. 'I suppose so,' he finally said. 'I don't go in much for fancy food.'

'I hardly call boiled beef fancy,' Gross replied.

'Not something I care for,' the gardener said with a scowl.

Gross dismissed him after another desultory question about his duties.

When he was gone, Gross turned to Werthen.

'Not him. The man wouldn't know one letter from another. He's illiterate. Carp is on the menu for tonight, not boiled beef.'

And so they continued, through the parlor maid, the upstairs maid, the cook and the coachman, none of whom seemed anything less than honest, loyal and a bit plodding.

The kitchen assistant, Fräulein Anna, was a different matter, however. Twenty at most, she was a mousey little thing whose face went red at Gross's first question and blazed on through his questioning about keys and proper etiquette for the staff – all of it oblique, for none of the staff aside from Netty knew of the missing letter. They had been told they were being interviewed by two gentlemen of the press for an article about their famous mistress. Anna squirmed and fidgeted through the entire affair, making Werthen, for one, most suspicious.

But when she too finished the interview, Gross only commented, 'Simple soul.'

'You saw how nervous she was, Gross,' Werthen said. 'Definitely makes me wonder.'

'The girl would fidget if you said good morning. A simple country child.'

'From Floridsdorf,' Werthen insisted. 'Hardly the country.'

'Well, then, let us search her room. Netty will have to manufacture some excuse to get her out of the house.'

Once Anna was dispatched on an urgent trip to the market, Gross and Werthen went through her small room at the top of the house with the utmost care. Werthen was struck by the absence of anything of a personal nature – not even a Bible. And definitely no purloined letter from the emperor of all Austria.

'As I said . . .' Gross began.

'She could have already passed it on to an accomplice.'

'Accomplices now?' Gross said. 'Yes, I imagine there would have to be.'

He sat on the spare metal cot the young serving girl slept on. 'Time may be against us, but I am afraid that it is the only avenue we have.'

'Would you care to include me in this conversation, Gross? What avenue?'

'I believe we need to insert someone into the staff. Someone who will pose as one of them, who will be able to gain the trust of the others. Someone, in short, who will be our spy.'

'You were right with your first statement. We don't have the time for such a maneuver. This could hit the newspapers at any moment.'

'Which we cannot stop at any rate if the letter has already been handed on to your accomplice.'

'Not my accomplice, Gross. Merely my assumption.'

'At least it is a course of action, Werthen. What do you propose – thumbscrews for Fräulein Anna?'

Neither Frau Schratt nor Prince Montenuovo were enthusiastic about the plan, but finally agreed when Gross assured him that it would not be their sole means of investigation. He promised that he and Werthen would continue to look into the backgrounds of each of those on the staff and continue to collect any information from their associates – meaning connections Gross and Werthen had in the underworld who might have heard of someone trying to shop such a high-profile letter.

They returned to Werthen's law office in the afternoon and began going over plans to insert someone in the Schratt household. Young Franzl brought in the afternoon papers as usual and listened in on their conversation for a moment.

'I'll do it,' he said brightly. 'Sounds like fun and I wouldn't be in the office all day long.'

'I didn't know it was so painful for you to be here,' Werthen teased.

The boy did not catch Werthen's tone, however. 'No, I didn't mean it that way. I love being here. It's just that this is a way I can really help out. Carry my own weight.'

Werthen had a sudden flash of panic, remembering their other office boy, the street urchin, Heidrich Beer, who they had dubbed Huck. He too had become involved – quite by accident – in a case Werthen was investigating and had ended up under the wheels of a train.

'I think it is a marvelous idea,' Gross said, fixing Werthen with a stare that let the lawyer know that he, Gross, was aware of his thoughts. 'Franzl here is an observant and outgoing young chap, and that is exactly what we need. Someone to make friends inside the Schratt household and to keep his eyes open.'

'I can do it, I know,' Franzl said earnestly.

'It's hardly a risky affair,' Gross said. 'We're not investigating a crime of violence, after all.'

Werthen thought about it a moment longer. 'Well, if you really want to,' he said to Franzl. 'But let's set some limits as to what you attempt to do.'

For the next hour the three of them huddled in conference at Werthen's desk, mapping out Franzl's role in the household. They wanted him in particular to get close to the kitchen assistant, Fräulein Anna; they would have Frau Schratt insert him as scullery boy to aid the aging cook. By the looks of her legs wrapped in heavy gauze, it was apparent the woman was suffering from varicose veins and could thus use an extra pair of hands. It was further determined that Franzl would not go snooping about in other people's rooms. He was simply to make friends with those he could and not be too obvious about it. To become a confidante, if possible. To keep his ears open.

'I could do that,' Franzl piped in. 'The captain showed me how to make nice with the other riders at the stables and not to make them suspicious of me.'

He was referring to his association with the lead rider of the Spanish Riding School, a man of meager background who was able to rise above his class and who had taken Franzl under his wing. Captain Putter was an honorable man; too honorable, as he took his own life over the discovery of a scandal with the famed Lipizzaners.

'I am sure you can, Franzl,' Werthen said. The boy had lost both parents when he was nine and his beloved mentor, Captain Putter, at ten. He had had enough troubles already in his short life. Werthen only hoped that he was not creating more for him.

# NINE

He was pleased to be back in Vienna.

He never thought he would say that, not even to himself. After all, Vienna was the scene of his disgrace, of his undoing. It had spelled the end of his career as a Russian agent.

But now it would be the scene of his rebirth, of his greatest achievement as a freelance agent.

*Freelance.*

He liked the sound of the word, for he was indeed a medieval mercenary warrior.

He pulled the comforter up over his left ear. He slept on his side, always his right side. To sleep on the left would mean cutting off the blood supply to the heart, slowing down his reaction time. He would not be slow to react ever again.

The landlady, Frau Geldner, ran a pension not far from the Empress Elisabeth West Train Station. She smoked a meerschaum pipe and affected a rough working-class accent, but she was as clandestine as he was. Far from being uneducated, she wrote for the anarchist papers throughout Europe and knew how to be discreet with her guests. The Pension Geldner was a byword in his profession. Indeed, he had stayed here the previous time, as well, but Frau Geldner was perfectly content to pretend that she did not recognize him.

*Freelance.* He closed his eyes and thought once again of his return to St Petersburg in disgrace, of being condemned to the Siberian camps. But most of all he could see each movement of his escape en route to the camps.

I will call myself Wenno, he thought as the guard slumped at his feet. Wenno, the famous master of the thirteenth-century Livonian Brothers of the Sword, the warrior monks who, like the Order of the Teutonic Knights, battled to convert the pagans.

Looking down at the man at his feet, he figured that this was one pagan who would not eat his borscht tonight. He leaned over, though, putting a manacled hand to the man's jugular to be sure. He was a thorough agent, trained in such things. The bruising at the neck where he had strangled the guard with his chains was already showing.

There was little time now for reflection. He searched the dead man's pockets, found a ring of keys, fitted several in turn into the lock of his manacles until he found the one that fit and freed himself.

He rubbed his wrists and ankles. He would never allow himself to be put in chains again. Ever.

It took him only three more minutes to strip the guard in the station bathroom – for he had feigned illness as the train pulled into Omsk station – and exchange clothing. His luck held. No one came in the bathroom during these critical moments. Just as he finished dressing, he heard footsteps approaching the door. He quickly dragged the dead guard into a toilet stall, propped him on the seatless toilet then counted a beat, waiting for the newcomer to enter the bathroom and find another vacant stall before he opened his stall door and left.

Back on the platform, he decided he would need to find a change of clothes soon; something that fit him better, and something that bore no connection to the Russian army.

Agent 302 no longer had any loyalty to that service.

The uniform earned him free passage in a third-class carriage to St Petersburg. A widow with a lunch basket on her way to relatives in Moscow took pity on the poor soldier and shared her food with him for over two days, and then left one scrap of sausage as she disembarked at Moskovsky station. Half a day later he reached St Petersburg and there, hungry and broke, he took up watch across the street from the massive Ministry of Agriculture on St Isaac's Square. It was Friday, pay day, and he was waiting for early leavers which would indicate higher-ranking bureaucrats and thus those with a fatter pay packet.

He let over a dozen men pass him without following them as they were larger than he was – the wrong fit. Finally, late in the afternoon, he saw the perfect victim crossing the square, tapping the left breast of his long-tailed suit coat as if making sure that his pay packet was safely tucked away. He let the man get beyond the equestrian monument to Nicholas I in the middle of the square, then took up the tail a discreet distance behind. It required great effort to restrain himself as the man headed for an inn on a side street off the square. How much would he spend in there? What fine food and drink would he partake of?

But agent 302 was disciplined; he knew he had to wait for the welcoming darkness of night, knew he could not follow the man into the inn, for he had no money to buy so much as a glass of vodka. He bided his time, strolling with hands behind his back like a soldier on patrol. A civilian now and again saluted him and he wished he could reach out and strangle the person, the dumb satisfied oxen that passed for much of humanity. Those people with their simpering wives and mewling children awaiting them in cramped flats; how he loathed them and their smug, secure lives. Lives that held no risk, no thumping of the heart, exhilaration at the kill. Those who lived their small lives in quiet, senseless anonymity.

Soon his quarry came out of the inn, a toothpick in his mouth, and headed north along the quay of the Moyka River. Suddenly it struck him that darkness would not fall for another number of hours, at least eleven at night at this time of year. Could he wait that long? How much of the man's pay packet would be left by then? And if, as he suspected, the man was headed for the shops of Nevsky Prospect, there might be precious few rubles left by the time darkness fell. He must improvise and quickly before more of the money was spent, for he noticed as well that the man, formerly wearing a wedding ring, had taken it off, which could mean only one thing: an amorous assignation was in the offing. Most likely one that dealt not only in an exchange of bodily fluids, but also in currency.

When they reached the Red Bridge, where Gorokhovaya Street crossed the Moyka, he determined to act. He caught up with the man and put a strong grip on his shoulder. The man spun around, muttering, 'What the—'

He cut him off. 'Citizen, your section chief at the Ministry of Agriculture hoped that I could track you down. It is imperative that you meet with him.'

'Proschkova? What could he want at this time of day?'

'Privy Councilor Proschkova,' he said, improvising, 'requests that you meet with him at a house quite near here, as a matter of fact. He sends his apologies, but deems it quite urgent.'

'Urgent? But how?' the bureaucrat said.

'That is not for me to know, Councilor.' He figured he was giving the man an upgrade in title, and noticed with satisfaction a trace of a smile on the man's thick lips, still working the toothpick.

'Well,' he finally sighed, 'I had other plans, but if Proschkova commands I must obey.'

He set off quickly across the bridge to the other side of the Moyka, making the bureaucrat scramble to keep up with him, giving him no time to think how irregular this all was.

He went several blocks toward the River Neva before he found a quiet street filled with large old apartment buildings. An elderly tenant was just exiting the front door of one and he quickly caught the door before it locked again. He held it politely for the bureaucrat.

'But Proschkova lives nowhere near here.'

'It is the house of a colleague,' he explained, leading the man deeper into the large entryway. His instincts had been right; the apartment building had several staircases leading to different landings. The third staircase was deepest in the central foyer and it spiraled up to the left, creating a hidden space in the corner beneath.

'The privy councilor said he would leave the key here,' he said as he ducked under the staircase.

The bureaucrat waited by the staircase instead of following as he had hoped. More improvising, acting as if fumbling in the gloom of the stairwell.

'Sorry, sir,' he said. 'My eyes have never been the same since Manchuria.'

This seemed to interest the man. As he ducked under the spiraling staircase, he said, 'So you fought during the Boxer Rebellion.'

But he never heard the response to his question, for agent 302 struck him a sudden blow to the sternum in just the right place to disrupt the rhythm of the heart. The man made a grunting sound as he crumpled to the cobbled floor and was dead by the time the agent leaned over to check for a pulse. Now came a frenzied change of clothing; he had been right about the man's size, for the clothes fit well. He left his old clothing and the body of the man – Nikolai Petrovich, as his document pouch identified him – under the stairs and quickly made his way out of the building without encountering anyone.

You make your luck, he told himself. You act with courage and fortitude and no one can stop you.

The rubles in the dead man's pay packet purchased him a first-class seat on the Tallinn express; the suit of clothes guaranteed his continuing anonymity. He took a much-needed bath at the station before departure.

Soon he would be free.

As the train sped along the flat farmland, he peered through his own reflection in the glass, an instant doppelgänger. It had been so for many years. Born Pietr Klavan, an Estonian who at one time had prospects of a career as a concert violinist, he had assumed numerous identities over the years. In Vienna he was Schmidt, representative of the Heisl Parfumerie; in Berlin he was Erlanger, a Hungarian rail engineer; in Warsaw he was de Koenig, the agent of a Dutch mining concern; in Zurich he was Axel Wouters, rubber merchant; and in Prague he was Maarkovsky, an importer of Polish vodka. He had posed as policeman, actor, wine grower and noble.

In each of those cities he had left dead bodies behind. Dead at the behest of his Russian handlers.

And it had been those same handlers who had turned against him, who had sent him off to the slow death of the *katorga*, the work camps in Siberia. They had to save their own careers for the death of a certain double agent in Vienna, and he was the sacrificial lamb.

But no longer.

Now he had another new identity: Herr Wenno.

He smiled at the thought. Wenno the warrior knight who would no longer fight the secret battles for the Russians but who would engage as his own man, his own warrior. An assassin for hire.

It was what he was best at; now it would be in his own service.

He awoke in the middle of the night, a troubled thought teasing at the back of his mind. Something left undone. A loose thread that might come unraveled. He turned onto his back; he would not sleep until he parsed this puzzle. And then it came to him. The under waiter; the colleague and perhaps the protégé of the older man. Had those two spoken of him? Had the Herr Ober taken the younger man into his confidence?

There was no way to discover that. At least not quickly, and time was of the essence now. But he did know the other waiter was watching him when he spoke to Herr Karl. He could provide a description.

No. This was not a time for subtlety.

It was a time for action. His handler at the Russian training school had taught him that axiom: when in doubt, strike.

# TEN

'**B**etween Frau Schratt's old rivals at the Burgtheater and those at court, I think there are enough suspects to go around,' Gross said, finishing his brioche with a flourish.

There had been no opportunity to talk about the case last night, for Werthen's parents had joined them for dinner and they had been sworn to secrecy.

Berthe, however, was a different matter.

'And what about the son?' she offered. 'He may have issues with the emperor. There could be jealousy or anger at the man who has taken so much emotional charge from his mother, who did not come to her aid after the death of the empress. And there is the fact, as I learned from Herr Sonnenthal, of the grandfather executed long ago on the order of a very young Franz Josef.'

'It's a possibility,' Werthen allowed. 'But it is also dangerous ground, questioning the son of Frau Schratt.'

'In fact, I have him on my provisionary list,' Gross said, eyeing the remaining brioche in the basket. Frau Blatschky had gone out early this morning to the Elias Bakery to fetch the criminologist's favorite breakfast rolls. 'However, from what one hears, the emperor has treated the young man rather well, seeing to his education and to prospects in the foreign service.'

Berthe had a sudden inspiration: thinking of Toni Schratt reminded her further of the seance she attended over the weekend. It was a performance that seemed guaranteed to embarrass the young man. And according to Berthe's friend, Rosa Mayreder, it might very well be part of a concerted effort on the part of Princess Dumbroski to undermine Frau Schratt's role as the hostess of choice in Vienna.

She mentioned the princess and was met by dumbfounded stares from the men.

'You actually think the woman would hire someone to steal a compromising letter from Frau Schratt just to gain a social advantage? And risk having the emperor turn against her?' Werthen was appalled at the idea.

'She fought a duel over a flower arrangement,' Berthe said flatly. 'Yes. Where Princess Dumbroski is concerned, I think anything is possible.'

'Well,' Gross said, finally giving in to temptation and taking the last roll. 'It looks like we all have our hands full, then.'

'I was rather hoping you could follow up on the Herr Karl affair,' Werthen said to his wife. 'Perhaps approach the archduke or Prince Montenuovo to get an appointment with Czerny at the Hofburg.'

'I could do both,' she said.

'It's settled then,' Gross said. 'We each have our tasks. But may I recommend, Frau Meisner, that you begin with the princess. Time is of the essence.'

Gross said her name with a slight lilt of sarcasm as he always did. The criminologist did not approve of modern women who kept their maiden names when marrying.

Werthen was not sure, but he thought he also caught a hint of insincerity in Gross's tone about time being of the essence.

Franzl thought it was a treat to be decked out in knee pants and apron. He was assigned the potatoes his first morning. He had to scrub them clean. Beautiful little round golden things, first of the season. It seemed Frau Schratt fancied her potatoes with the skins on, so it was Franzl's first task in the household to see to it there was not a speck of earth left on them.

He worked away in a corner of the large and gloomy kitchen downstairs from the main rooms. It had been a busy day so far, he thought as he scrubbed away at the potatoes with the wooden-handled brush. They'd been delivered at six a.m. promptly by a fiaker. Frau Schratt had introduced him to the cook, who'd seemed unimpressed, and to Fräulein Anna, the other kitchen helper, who'd given him a sweet smile. It was she that Advokat Werthen explained they especially wanted him to watch. But now that he'd met her, Franzl could not understand why. Anna seemed like someone who wouldn't even hurt a fly. She kindly showed him the proper way to clean the potatoes: not so hard as to disturb the skin, just the right pressure.

'Frau Schratt's very particular about her potatoes,' she told him.

'I'm sure you've got other things to do, Anna,' the cook said then. 'The boy's come to make our lives easier, not more difficult.'

Anna winked at him as she scurried off to feed the boiler more coal. He was amazed; the house had what they called central heating. This was the life.

Berthe met Rosa Mayreder at the Café Eiles just down the street from her apartment later that morning. They had tea and Berthe explained as much as she could to her friend about her reasons for wanting to get to know the princess better.

'This mysterious investigation of yours had better be important,' Rosa said. 'The princess is not someone you want as an enemy.'

'I can see that,' Berthe said. 'If you could just introduce us formally . . . I had no chance to meet her last Saturday.'

'She likes it better that way. Fans not friends.'

It had been several years since Werthen last spoke with Alexander Girardi, famed actor, comedian and tenor. Werthen and Gross's first case, investigating the murder of Gustav Klimt's model, had taken them to the dressing room of the actor, for he, like Klimt, had been carrying on an affair with the unfortunate young woman. Girardi had not been implicated in the murder, nor had he been able to supply any valuable information. Werthen was hoping that this time things would be different.

Frau Schratt and Girardi were old friends; some said one-time lovers. What Werthen knew for sure was that Girardi was in Frau Schratt's debt, for it was she who interceded with the emperor in 1896 when Girardi's estranged wife attempted to have him committed to an asylum. Now, happily divorced from said wife, Girardi was once again the uncrowned king of Vienna, copied in dress and manner by the stage-happy populace, and Werthen was hoping the man could tell him who Frau Schratt's professional enemies might be.

Girardi's home in the cottage district north of Vienna in Döbling belied his humble roots, the son of a locksmith in Graz. The villa looked large enough for several families; a bachelor like Girardi could get lost in its many rooms.

Frau Schratt had arranged the interview for Werthen; a servant let him in at the appointed hour and took him to a small music room where Girardi was busy working on the role of Kálmán Zsupán, the wealthy pig farmer from Strauss's operetta, *The Gypsy Baron*. It was one of the few operettas Werthen – no fan of light opera – had ever seen. Werthen was astounded to find Girardi in full costume with a ridiculous fake beard, moustaches spit-turned at the ends and a comical hat perched atop his head, its brim turned upward like a breakfast roll.

He stood in the doorway without interrupting as Girardi finished the scene, a recording of the orchestral version playing on an Edison phonograph. Werthen was struck by the consummate professionalism of the man. Girardi had premiered the role of Kálmán Zsupán and had perfected it: he *was* Kálmán Zsupán. Yet here he stood in full costume working on it as if he were fresh to the stage.

Girardi, aware of Werthen's attention, ended the rendition with a flourish, bowing deeply to his audience of one.

Werthen could not stop himself from clapping; the actor's impish enthusiasm was infectious.

'Yes, I do recall you now,' Girardi said as they sat opposite each other at a small, delicately inlaid table freshly laid with a silver pot of hot coffee. Girardi laid his comical hat on the table and poured himself a cup. Werthen declined.

'That sorry business with Liesel,' Girardi said.

Fräulein Elisabeth Landtauer was the model whose death had spurred Werthen's first investigative efforts. He was happy to note that Girardi had not forgotten the young woman; it made him seem more human. More human also was his reversal to the twang of Viennese dialect, which the actor had perfected so well.

'Yes, quite sad,' Werthen said, not wanting to go too deeply into that affair, as it had ultimately led to the very gates of the Hofburg. 'About Frau Schratt . . .'

'Is she in danger? Just what is this about?'

'I am not at liberty to discuss the details of the investigation, Herr Girardi. I do not believe she is in any physical danger, but

it would seem she has an enemy or enemies that wish her ill.
Let us leave it at that.'

'How can I help? Kathi is the dearest friend. She has been
there for me when I've needed her. I'll gladly return the favor.'

For once the actor sounded as if he were not on stage.

'Who might wish to see her harmed, discredited? We are not
talking about petty jealousies here but real animosity.'

'Does this have to do with the emperor?'

Werthen ignored the question. 'Can you think of anyone that
might fit that description?'

Girardi shrugged. 'In the theater? There are several. In real
life,' he swept his hand dramatically as if implying that his
Döbling villa represented reality and not the stage, 'very doubtful.
Kathi is the kindest woman I know. She is the sort to take in
strays, to help out complete strangers.'

'In the theater, then.'

'One makes enemies in such a hothouse environment,' Girardi
said. 'There are only so many roles, so many good parts.'

'But she's virtually retired.'

Girardi smiled at this. 'Actresses never retire, Advokat. They
may perform less, but they never take a final curtain willingly.
Also, Kathi has *Protektion* – connections.'

'The emperor?'

The actor nodded. 'She is loath to use this influence, but those
who are against her do not believe that. They see her standing
in the way of progress at the Burg – keeping the young actresses
back, interfering with the management of the house.'

'Names?'

'Surmise, Advokat. Merely that.'

'Understood. I am not assuming guilt, merely looking for a
direction in which to move forward.'

'Two people come immediately to mind. Fräulein Maria
Theresa Greilin and Herr Director Schlenther. The one is a
budding star at the Burg and the other—'

'The director of the Burgtheater.'

'He and Kathi have been at each other's throats since he
arrived in Vienna in 1898. Up to then, Kathi had been the queen
of the Burg, the people's favorite and the emperor's special
friend. She had her pick of roles, some of which might have
been more appropriate, truth be told, for younger actresses. She

advocates for her friends and, when under contract, had leave time that left most wishing they knew an emperor. That changed with Schlenther's arrival. He's a stolid Prussian and could not tolerate interference in the affairs of the Burg. Subsequently, Kathi's contracts were brought more in line with others at the Burg. But it bred animosity and led to Kathi attempting in every way possible to dislodge the director. She is a very powerful woman, our Kathi, and she has very powerful friends. The one thing saving Schlenther is Prince Montenuovo's dislike for Kathi.'

In addition to his other roles at court, Werthen knew that Montenuovo also was in charge of the court theaters.

'And Fräulein Greilin?'

'She is a Schlenther protégé. Quite talented, really. But not favored by Kathi. I fear Kathi has another favorite, young Fräulein Minter, born in Baden bei Wien and the daughter of a grocer, just like Kathi. The girl has become something of a surrogate daughter, and Kathi does campaign for her. She may be officially retired, you see, but she keeps her hand in the thespian ring. There was a public altercation between the two . . .' Girardi sighed at the thought. 'Very unprofessional on the part of Fräulein Greilin, but she is young and feels that her career is threatened.'

Werthen made note of both of these. 'No others?'

A shaking of his head. 'As you say, petty jealousies.' He rose, putting his comical hat on once again, his features transforming before Werthen's eyes. He was Kálmán Zsupán.

'And now, I fear, I must return to my rehearsal. There is a performance in three days' time. Do give my best to Kathi. And if there is anything else I can do . . .'

'You've been more than helpful,' Werthen said, taking his cue to leave.

They arrived at the Ringstrasse apartment of Princess Dumbroski at exactly one in the afternoon, as arranged. Frau Mayreder used the excuse of a forgotten reticule from the Saturday seance for this appointment.

As they ascended in the elevator to the third floor, Frau Mayreder said, 'I still do not know what you hope to accomplish by such a visit. You are being awfully closed-mouth about it all.'

Berthe smiled at her friend. 'You'll have to trust me, Rosa. It is a matter of state, but that is all I can tell you.'

'What an exciting life you live with that investigator husband of yours. I assume it is some sort of private inquiry.'

Another smile. 'And how do you know it is not my own case?' Berthe said, which brought a shade of pink to the cheeks of Rosa Mayreder, the great proponent of women's rights.

Berthe patted the woman's forearm. 'It's quite all right, Rosa. I am guilty of the same. Remind me I have a doctor's appointment and I imagine an imposing male figure in white coat.'

'And if *we* do it, think how long it will take to change the world.'

The lift reached the third floor with a sudden jolt, rocking them as they stood by its door.

A maid answered the door of Princess Dumbroski's apartment on the second knock. Rosa Mayreder supplied their names and the woman said, 'She is expecting you. This way.'

The apartment proved to be rather cavernous, with a number of white lacquered doors leading off a main hallway. As they proceeded they could hear a metallic clinking as of small imperfect bells being sounded. The maid finally stopped in front of a pair of doors behind which the clinking sound seemed to emanate.

She threw open the doors to display a scene out of a mad painting by Bosch. There in front of them was Princess Dumbroski, attired in tights and fencing mask, a foil in her hand and nothing on her torso. She was circling a young woman in the same attire, or lack thereof. Blood streamed from a wound on this woman's left bicep. Their bare breasts heaved as they circled and parried, taking deep breaths. The foils had no *fleuret* at the tip to blunt the sharp point; they were fighting, it appeared, for real. The princess made a sudden thrust which the other woman blocked, but it was merely a feint, for Princess Dumbroski quickly brought her blade to the left now, slashing at the woman's upraised forearm, cutting and bringing more blood.

'*C'est tout!*' the princess shouted. 'I have scored twice. Sufficient for today.'

She lifted her mask up; her face was filled with a fierce animal passion.

The other woman also lifted her mask. 'My apologies, Princess.

I lost my concentration.' She glanced at Berthe and Rosa Mayreder standing in the doorway, slack-jawed as if to blame them.

'Yes, but the first cut came *before* our visitors. Enough. Have those wounds attended to.'

She approached the other, gave her a formal kiss on each cheek and then, pausing, kissed her on the lips.

The other fencer passed by Berthe and Frau Mayreder, making a low, undecipherable sound as she did so. It was clear to Berthe that this woman did not appreciate their presence.

Princess Dumbroski made no attempt to cover her breasts as she turned her attention to them.

'How do you like my little gymnasium?' The princess, still holding her foil, swept it about the large room proprietarily.

It was indeed appointed as a room for gymnasts with its floor mats, balance beam, leather-covered horse and dangling rings. In one corner lay a set of dumbbells.

'What's good enough for the empress is good enough for me,' the princess said breezily.

The Empress Elisabeth, assassinated four years earlier, had been an enthusiast of physical exercise, outfitting rooms at the Hofburg and at Schönbrunn with similar exercise paraphernalia.

'And like the ancient Greeks, we prefer to take our exercise *au naturel.*'

Berthe, who had made a study of Greek, understood the implied joke, for the word was derived from *gymnos*, which meant naked: ancient athletes trained in that state. The irony was that the word gymnasium in German referred to a preparatory high school. Berthe could hardly imagine the young scholars at the elite Theresianum Gymnasium going about their Latin studies *au naturel*.

'She was bleeding,' Rosa Mayreder said, still somewhat shocked at the scene.

'Just a knick. I know when to stop.' She fixed her eyes on Berthe now. 'And I know when to inflict pain.'

Berthe felt herself redden at the comment. She could never control this blushing that would start at her chest and blossomed up her neck. Fortunately, she was wearing a high lace collar today.

'So, Frau Mayreder, you have misplaced your reticule. We are no train station maintaining a lost and found, but I am sure Elise will do what she can to look for it.'

The princess pulled a bell rope on the wall in back of her, next to a window looking out on the Ringstrasse. The maid who had let them in promptly came to the door.

'Elise, perhaps you can assist Frau Mayreder. She seems to have misplaced a reticule.'

'Madam,' the woman said by way of response, nodding her head.

'And while you are about your business, perhaps your young friend and I can get to know each other.'

It was what Berthe had been hoping for, but suddenly she was not so sure she wanted an intimate tête-à-tête with the princess. She felt out of her depth, on her guard.

But Rosa Mayreder did not sense this, leaving the two to their discussion as she searched for the fictional reticule.

Once the door was closed, Princess Dumbroski looked closely at Berthe. A towel hung from the back of a chair, but still the woman made no effort to cover herself. Berthe tried to focus on her face.

'Now, Frau Meisner, perhaps you can tell me what this little farce is all about?'

'Berthe, please,' she said, still trying to follow her original plan of somehow becoming friendly enough with the princess to discover helpful information.

The woman tilted her head to the side as if to examine a rare art work.

'I use Christian names only with those I am intimate with, Frau Meisner. And you should know that I really do not have friends. Allies, yes. Friends, very sparingly. Is that what this little ruse about the missing handbag is about? You want to be my ally?'

She took several steps toward Berthe, who still stood by the door.

The princess was now only a step away from her as she spoke: 'Or do you seek something more intimate?'

Berthe tried to laugh it off. 'You have caught me out, Princess. I am one of those curious Viennese who wishes to know more about a woman who duels, who holds seances.'

A half-step closer. Princess Dumbroski shook her head.

She was close enough now for Berthe to smell the sweat on her. She swallowed hard.

'I think not,' Princess Dumbroski said. 'You know what I do think, though, Frau Meisner? I think you may be working with your husband, Advokat Werthen, in a desperate attempt to find a missing letter belonging to a certain washed-up actress who has an inflated opinion of her importance to an aged ruler.'

Berthe struggled to keep her expression from giving her away, but it was not her expression that did so.

'I see by the extreme coloring rising from your neck and spreading to your cheeks that my surmise is correct.' She reached out with her left hand and brushed Berthe's cheek as proof. The foil still remained in her right hand.

'You see, I have my allies in many places. There is not much that happens in Vienna that I am not aware of. Of importance, that is.'

Another half step closed the distance between them. Berthe made to move back, but her back was against the doorjamb. Princess Dumbroski's face was next to hers. She could feel the woman's breath on her.

'I could always use another ally,' she said. 'Or another intimate. A beautiful woman like you must have allies, too. Or intimates.'

She kissed her on the mouth before Berthe could move her head.

'I think I had better leave,' Berthe finally said, finding her voice.

'As you wish,' the princess said, stepping back now and whipping foil in the air like a riding crop. 'Next time you come, don't bring the old woman.'

Berthe wanted to strangle her. Rage built like damned-up waters ready to break through. She turned to go.

'And Frau Meisner, for your troubles, I had nothing to do with the missing letter. But that woman has plenty of other enemies. Don't forget the son. Family revenge is a powerful motive.'

Berthe could listen to the woman's insidious tone no longer. She burst through the double doors and into the hallway, eager to find Rosa Mayreder and be gone. Laughter followed her down the hall as she brushed the despised kiss from her lips.

# ELEVEN

Gross was in no hurry. For him, this was an exercise in futility, but the emperor requested it and there was an end to it. It needed to look like a formal investigation. Mundane, though. And a pity. It would all end badly.

He needed a bit of exercise, hoping to work off the lunch of *blutwurst* and *knödel* he had just consumed, so he strolled along the Ringstrasse, headed toward the Third District and Favoritengasse. Yesterday's snow was already turning into a slushy mess.

It took him a half hour to reach the Consular Wing of the Theresianum on Favoritengasse, location of the elite Consular Academy, formerly the Oriental Academy, where the empire's best and brightest were trained for the diplomatic corps. Gross had no intention of interviewing Frau Schratt's only son, Baron Anton Kiss, in her premises or in her presence; he would much rather conduct such a discussion on the neutral grounds of the school where he was in training.

A liveried servant in white gloves stood at the entrance to the Consular Wing. Gross introduced himself and his reason for visiting and the servant led him into an interior courtyard and up a flight of stairs to a suite of rooms appointed in proper imperial style.

The servant led Gross to a waiting area. 'I will announce you to the director,' he said, and then scurried off to the largest corner office.

Several minutes later he was ushered into the director's office, whose door held a brass plaque announcing its occupant: Michael Pidoll von Quitenbach. The director was an austere-looking man, bald, with white fringes and a Van Dyke beard and moustache of the same whiteness. His skin was also of a powdered pallor; the only bit of color on his face was his defiantly black eyebrows. He was dressed formally in the black cutaway of the foreign service, standing behind a vast cherrywood desk as Gross entered.

'And how may I assist the eminent criminologist?' von

Quitenbach said, his accent more high German than Austrian. As always, Gross was pleased by his name recognition, but it did not appear the director was any too pleased to greet him. A dyspeptic scowl appeared to be his standard facial expression, even when talking, which was, Gross thought, quite an achievement.

'I need to talk with one of your young scholars,' Gross said, taking the chair opposite the director. 'Baron Anton Kiss.'

Von Quitenbach's eyebrows lifted. 'The baron. May I inquire why you wish to see him?'

'I'm afraid not, Herr Director.' He reached into his breast pocket and brought out the authorizing letter Prince Montenuovo had given to him and Werthen. The man read the brief note without expression.

Handing it back, von Quitenbach asked, 'Where would you like to meet with the baron?'

'This office should suffice,' Gross said with a degree of impish satisfaction. That'll teach the fellow to scowl at me, he thought.

Von Quitenbach stiffened at the suggestion but, a loyal bureaucrat, he made no protest.

'I shall await you in my assistant's office.'

Gross imagined a game of musical offices as the pecking order came into play, dislodging one underling after the other from his office.

It took several minutes, but finally Baron Kiss was shown into the room, a young, good-looking boy-man with the rosy cheeks of a youth from the Alps via Vienna's exclusive Hietzing district.

Gross by this time had made himself comfortable in von Quitenbach's chair. Introductions were briefly made and Gross nodded at a chair across the desk from him, but the youth ignored the gesture. Instead, he said, 'What is all this about? Am I to be disturbed in the middle of my economics class? Couldn't this wait until the end of the day?'

'As your classes go on until eight in the evening, I think not,' Gross responded. 'I have been commissioned by the highest authority, I assure you, Herr Kiss.'

He let the comment sink in as well as his intentional dropping of the youth's title.

'Uncle Franz Josef, that would be, then,' Kiss allowed. 'And it is probably about this wretched missing letter business.'

Gross knew the youth was aware of the missing letter, for his mother had informed him and Werthen that her son had checked the doors and windows for a possible break in. But he was hoping Kiss could inadvertently offer some evidence to bolster a theory he was developing.

'Your assumption is correct. And please do take a seat, Herr Kiss.' He waited for the young man to do so before continuing. 'Is it possible your mother might have mislaid the letter?'

'You'll have to ask her about that, but I assure you my mother is a very organized woman. She has compartmentalized her life to exacting standards.'

The comment sounded more like complaint than praise; an actress such as Frau Schratt must have had to leave a young boy much on his own when touring and when ministering to the emotional needs of an emperor who liked to pay six a.m. morning visits to his mistress.

'Yes, to be able to memorize all those lines,' Gross said. 'Quite a talent.'

'If you say so. Really, is all this necessary? It seems much ado about nothing. All of Vienna knows that mother and Uncle Franz are special friends.'

'There may be more to it than that,' Gross replied, 'but the contents of the letter are not my concern. I have been tasked with ensuring that it is returned to its rightful owner.'

'Does that mean the emperor? And what a bloody silly comment. Of course the contents are your concern. If someone or something is mentioned therein that might prove inflammatory, then it is highly relevant for investigators to know about it. It would help narrow down those who might profit from such disclosure or threat of disclosure.'

Gross nodded appreciatively at this comment. The young man, he decided, stood to have a formidable diplomatic career. His reasoning was impeccable, but Gross had to remain circumspect. He could hardly make the slight against the German Kaiser in the letter public knowledge.

'Let us say there may be sensitive material in the letter, not as regards your mother's friendship with the emperor, but about a third party. However, I hardly think the person in question would have knowledge of such a letter. I understand you examined all possible points of entry to your mother's villa and found nothing untoward.'

'That is so,' Kiss said.

'And from that you concluded . . .?'

'Exactly what I assume you concluded: that it was someone in the household who took the damned thing. Someone most likely in the pay of one of mother's enemies.'

'She has a number of those?'

'Famous women always do. Famous women who are the mistress of an emperor, even more so.'

He pronounced the word 'mistress' with a degree of venom.

'You do not approve of your mother's relationship with the emperor?'

'Is that any of your business?'

'I have been commissioned to be thorough in my investigation,' Gross said.

'Which means I too am a suspect, I suppose.'

Another nod from Gross.

'Am I to provide an alibi, then? This is absurd. Why don't you use this fancy dactyloscopy one reads about in the papers?' He cast Gross a challenging grin.

'In fact, we did take fingerprints of the handle to the drawer as well as the interior. But I am afraid there were a mass of such prints, all indecipherable. Besides, if one were aware of the science of fingerprinting,' he cast Herr Kiss a meaningful glance, 'then all one need do is wear a pair of gloves to avoid detection.'

Herr Kiss had now stopped smiling. 'What is it you want to know from me, other than the fact that I did not take the letter in question?'

'A shortlist of enemies would be helpful. Also, any of the staff who you think might be capable of such a deed.'

Kiss looked upward as if searching for inspiration. He sighed deeply. 'I highly doubt any of the staff is involved,' he said.

This comment gave Gross a sudden jolt but he did not show any emotion.

'Enemies then,' he said.

'I can do you one better. Why not visit the count?'

'Which count would that be, young man?'

'Count Johann Nepomuk Wilczek. Uncle Hans and mother were . . . well, they have been friends for years. Longer even than Uncle Franz Joseph. He may be able to help you.'

The Baron Kiss appeared to have a quantity of 'uncles.' It was also clear to Gross that he was withholding information. Kiss had not yet learned the fine art of dissimulation, so vital in the diplomatic trade.

'You surely do not put him in the category of enemy, then.'

Kiss shook his head. 'Uncle Hans has an island named after him.' He said this *non sequitur* earnestly as if it provided some sort of testimony for the man. 'He can tell you all about mother. No one knows her better.'

Gross squinted at him; he felt that same jolt of uncertainty Kiss's earlier remark had elicited.

'Is that all?' Asked like a young school boy of an older prefect.

'I think that should suffice,' Gross said. 'I thank you for your time and hope that I have not too greatly disturbed your studies.'

Kiss rose and left the room without an adieu.

The school director, Michael Pidoll von Quitenbach, must have been watching the hallway, for he appeared in the doorway not half a minute after Baron Kiss's departure.

'I hope that little visit helped,' he said. There was more than a trace of irony on the word 'little'.

'It all helps,' Gross said. 'Each of the fragments adds up, you see. Individually they are simply shards, tile chips. But correctly assembled . . .' Gross snapped his fingers, '. . . and *voila*, we have—'

'A mosaic!' Von Quitenbach beamed, proud of himself.

'More of a collage, Herr Direktor. Sometimes a mere tessellation. And that is where this comes into play.' He tapped his right forefinger against his temple. 'The facility to interpret the patchwork, to make your mosaic out of a variegated montage is more than a guessing game. For that, you need training, diligence, experience, but most importantly talent.'

He found himself glaring at the man whose ironic intonation of the word 'little' had spurred this invective. But apparently its intended target was completely unaware of the hedged hostility in Gross's comments, for which the criminologist was happy.

This fit of pique bothered Gross. What has got into me that the smallest perceived slight can set me off so? he wondered. But he knew.

Baron Kiss had said it himself: *this wretched missing letter business*. He might as well be investigating a case of infidelity.

\*     \*     \*

He returned to his room at one-thirty in the afternoon. He checked the tell he left at the bottom of the door. Before leaving, he had stuck one of his black hairs to door and jamb with a bit of grease. It was still in place.

Young Dimitrov was at his side; he could feel the man's anxiety. It oozed from his pores like stale sweat.

'What are you looking at?' Dimitrov said in badly accented German.

'Nothing for you to worry about.' He bent down and retrieved the hair, then opened the door.

'It's small for two of us,' Dimitrov said, surveying the room with its pair of cots separated by a scarred deal table and a pair of rickety chairs. Wooden pegs hung on the walls at the head of the cots in lieu and a wardrobe stood against the wall between them.

'We won't be here long,' he replied.

'I won't be, that is for sure.' Dimitrov made an attempt to laugh; it trailed off into a thick cough. He dropped his case to retrieve a soiled handkerchief from his breast pocket.

The hairs on the back of Wenno's neck bristled as the suitcase struck the floor. He shut the door behind Dimitrov. 'You should be more careful with that case.'

Dimitrov coughed blood into the handkerchief, sniffed once, folded the rag and stuck it in his breast pocket once again. He shrugged at Wenno's suggestion.

They had promised him a volunteer; they said nothing about the mental condition of the man.

'What kind of a name is Wenno anyway?' Dimitrov asked.

He didn't bother answering this. 'We have a little over a week for preparations. They say you are willing to give your life for your homeland. Are you a patriot?'

'I'm dying anyway. They're paying my wife.' A snarl of a grin. 'My widow soon enough.'

Wenno had worked with all sorts of agents: those who did it for love of country, those who did it for love of money, those who were forced into it either by their rank or by blackmail. He preferred working with those who – like himself – were paid. Paid professionals.

Dimitrov was being paid. Period.

'Did they give you any training before sending you to me?'

'They said you would handle that end. Look, I'm all in. I was on that stinking train for twenty hours. Twenty hours on a third-class wooden bench. You'd think they could afford first class.'

'It's a matter of discretion,' he told him. 'You don't need unwanted attention with what you're carrying in that case.'

'Which translates that you don't figure I look like the first-class sort.'

He had not taken Dimitrov for the introspective sort, but obviously there was some organ at work between the man's ears. 'It's how your controllers would think. Not my decision.'

'Well, thanks for that, at least.'

'Did you eat?'

'I ran out of cheese and salami somewhere in the miserable flatlands of Hungary. You got something here?'

'We can go out. There's a good *gasthaus* at the corner.'

Dimitrov's face suddenly paled. He grabbed the handkerchief out of his pocket and put it to his mouth as another fit of coughing gripped him. His eyes teared and he breathed deeply as he again folded the cloth.

'Does that go on most of the time?' Wenno asked Dimitrov. A curt nod. 'Worried about your sleep?'

He shook his head. 'Worried that you make it to next week.'

# TWELVE

'What are you doing, little poppet?' Franzl looked up from the sketch he was making. 'Nothing.'

'I didn't know you could write.'

The dinner dishes were cleaned up and the cook and Fräulein Anna were sitting at the kitchen table having their meal. Franzl had finished his quickly and discovered a bit of scrap paper and a pencil in the small writing desk in one corner of the cavernous kitchen where the cook planned her menus and shopping lists.

'I can write,' he said, looking up briefly. 'But I'm not writing now.'

Anna smiled at him. 'Well, what are you doing then? Doodling?'

'Sort of.'

She shot him another impish grin, hopped out of her chair and came over to where he was sitting on a low stool, using the seat of a chair as his desk.

'Well, you are a clever little poppet, aren't you!' She snatched the sketch and went back to the cook. 'Look what he's done. He's made pictures of us eating.'

Cook glanced up from her kraut and pork long enough to make a grunting noise, followed by, 'Be better off learning to clean the skillet properly.'

'I think it's wonderful,' Anna enthused. 'A regular artist is our Herr Franzl.'

'And he's going to be a regular sleepyhead tomorrow if he doesn't get to bed,' Cook said. 'You, too, you flighty little bird.'

Anna rolled her eyes at Franzl, making him giggle.

'And what's so funny about that?' the cook thundered. 'Tomorrow's another day just like this one. You need to be up and working by six, so off with you both.'

Cook stood and swept the plates off the table, plunging them into the sudsy water of the deep porcelain sink.

'I need to clean the last of the dishes,' Anna said.

'Off with you. I'll see to these, you see to your little "poppet."'

It came as a surprise to Franzl that he was sharing lodgings with Fräulein Anna, but he figured if it was all right with her it was for him, too. Truth was he liked her. She treated him like a little brother.

They went up the back stairs to the top of the house where the servants' rooms were. It was a small room, but they had hung a blanket over a rope as a divider.

'Sorry to be crowding you,' Franzl said as he went to his side.

'No. I think it's just fine. It's nice to have someone to talk to before going to sleep. When you get bigger they'll give you your own room, but for now we can be roommates.'

She pulled the blanket across the rope, providing a degree of privacy. He listened to the rustle of her clothes as she changed into her nightgown. Then he hurriedly hopped into pajamas as she turned down the gas lamp.

'Cook is right,' came her disembodied voice from the other side of the blanket. 'Tomorrow's another day and it's up early around here, I can tell you.'

'She likes to yell,' Franzl said.

'Cook? Yes, but she doesn't really mean anything by it. She's got a big heart, really. Just likes to act bossy. I mean, look at her tonight cleaning up after us.'

Franzl considered this and decided Fräulein Anna was probably right.

'You just do your job and it'll be fine,' she said. 'Besides, she's a little nervous. We all are.'

'Why is that?' he asked.

'About the letter, of course. But then you wouldn't know – you just got here. Cook says we're not to know, but she overheard some fancy gents the other day who came asking questions. Acted like they were newspaper writers or some such, asking us all questions – could we read, did we know where certain keys were . . . Cook says they were investigating a letter that's gone missing.'

Franzl felt his pulse quicken. 'What kind of letter?'

'An important one, I guess. No wonder, we've got important people calling at this house. I suppose you don't know about that, either.'

'Actors and such?' Franzl said. 'I know Mistress is a famous actress.'

'A whole lot more important. The emperor himself is a special friend. He sometimes comes to visit for breakfast. You might even see him one day.'

Franzl whistled low to let her know he was impressed. But he didn't like trying to fool Fräulein Anna.

'Cook says it's all a lot of hogwash, pardon the expression.'

'Why is that?'

'Promise not to tell?'

Franzl crossed his fingers. 'Promise.' And he hated himself.

'Cook thinks that letter did not really go missing. There wasn't much activity around this house for a month or so, I can tell you. And then this letter disappears and suddenly there are visitors from Schönbrunn and fellows who call themselves newspaper reporters and now the mistress is in the spotlight again. That's what Cook thinks, anyway.'

'You mean that mistress made it all up?'

'Remember, you promised not to tell.'

\*       \*       \*

'I think we should be going, Emile,' Frau von Werthen told her husband. 'I believe our trio of intrepid investigators has things to discuss.'

Werthen's father, having taken a glass or two of the Gewürtztraminer beyond his usual quota, looked crestfallen at the suggestion. 'But we just got here.'

'Yes,' his wife teased, 'and we just ate one of Frau Blatschky's best plates of boiled beef, fresh horseradish and parsley potatoes. And a double helping of rice pudding for someone I know to top it all off.'

Gertrud von Werthen got up and lifted her husband by the arm. Before rising, Emile von Werthen quickly quaffed the last drams of the wine in his glass.

Werthen and Berthe exchanged smiles. They made no polite protests: they *did* in fact have matters to discuss. Gross sat across the table from them enjoying his own second helping of the rice pudding, evidently oblivious to the imminent departure. At the last moment he mustered a modicum of politesse, rising from his chair to wish the older couple a good night. He would be following them soon, for he was staying at the same lodgings, the Hotel zur Josefstadt in the nearby Langegasse.

They saw Werthen's parents off at the door and then he and Berthe returned to the dining room where Gross was still worrying his rice pudding.

Werthen went first. He outlined his discussion with Girardi and how he had started to follow up on the enemy list the actor had given up.

'I sat in Herr Director Schlenther's outer office at the Burg for a good half hour waiting to speak with the man, then I finally realized it would be a fool's errand. After all, what would I ask him? "Did you hire someone to steal a letter from Frau Schratt?" Nonsense. Finally I decided it was enough to know who the possible enemies might be, but there is precious little to be gained by interviewing them other than watching for guilty reactions to probing questions.'

'I'm afraid I came to the same conclusion,' Berthe said. 'The one thing I did learn from Princess Dumbroski was that she already knew of the missing letter. She seems to have a network of allies in high places. And she swears she had nothing to do with the theft.'

Berthe unconsciously wiped her lips with the linen napkin.

'That's all?' Werthen intuitively sensed that his wife was holding something back.

Berthe shook her head. 'Nothing else worth sharing. She is an odious woman. And clever to boot.' She was not about to tell her husband of the shaming kiss.

They sat in silence for a moment, waiting for Gross to share his information.

'I may have had more luck,' the criminologist began, leaning back in his chair and folding his hands over his well-fed stomach. 'Anton Kiss is doubtless conflicted about his mother and her relationship with the emperor, but I do not believe he is responsible for the missing letter. There was something, however, that I felt he wanted to say but could not bring himself to do so. Instead, he directed me to another of his mother's admirers, Count Wilczek.'

'The leaping lord,' Berthe said brightly. The count had been a high jumper of international repute in his youth and was known to practice his jumping prowess at any moment. Those strolling down the Herrengasse might very well be treated to the sight of a tall, lean man in his sixties leaping from the second-floor window of his city palace to the cobbled street below instead of using his front door to exit.

'I was not aware of that distinction,' Gross said, irritated at Berthe's comment. 'I know of him only as a rather rare form of nobility – a man who actually exhibits noble behavior. You know he fought as a common soldier at Königgrätz when he should have been officer class. Carried a wounded captain out of a hail of bullets, they say. Awarded the Medal of Honor for his troubles. He personally funded the Austro-Hungarian North Pole Expedition—'

'Yes,' Werthen interrupted, 'and he served at court, formed the first volunteer ambulance society and is refurbishing his castle at Burg Kreuzenstein. All very well, but what did the good count have to tell you?'

'We are skittish tonight, aren't we?' Gross said.

Werthen pulled a face at this.

'Very little and quite a lot,' Gross said, assuming his irritating mysteriously imperious air.

'Oh, come now, Gross,' Berthe chided. 'No reason for cryptic statements. Did you discover anything or not?'

'You tell me. The count merely stated that Frau Schratt is the most wonderful, sincere and sensitive person it has ever been his good fortune to know. He also said she was most grievously disappointed following the death of the empress.'

Werthen thought about this for a moment. 'Because of the subsequent intrigue at court against her?'

Gross shook his head.

Berthe gasped as if seeing a ghost. 'My God,' she said. 'She expected a marriage proposal.'

'Don't be absurd,' Werthen began, but then he saw the smile on Gross's face.

'Too true, Frau Meisner. The poor woman actually expected a morganatic marriage.'

'She must have been horribly disappointed,' Berthe said. 'After all those years . . .'

'Indeed,' Gross said. 'She has been out of the emperor's life for a pair of years, only lately returning to Vienna from her travels.'

'Revenge?' Werthen asked, understanding the import of the count's information.

'Perhaps,' Gross allowed.

'Or a cry for attention,' Berthe added.

Werthen could only think of how incestuous all such matters were in Vienna. He had not been aware of the liaison between Frau Schratt and Count Wilczek, but it was merely one more indication of the village-like nature of Vienna. The count's wife had been the former maid of honor to the Archduchess Sophie, mother of Emperor Franz Josef, the very man who the count had cuckolded with Frau Schratt. Plus, it was rumored that Count Wilczek had the ear of the willful Crown Prince Rudolf, son of the emperor, who would not listen to a word of advice from his own father.

Werthen imagined there was little love lost between the emperor and the count.

# THIRTEEN

The man who now called himself Herr Wenno, Pietr Klavan, was most at ease in the night, even one as bitterly cold as tonight. The darkness suited him. He sheltered in the doorway of a tobacco shop across and just up the street from the Café Burg. The street had electric lighting, but Klavan had made sure his sentinel position was between the lights; he was in the shadows in the recessed doorway with an unobstructed view of the café entrance.

He had been here for almost an hour. He could not read his pocket watch in the gloom, but intuiting the time was one of those skills he had, like sensing where a man carried a hidden weapon or knowing how long a man's reach was before engaging him in battle. One of those skills that cannot be trained. Enhanced. Polished. But never trained.

He had left the unfortunate Dimitrov at the pension, sleeping and fitfully coughing. The man took enough cheap Spanish brandy to put an elephant to sleep. Klavan had aided the process by slipping laudanum into his drink.

It felt good to be away from the walking corpse. The outdoors smelled fresh tonight with the slight breeze off the Danube Canal. It was near freezing, but Klavan was not uncomfortable. He kept his hands in his pockets, felt the revolver in the right one and the garroting noose in the left. There was a blade strapped to his left leg.

Light spilled out into the street from the café doors opening. He tensed, ready for action, but it was only the last of the customers leaving for the night. His man would be coming presently, he hoped.

This was not his usual method of operation. Klavan was someone who planned well and wisely, who knew the lay of the land, who appraised himself of routines, timetables and routes in advance.

Christ, he was not even sure that the junior waiter would be closing up tonight, but it made sense: if he was second to Herr

Karl, he would be taking over that man's responsibilities. So much for his usual operating methods.

This was no longer a usual operation, however. Since realizing he had left a possible loose end, he knew he had to sew it up or cauterize it. There was no time for subtlety. But the one thing he had to avoid at all costs was drawing attention to the man's death. This *must* appear accidental. It must go unremarked. Or undiscovered.

It would be soon now, he thought. He needed to be ready, to strike like a snake and disappear into the night like shade. This was a test mission for him and for future employers. Botch this and he would be hard pressed to find such work again. Klavan had gone from government agent to freelance, and the generals in Belgrade were his first employers.

After making his way out of Russia, Klavan had wanted to stop off for a time at his home by the Baltic, but he had been warned off. His old grandfather was outside the house playing the role of living beacon, wearing a red vest he reserved only for funerals. This let Klavan know something was amiss before approaching; then he had seen the Russian soldiers tucked away behind outbuildings in the nearby ditch. He made no attempt to turn into the lane to his family home, his heart aching to say farewell properly to his people.

He'd robbed a bank in Riga, taken a train through Poland and ultimately made his way to Brussels, where Monsieur Philipot ran his little business. During his years as a Russian agent, Klavan had used Philipot's men several times when short-handed on operations. They were generally reliable though not always the best at their job – killing. He'd had to step in for the third such young freelance and finish the job, wringing the neck of a dowager of seventy. But she was a woman with a head full of secrets she was trying to flog to the highest bidder.

Monsieur Philipot, a man as round as he was tall, was not happy to see him, knowing that he was on the run from the Russians. But when he learned that Klavan had come to him for work and not for help, the man brightened.

'I have just the thing for you,' Monsieur Philipot said.

They were in his watch shop which sold very few watches. 'This one requires someone of your skill level. As I understand it, there has been an attempt already on the target, but it was poorly conceived and the execution was even worse.' He laughed out loud at his unintentional pun, spitting a damp crumb of cheese onto Klavan's coat. Philipot was the sort to snack most of the day; he always had a plate of cheese and wurst handy.

When Philipot told him who the target was, Klavan could only marvel at the audacity of such a deed. Then, learning who his prospective employers would be, he better understood.

He took the train that very night for Paris, where he was able to catch the Orient Express to Vienna and from there through Budapest to Belgrade. He found a hotel and bathed, arranged his materials, and then went to the address supplied by Philipot.

It was on a quiet backstreet in the center of Belgrade. There, in a third-floor walk-up, he met four young Serbian military officers, their leader a captain in the General Staff of the Serbian Army. He went by the code name of Apis; the others were not introduced. They spoke in German, though it was clearly a language Apis hated. He knew of Klavan's history, and that he was on the run from the Russians.

'We sometimes look to Mother Russia for support,' Apis told him. 'At other times, we use whatever agencies are available to us. Our Black Hand has a long reach.'

It was the first Klavan had heard of this secret organization. He eyed the mustachioed Apis carefully. Fearing a trap, he had wired himself with explosives at the hotel, for he would not be taken alive. The Russians would not send him off to one of their godforsaken work camps.

'So, Herr Klavan, you can trust me. I assume you prepared some sort of insurance for this visit. You may rest assured that you are worth more to us alive than dead or in the hands of the Russians.'

He snapped his fingers and one of the other officers handed him a black satchel. Apis opened it to display fresh bank notes: French francs and British pounds.

'Our down payment. The rest will be made available to you via Monsieur Philipot upon the successful completion of your mission.'

Apis named the target and the final price.

'The means are up to you. We will provide what support we can, but you are on your own. This affair does not come back to Serbia. If captured there is no one who will believe a word you tell them. Your previous exploits in Vienna have seen to that. And if you decide to simply disappear with our money without fulfilling our little contract, I would advise you simply not to try it.'

'The long reach of the Black Hand?' Klavan had said it with a slight smile, but he knew there was nothing humorous about Apis.

'Exactly, my friend. I believe we understand one another.'

The café door opened once again, cutting these thoughts short.

'Goodnight, Kleinman,' a tall, thin man said to another person inside as he closed the door and locked up.

Klavan sighed in relief. It was the under waiter.

The waiter headed north out of the Inner City toward the Danube Canal. Klavan kept a half block behind him. The waiter had the demeanor of a man headed home after a hard day's work, which might make Klavan's job easier. It was just after ten at night, and there were few pedestrians about, especially with the cold. A sharp blast of chill wind bit into him as they neared the canal. The waiter suddenly stopped as he approached the broad expanse of the Franz-Josefs-Kai paralleling the canal. Klavan quickly ducked into a doorway as the waiter looked in back of him. A late horse-drawn tram made its way along the broad boulevard that also served as a dockland for produce. The waiter made his way across the street toward the Stephanie-Brücke, obviously on his way into the Second District across the canal.

Klavan needed to make his move now. There were no pedestrians about and he made a dash across the street, catching up to the waiter as he began to cross the bridge. He had his pistol drawn and had it to the man's head before he could react.

'Make a sound and you die,' he said.

The man's eyes grew bigger, the whites showing as they stood under the lights at the foot of the bridge.

'Cooperate and you live,' Klavan said, his voice controlled. He jerked his head to a flight of stairs leading down below the bridge to a promenade and docks closer to the water level.

'What do you want?'

'Your money. Now move and no one gets hurt.'

The man's eyes surveyed the scene, but there were no other pedestrians about, no street traffic.

Luck is with me, Klavan told himself. 'Move or die here,' he hissed.

The waiter shuffled toward the steps, Klavan in back with the gun against his back.

Reaching the bottom of the steps, Klavan shoved the man to the right, under the bridge and out of sight. He felt more confident now. Halfway home.

'Here,' the man said, pulling out a crumple of bills from his pants pockets. 'Take it. That's all I have. I don't carry a wallet.'

Klavan said nothing, merely fixing the man with his icy gaze.

'Take it,' the man pleaded, holding out the bills. Klavan's silence unnerved him. Then his eyes went to Klavan's hands and a sudden recognition struck the waiter. 'Mother of God, it's you. The man from the café talking to Herr Karl the day he died. You were the one who killed Herr Karl. I saw you. I followed Herr Karl that night. You must be the one.'

The words chilled Klavan more than the wind off the Danube Canal.

'Who have you told?' The words were uttered with almost a sweetness that again caught the waiter off guard.

'You'll never get away with this. Werthen will see to that. I swear—'

He was about to scream out when Klavan clapped his hand over the man's mouth, his left cupping the back of the man's skull. A quick twist and he broke the waiter's neck.

He let him drop to the cobbled promenade, a lifeless rag doll.

Focus, he commanded himself. No way to make this look like an accident now, not with a broken neck. So concealment was the thing. He looked around and found a stack of heavy cobbles under the bridge left for repairs. He stripped the long coat off the man, found no belt but there were suspenders. Even better. He took out the knife from its leg sheath and cut the suspenders in two. Then he trussed several of the heavy cobbles in the man's coat like a satchel, binding it at the top with one of the suspenders. The other he tied to this bundle and wrapped it around the man's waist, tightly securing it.

There were voices overhead – a woman and a man.

'Come on, dearie,' the woman said. 'We can go below. Nobody will see. A nice fast one for you.'

He would have to kill them as well. Which actually might

be a good idea. It would surely take attention away from a waiter gone missing.

'No, I don't think so,' the man said. 'Too cold for outdoor sports.'

'Oh, you're a comedian,' the woman said in a shrill tone. 'Feel this. It'll warm you up.'

'Give it a rest, will you?' the man replied. 'I've got a wife waiting for me at home.'

'But she won't do what I could do for you, dearie.'

He heard footsteps clapping on the bridge overhead, moving away, crossing the bridge. One pair only.

'Go ahead!' the woman shouted at him. 'Go home to your sweet little frau. You don't know what you're missing.'

Soon, he heard her leaving the bridge and going back to the quai. He waited another five minutes before moving the body over to the edge of the dock and letting it down gently, without a splash, into the murky waters of the canal. It sunk immediately.

He did not go back up to the Stephanie-Brücke, but instead walked north along the docks to Maria Theresien-Brücke, where he went up a flight of stairs again to street level.

It would be a long walk back to his pension, but he had much to think about.

He was sure of the name. The waiter had said *Werthen*. He knew the lawyer and his friend Gross from his earlier mission in Vienna. It was they who caused his fall from grace with the Russians. They who made him a man without a home.

How much did they know? What had the waiter told them? Did they know of his blackmailing Herr Karl? Of the request to Oberstabelmeister Johann Czerny to put Postling on the list?

It had been an intricate, beautiful plan he had constructed after the heavy-handed and botched work of his predecessors. Discovering the weak link in the Oberstabelmeister's life, examining and then exploiting that weakness: his friendship with Herr Karl. And then, the night of Herr Karl's death, when all seemed lost, his sudden inspiration, and he was in control again.

And now, to have it suddenly put in jeopardy once more. It was too much.

He would need to double-check everything, beginning with the old man, Hermann Postling. Had he been traced to the men's hostel? That would be easy enough to check on.

And then there was the meddling Advokat Werthen and the pompous Doktor Gross to deal with. He smiled at the thought. Actually, this might be a stroke of luck, if he looked at it in the right way. To finally get pay back on those two: that would be a fine thing.

And one further thought: he had neglected to go through the waiter's pocket. Perhaps there was some incriminating bit of information there. But he consoled himself that it would be some time before the body was discovered, if ever. His mission would be accomplished by that time and he would be on to a new life.

Still, the oversight rankled. It was an error he would not have made several months ago.

# FOURTEEN

Werthen was not looking forward to the appointment. Netty was wearing the same blue linen shirtwaist and scowl on her face that she had when they had first come to talk with Frau Schratt.

'She's expecting you,' the housekeeper said abruptly. 'You know where to go.'

She left them to find their own way to the conservatory once again. Werthen and Gross exchanged glances but said nothing. As they made their way down the long hallway, a hand reached out from a dark recess and grabbed Werthen's arm. It startled him, but his eyes were adjusting to the gloom and he could make out the features of Franzl.

'Advokat,' the boy whispered. 'I've got something to tell you.' He tugged at Werthen's arm and the lawyer moved into the recess of the doorway while Gross stood watch in the hall.

'What is it, Franzl?' Werthen said, his voice lowered.

'Fräulein Anna and I were talking last night,' Franzl said, his eyes wide and almost frightened-looking. 'She says Cook thinks the letter really didn't go missing after all. That maybe the mistress wants some attention from the emperor.'

Werthen nodded at this confirmation of his own theory.

'I feel awful,' Franzl said. 'She swore me to secrecy.'

'Who?'

'Fräulein Anna. I lied to her and after she's been so good to me.'

Werthen put his hand on the boy's shoulder. 'Don't worry, Franzl. We already decided the same thing, so it's not really like you betrayed her. That's why we are here today – to talk to Frau Schratt. Besides, I think your services will not be needed here after today. We'll take you with us when we go.'

'They've got central heating here, did you know that? Every room has a little heater in it. No fires to build except in the boiler.'

Werthen squeezed Franzl's shoulder. 'You've done well. Don't feel guilty.'

He moved back into the hall and told Gross what Franzl had said. The criminologist grunted in assent.

'Still, it needs to be handled gently,' Gross said.

Frau Schratt was seated in the same chair as on their last visit. She greeted them with a question: 'Has there been progress?'

Gross and Werthen sat across from her.

'Not really, Frau Schratt,' Gross said.

Her eyes squinted at him. 'Then why the urgency of this meeting? You could very well notify that creature Montenuovo of your failure. Why bother me?'

Gross sighed. 'You misunderstand me, Frau Schratt. I think we may have found the letter, but as to progress, that remains to be seen.'

Her squint narrowed now to a look of suspicion. 'You are speaking in riddles, Doktor Gross.'

He tilted his head at this. 'I have been accused of that before, Frau Schratt.'

She glanced from Gross to Werthen, but he gave nothing away, either.

They sat in silence for a moment.

'And just where is this letter now?' she finally said.

Gross smoothed his moustache with his right forefinger. 'I believe if we examined your escritoire one more time, we might just discover that the letter somehow became lodged behind another folder or perhaps in the join of the wood.'

'I told you, I examined the drawer thoroughly,' Frau Schratt began, and then looked at Gross's expression, his eyes fixed on

her. She shifted her gaze to Werthen, but he also had his courtroom face on.

She sat upright in her chair, clasping her hands in her lap. 'I
see. You believe I deliberately sequestered this letter. To what
end?'

Werthen remarked the false note, as did Gross. An innocent
person would demand their heads, not question possible motive.

They did not reply.

'This is absurd,' she spluttered.

'Yes, absurd accidents happen,' Gross replied. 'Absurd or not,
just think how relieved everyone will be, the emperor in particular,
when it is learned that the letter is safe. I am sure he will thank
you personally. After all, there is no blame to simply mislay a
letter. And it was wise of you to sound an alarm when such an
important document appeared to have gone missing. It demon-
strates due diligence on your part.'

He was offering her a way out and Frau Schratt was apparently
considering it.

She stood with a suddenness that caught them off guard.

'I will take one more look at your insistence,' she said as they
were rising. 'You may wait here.'

She swept out of the room and Gross and Werthen sat again,
saying nothing. Werthen doubted it would take very long.

He was right. Five minutes later she was back in the room, a
letter in her hand.

'I feel such a fool,' she said, her Burgtheater voice ringing in
the conservatory. 'You gentlemen were right. I do not know how
I could have missed it. The letter somehow got into the file of
Burgtheater contracts.'

She handed it to Gross. 'You may return it to the emperor,'
she said grandly.

Gross held his hands to his chest palms out. 'No, no, my lady.
I leave that for you to do in person if so requested. I am only
happy to report that things have been resolved so nicely. And
now, Frau Schratt, we will take up no more of your valuable
time.'

She half bowed at this. 'I suppose you will be taking your
little protégé with you,' she said, obviously referring to Franzl.
'Too bad, for Cook tells me he is a fine addition to the kitchen.'

'Yes,' Werthen said. 'Franzl will come with us.'

She nodded, feigning a smile. Werthen hoped she did not attribute their deduction to Franzl's actions and take out retribution on the staff for perceived loose tongues.

'Count Wilczek sends his regards,' Werthen said, 'as does Herr Girardi.'

At least that will give her someone else to wonder about, Werthen thought.

'You gentlemen have been busy,' she said, putting out her hand to be kissed. 'The emperor is fortunate to have such clever fellows in his employ.'

In turn, Gross and Werthen kissed the air an inch above the proffered hand and took their leave. Franzl was waiting in the front hall, his small satchel of belongings at his side. As they were leaving, Fräulein Anna came tripping down the hall.

'Off so soon, poppet?' she said, a look of surprise on her face.

Franzl looked confused.

Werthen tried to cover for him, saying, 'Frau Schratt has decided she needs an older assistant in the kitchen. We agreed to take him back into town.'

A vacuous enough explanation, but it seemed to satisfy Fräulein Anna, who bent over and gave Franzl a hug and kiss on the cheek.

'Take care of yourself, poppet.'

He sniffled. 'You, too.'

Franzl did not speak a word the entire ride back to Habsburgergasse.

They meet at the Hofburg that same afternoon. Gross was last in Montenuovo's city office on the matter involving Court Opera Director Gustav Mahler. He was joined this time by Werthen, who was gazing out of the fine lace curtains covering the floor-to-ceiling windows, through the embroidered Habsburg eagle in the center of the curtain to the Imperial Chancellery across the courtyard. The emperor had his town apartments there. Gross wondered if he were at the Hofburg or at Schönbrunn, or perhaps even at Frau Schratt's paying the good lady the attention she required.

As he was mulling this over, the hidden door in a wall of bookcases opened and Montenuovo made a dramatic appearance. Today he was dressed in the quasi-military style of his office with embroidered blue tunic and sword at his side, supported by a broad red sash from his right shoulder to his left hip.

'Gentlemen, gentlemen, please be seated,' the diminutive prince said as he took the large chair on the opposite side of a massive rosewood desk. 'I understand from my aide that congratulations are in order. Splendid work.'

'Rather mundane, actually,' Gross said, again taking the lead and leaving Werthen in the role of Greek chorus. 'The letter had merely been misplaced.'

Montenuovo formed a steeple with his fingertips touching upraised in front of his chest. He tapped the fingertips together rhythmically.

'Misplaced?'

'Put into another folder by accident.'

'I see.' He said it as if he were blind.

Silence for a moment.

'You brought the letter, I assume.' The prince reached across the desk as if to take it in hand.

'Actually, I left it with Frau Schratt. She and the emperor can determine what is to be done with it, I imagine.'

Montenuovo drew his hand back in. '*If* it does not go missing again in the meantime.'

Gross shook his head. 'I do not believe that will happen again. And now perhaps, Prince Montenuovo, you can tell me what this is really about. In lieu of payment, I would greatly prefer the truth.'

The prince leaned back in his chair, smiling at Gross. 'I see why they call you the father of criminalistics. Tell me, what leads you to this deduction?'

Werthen eyed Gross: he would like to know, as well, for it was the first that he heard of this.

Gross cleared his throat as if preparing to deliver a university lecture.

'It was patently obvious from the first day we met. You told us that the emperor needed our services because of the delicate nature of the missing letter and because he did not want to appear to have feet of clay to his junior officers. Nonsense and piffle. He is the emperor: he commands, the others obey. No, there is only one reason that he would call in an outsider such as myself . . .'

Werthen noted his absence in the outsider category. Gross might be a great criminologist, but he was even a greater egotist.

'And what would that be, Doktor Gross?' Montenuovo obligingly queried.

'That he cannot trust even his inner circle. That there must be a reason for such distrust—'

'But you are assuming that he does trust me?' Again the steepling of the fingertips.

'Most certainly. You are the one man he can trust, Prince. You would have the most to lose in professional status were anything to happen to the emperor.'

Montenuovo displayed no reaction to this rather demeaning comment: no one else would have the prince.

'And that is what this is all about, is it not, Prince? Something happening to the emperor. As with the unfortunate accident with his royal carriage two weeks ago.'

The fingertips bounced with increased tempo until the hands intertwined and were lowered to the desk.

'Very good, Doktor Gross.'

Werthen had finally had enough. 'What's all this about, Gross?'

The criminologist turned to him. 'A theory, my dear Werthen. A theory.'

'Would you care to appraise me of it? As usual, I had the mistaken notion we were working together.'

'I should rather the prince do that,' Gross said with that irritating superciliousness that made Werthen want to crush the man's hat.

Gross turned to Prince Montenuovo. 'Am I correct, Prince?'

An appreciative nod from the small man. 'There was an unfortunate incident a couple of weeks ago, yes. The royal carriage was overturned when a fiaker ran into it.'

'There was rather more to it than that, as I understand,' Gross said.

'But how could you know any of this, Gross?' Werthen asked. 'You were in Prague two weeks ago. I live in Vienna and had no knowledge of such an accident.'

To which remark Gross merely rolled his eyes.

'So you keep informants about,' Werthen said.

'Otherwise known as assistants. Clever journalist chaps who are kept from publishing the news they gather but who

do not mind earning a few crowns to pass on valuable information to me.'

'It seems you have your own network of spies at work, Doktor
Gross,' Montenuovo said.

'Assistants,' he repeated.

Werthen wondered if one of these assistants might not be
his secretary's beau, Herr Sonnenthal, journalist for the *Arbeiter
Zeitung.*

'All the better,' Montenuovo said. 'You will need them. You
are absolutely correct that the emperor does not trust his inner
circle. He has even begun to worry that there may be a traitor
in his Trabant Life Guards. The incident of the royal carriage
was a bit unnerving. One can only thank the Lord that, at the
last moment, he decided to walk. That is why, when this letter
went missing—'

'The emperor thought it was another plot to do him harm,'
Gross finished.

'Quite,' the prince said.

'Please forgive this poor benighted individual,' Werthen interrupted, exasperated at being excluded from the facts. 'But are
you saying that someone is trying to kill the emperor?'

'Concision, Werthen,' Gross said as a proud parent might to
a ten-year-old. 'You are its master.'

'It would appear so,' Prince Montenuovo affirmed. 'The
carriage incident was, as Doktor Gross indicated, rather more
complicated than a mere accident. Armed men stormed out of
the fiaker in broad daylight at the gates of Schönbrunn, threw
open the imperial carriage doors and, discovering it was empty,
killed the driver and lone guard instead. They most brutally and
brazenly emptied their revolvers into the two men, then reloaded
and fired off a fusillade at approaching guards from the palace.'

'Why an empty carriage?' Werthen said.

'Pardon me?' the prince asked.

'He means,' Gross said, 'why would the carriage proceed when
the emperor had decided to go on foot to his nearby destination?
One assumes he was on his way to Frau Schratt's?'

A curt nod from Montenuovo. 'And it is standard protocol to
vary the means of transport.'

'In other words, when the imperial carriage draws down a
Viennese street it might very well be empty.'

'Yes, Werthen,' Gross answered for the prince. 'Standard security methods.'

'Guards from the palace witnessed the incident at the gates,' Montenuovo continued, 'but by the time they ducked the salvo of bullets and had raced to the scene, the fiaker and assailants were long gone. We, of course, covered up the incident. Passersby were told it was a military exercise, and newspapers were forbidden to print any mention of it.'

Montenuovo nodded at Werthen. 'It appears our silencing methods functioned.'

Werthen tilted his head in assent. One could not keep secret the fact that a certain princess was carrying on an affair with the captain of the guards, but when there was an attempt on the emperor's life, all was silence.

'I am actually delighted that you have discovered the true motive behind your commission, Doktor Gross.'

'And why would that be, Prince?'

It was now Werthen's turn to be one step ahead. 'Because he wants to continue our commission in order to find out who was behind the attack.'

Gross pursed his lips. 'Don't be absurd, Werthen. No. Prince Montenuovo wants nothing less than that we prevent the assassination of the Emperor of Austria and King of Hungary. That we, in fact, save the empire.'

# PART THREE

PART THREE

# FIFTEEN

He would have to take Dimitrov with him. Klavan could not trust him on his own. Dimitrov was in even worse shape than when he had arrived, if that was possible. 'You've got to stop drinking,' he told the man after he had shaken him awake this morning. 'You're a mess.'

Dimitrov smirked at this. 'Perhaps a new suit of clothes will do the trick,' he said.

'It is rather too early for gallows humor,' Klavan retorted. Why had the idiots in Belgrade sent him such a specimen? Did they want him to fail?

Had he under- or over-estimated Apis? Is the man a preening fool or a canny stage manager somehow setting me up for a fall? Klavan wondered.

But it was too late for such second thoughts. He knew this from long experience: the soft part of you, the piece some called cowardice, was always looking for a way out, always seeking excuses for inaction.

'Get dressed,' Klavan ordered him. 'We've got a busy day. You can have coffee on the way.'

'But I do enjoy the cup Frau Geldner serves.'

'You haven't been talking to her, have you?'

'I've displayed good manners, Herr Wenno. Nothing more.'

'She's not the bumpkin she appears,' Klavan said. He himself had stopped taking morning coffee his second day in Vienna; he didn't like the questioning looks the other boarders were giving him. Anonymity was his only friend. There was one especially interested fellow. Klavan heard he was the nephew of Geldner. He had little piggy eyes that sized Klavan up like maybe he was fitting him for a prison suit.

They took the elevated train from the west train station along the Gürtel, or outer ring road, to the Josefstädterstrasse stop, and then headed by foot down Neulerchenfelderstrasse to the Kubit Men's Hostel. Klavan had actually stumbled on his plan, but regardless of how it had been developed, it was a thing of wonder.

And it all depended on one old man – Hermann Postling.

They stopped outside the hostel for a moment, then headed in.

'Jesus,' Dimitrov muttered as they entered the dingy building. 'Is this where they store you when you get old?'

'Only if you're lucky,' Klavan said. There was a front desk where Klavan signed in as a supposed nephew of Postling.

They proceeded to the second floor, to the reading room where the old man usually passed his days. He was there, in his corner seat, a world atlas open on the table in front of him. None of the other men shared his table. Postling was the solitary sort and not quite all there. The atlas was open to a map of the Canary Islands, Klavan noticed as he and Dimitrov approached. The old man had a fixation on islands; he swore he was going to retire to one when his ship came in.

'It's nice there this time of year,' Klavan said, taking a seat uninvited next to the old man, who smelled unwashed.

Herr Postling looked at Klavan and then at Dimitrov, who was still standing.

'Fat lot you know about it,' he said. 'I doubt you've ever been on a ship let alone an island.'

'I could take you up on that bet, Herr Postling. I come from a long line of—'

Klavan had almost said 'amber fishers', but abruptly cut himself off. There was no need to share his life story, to give anyone a hint of his true identity. Dimitrov lifted his eyebrows as if beckoning him to finish.

'You are quite right,' Klavan said to the old man. 'I saw a reference to the weather in Tenerife the other day in a newspaper.'

The old man tapped his bulbous red nose. 'You can't fool Hermann Postling. I can smell shit a mile off.'

But he was incapable of smelling his own, Klavan decided. Postling was an unwashed and disagreeable codger, which made him even a better choice. Klavan felt no reluctance in using him and discarding him. There was no one to miss him, no one to question about poor old Hermann. The hostel keeper had seemed amazed the first time Klavan had come to call that the old man could actually have a nephew who cared enough about him to pay a visit.

'Is that where you're going when you get your twenty pieces of silver?'

Postling eyed him contemptuously. 'Not likely I'd tell you, is it?'

'And you haven't told anybody else, right? Like you promised.'

'Who would I tell? And why? Buzzards around here would probably just try to steal the invitation.'

'You keep it hidden. That's the idea. Can't trust anybody.'

Postling looked up at Dimitrov again. 'Your friend going to sit down?'

'He likes to stand,' Klavan said. 'We've got to go soon. I just wanted to drop by and see how you're doing.'

'I'm not sharing the silver, if that's what you're after.'

Klavan shook his head. 'Wouldn't think of it. I just don't want people pestering you. Nobody's come around asking questions, have they?'

'What kind of questions?'

'Just questions. Maybe about the invitation.'

The old man muttered something in such a thick Austrian accent that Klavan did not catch it.

'What's that?' he said.

'I said there's no damn misfit bothering me except for you.'

Back out on the street, Dimitrov asked, 'What was all that about?'

'Just my old uncle,' Klavan said, turning his collar up against a sharp wind.

'And the twenty pieces of silver?'

Klavan eyed him with a brooding sense of loathing that shut the other up.

It was, in fact, how Klavan had met old Postling: begging on the street near the water tower on the Wienerberg in Favoriten. It was a spot Klavan had taken a shine to, with a view over the city that made a man feel like he controlled things. He had been there several times, thinking and planning. He'd taken little notice of the old man before, but for some reason today he'd focused on him.

At first glance, Postling was just one more scrofulous old reprobate, with an aroma coming off him bad enough you'd think it would keep anyone at arm's length. But it didn't. This patch of ground was near playing fields and a park that attracted the Viennese, even in winter with skating. He did all right for himself as a beggar. Klavan could see there was something about the old man, a cast of the eye, a glum look that reminded him of his own grandfather, and he'd dropped a half crown in the man's filthy tin dish. The clatter seemed to wake the geriatric up; he'd spluttered to life.

'Don't have to make a racket of it,' he'd said. 'Now I suppose you expect me to tip my hat to the fine gentleman. Pah. When I get my invite and my twenty pieces of silver from the emperor there'll be no more begging for Hermann Postling.'

He'd had no idea what the ancient shit was talking about, but Postling was happy enough to fill him in.

And thus was born his plan.

A bit of charity that paid off handsomely. Or would, anyway, as long as Dimitrov put a cork in the bottle.

'Just a simple question,' Dimitrov said, still stung by Klavan's silence.

They walked on without speaking. Klavan needed a break from the man. He saw a poster on the side of a factory wall, garish red with huge black lettering and a pair of handcuffs dangling between the letters: 'See the Great Houdini Defy Death by Drowning!'

'I assume the bullets were at least recovered before burial,' Gross said, his voice inching toward petulance, Werthen noted.

The court coroner shook his head. 'I'll have to check with my assistant, but I cannot see the importance of that. The driver and the guard were killed. Shot down like dogs at the gates of Schönbrunn. The means of death is clear.'

Gross rolled his eyes; a low moan escaped his throat as if he were in pain.

Werthen knew he was about to explode and interceded quickly. 'I believe Doktor Gross was hoping to examine the spent rounds for any identifying features.'

The coroner stared at him as if he were speaking Mandarin. Finally he said, 'I will get back to you after I speak with my assistant.'

Gross wasted no time in departing the coroner's office in a discrete corner of the immense Hofburg complex; he stomped down a long hallway like a man bent on violence.

When Werthen caught up with him, Gross turned on him as if it were he, Werthen, who was about to receive said violence.

'Damned incompetent man,' he thundered. 'Just our luck the shooting took place on court property. Herr Doktor Starb, whatever his deficiencies in dress might be, is at least no fool.'

Gross, Werthen knew, was referring to the director of the city morgue at the General Hospital, Doktor Starb, with whom they had had dealings in the past. But as this killing took place at Schönbrunn, the subsequent autopsy was under the purview of the court morgue, which was not known for its scientific acumen. Likewise the investigation: the bumbling fools had no clue as to who might be responsible for such an outrage. He and Gross had read their report; they could not even come up with a consistent description of the two assailants. In one report they were described as tall, beefy criminal types, in another as dark and sinister-looking denizens of the Balkans.

'And now we are denied even the spent bullets,' Gross said in the same voluble manner.

'We don't know that, Gross. Perhaps this assistant . . .'

'Oh, bravo for the assistant. Another fool, most likely. Someone's damned incompetent nephew, I'll warrant.'

There was no use talking to Gross when he was in one of these moods. Werthen just walked on down the corridor.

'*Et tu*, Werthen? Turning your back on me, as well?'

'So what is this secret you so desperately want to share?' Berthe smiled as she said this, for she had an inkling of what was coming.

Fräulein Erika Metzinger, her husband Karl's secretary, moved her still-untouched schnitzel around on her plate. They were seated at a window table at the Café Frauenhuber, which Karl called his home away from home; his 'third place.'

'Erika?' Berthe prodded.

'He's asked me to marry him.' She did not look up from the plate.

'But that's wonderful,' Berthe said. 'Why the long face? You love him, don't you?'

Erika finally looked up. 'Of course I do. He's the most wonderful man I know.'

'We are speaking of Herr Sonnenthal, right?'

This comment finally brought a smile to Erika's face.

'Yes, Berthe. We are talking about Bernhard.'

'Well then, again I say that's wonderful. But you really must do something about his name. You can't whisper sweet nothings to "Bernhard."'

'At such moments I simply call him Herr Sonnenthal.'

Which brought a laugh from Berthe this time. 'He really is a fine young man, Erika. You two are perfect together.'

'That's just it,' Erika said. 'I think we are perfect now, without marriage. I'm afraid it will change everything.'

'Marriage?' Berthe said incredulously. 'It's been almost four years for me and I haven't changed into a werewolf yet.'

'Be serious, Berthe. You know what I mean. I don't know if I am cut out for the role of hausfrau.'

'Is that what he wants? Someone to boil his shirts and have a hot meal ready whenever he arrives home?'

Erika shrugged.

'Which means,' Berthe persisted, 'that you haven't even asked him about his expectations. It's a new world, Erika. Even for the men we love.'

'I hope so,' Erika said, gazing quizzically now over Berthe's shoulder.

Berthe turned and saw the head waiter standing nearby as if he wished to speak with her. It was one of the under waiters who had served them earlier.

'Hello, Herr Otto. How are you this fine day?'

He looked troubled. 'Not so good, Frau Meisner. You see, it's my nephew. He seems to have gone missing.'

'It's patently obvious what's happened,' Gross was saying that evening after dinner as they all sat around the littered dining table at Josefstädterstrasse. 'The fellow's done a runner. Shows he was guilty all along. He'll probably turn up as a mustachioed waiter in some out of the way place in Italy beyond the reach of Austrian law.'

Werthen finished his coffee, setting his cup down deliberately. For a man of such intelligence, Gross could make quite ignorant pronouncements from time to time.

'And leave his pregnant wife and young son in the lurch?' Werthen said.

'To keep his neck out of the noose,' Gross replied. 'A dead man is little use to wife and children. At least this way he could send support money.'

'But there was no direct evidence linking him to the crime other than his own testimony . . .'

'Which you yourself wondered about at the time, I believe you told me. An attempt to cover his tracks in case anybody had witnessed the cowardly crime.'

True enough, but Werthen had begun to discount such a theory. Herr Otto was one of the best judges of a man's character that he knew. If Herr Otto did not suspect his nephew, then the young man was surely innocent.

'I was only at the tip of the iceberg with that investigation,' Werthen countered. 'There are still numerous leads to follow before jumping to conclusions.'

'Well, Herr Advokat,' Gross said in his courtroom voice, 'then come up with an alternate solution for Herr Falk's sudden disappearance.'

'Perhaps he's had an accident,' Werthen said, but realized how feeble that sounded the moment he uttered it.

'Two days missing,' Berthe said. 'I agree with Doktor Gross. He's run away. Or else . . .'

'Quite,' Gross said. 'Or else he's dead.'

# SIXTEEN

Werthen felt torn: he wanted to go back to his initial investigation, yet no less a personage than the emperor himself requested – no, commanded – his services. The next morning he and Gross got an early start. He had promised his parents that they would all go out to the Vienna Woods with them this Saturday to further inspect progress on their new villa, but Gross was adamant.

'Time is of the essence, Werthen,' he insisted. We have already lost two weeks. The trail will soon grow cold.'

'How much colder can it grow, Gross? There are no leads to follow.'

Gross cast him one of his knowing looks, which infuriated Werthen even further.

They took the tram to Schönbrunn, each sitting in his little pool of brooding silence after a remark from Gross as they boarded.

'No reason to be glum, Werthen. Your crime is solved. Falk's disappearance proves that. Be thankful we have such a lovely new task before us.'

No word from Gross as to why they were traveling to the summer palace once more, and Werthen was damned if he was going to ask, like some schoolboy querying his teacher.

Thus, there was silence between them as the tram rattled along the standard gauge rails on Mariahilferstrasse. Yesterday had been the first day of spring, and for once Viennese weather obeyed the seasons; the day was sunny and quite balmy, bringing the Viennese out in droves to the sidewalks of the busy Mariahilferstrasse. It was still morning, and the shops were open before Saturday half-day closing. Could Herr Falk be among them, somehow lost in the city? Perhaps he had a head injury. They say such things can cause a person to forget his identity.

Grabbing at straws, he told himself. Perhaps Gross was right about Falk.

They arrived at the gates of Schönbrunn, at the approximate spot of the failed assassination attempt on Franz Josef.

Gross immediately began scouring the cobbled area.

'You can't actually imagine you'll find any here after two weeks have passed,' Werthen said.

Gross made no reply.

'You can be damnably irritating,' Werthen said in exasperation.

This comment appeared to reach the criminologist. 'What do you say, Werthen?'

'Nothing.' He shook his head disgustedly.

'Well, don't just stand there with your hands in your pockets. We have investigating to do.'

He struck off at a furious pace toward an outbuilding a few hundred yards from the main gates. Werthen rolled his eyes and set out after Gross, catching up only as they approached what appeared to be a workers' shed.

'The guns were reloaded,' Werthen said as he finally realized their mission. 'Montenuovo said they emptied their revolvers and then reloaded.'

Gross wheeled on him suddenly but his face was beaming. He clapped Werthen on the shoulder.

'Good man. Which means . . .?'

'That you're hoping to find a casing. Perhaps one swept up as a souvenir by one of the groundsmen.'

'Ah, your wife is a lucky woman, Werthen, to be married to such a clever man.'

'You could have appraised me of your intentions, Gross.'

'But that would have denied you the delights of discovery.'

Werthen very much doubted his old mentor was actually attempting a learning opportunity. It was more likely a matter of raw egoism.

Gross began vigorously rapping a knuckle on the door to the outbuilding, which had the sign *Platzwart* – groundsman, over the lintel. The door was opened suddenly by a squat man in the grey uniform with red piping of the groundscrew at Schönbrunn.

'Good day,' Gross said pleasantly. 'I've come to talk with your supervisor.'

'You're already doing so,' the man said in a thick Viennese accent. 'What do you need?'

Gross quickly produced his letter from Prince Montenuovo, which made the fellow stand up straight and take notice.

'I need to talk with the crew that swept the front entrance the day of the accident two weeks ago.'

The man squinted at Gross and then let out a sigh. 'I knew it,' he spluttered.

Werthen and Gross exchanged glances but said nothing.

The man rubbed his stubbled chin. 'I told Müller he should report it to the palace authorities, but no, he knows better. There's no reasoning with the man.'

'Herr . . .?' Gross prompted.

'Wilma,' the other said. 'Siegfried Wilma. I've been the supervisor here for five years and nothing like this has ever happened on my watch.'

'Herr Wilma, what should this Herr Müller have reported?'

'Let him tell you himself.' He turned around and yelled into the depths of the shed. 'Müller! You've got company.'

A bleary-eyed giant came lumbering to the door, towering over his supervisor.

Wilma looked up at the man. 'I told you so.' And then he left Müller to deal with Gross and Werthen.

'So what do you two want?' It was not so much a question as it was an accusation.

'We understand you found something at the entrance to the palace,' Gross said. 'Just after that unfortunate accident two weeks ago.'

It hadn't been stated, but this was a good working assumption, Werthen figured.

Now Müller's mouth turned down at the corners; he was a sulking bear of a man.

'Never did,' he said. The denial sounded so patently false that Werthen let out a low laugh.

'I don't think it's funny,' Müller said, spittle flying from his mouth. 'I didn't find nothing.'

'This "nothing" you didn't find,' Gross said evenly. 'Might it be a shell casing?'

Müller's eyes squinted into arrow slits on a castle wall.

'Herr Müller?' Gross prodded.

'I don't have them.'

'What did you do with them?'

A muscle worked in the man's jaw. Werthen could tell Müller was struggling to concoct a lie, but he continued to let Gross handle the interview.

'I'll know if you're lying,' Gross said. 'If you want to keep this job you tell us the truth, and now.'

His voice rose on the last word, making Müller's eyes now open wide like a frightened horse.

'Sonnenthal. That reporter fellow. He's got them. Paid me for them but not enough for this trouble.'

Gross looked stunned for a moment, then turned abruptly and stormed off toward the fiaker rank near the palace entrance.

Werthen caught up with him again. 'Sonnenthal,' he said. 'Our Sonnenthal?'

Gross grunted at the question.

So I was right about Gross's sources, Werthen thought.

'The man should have told me,' Gross thundered, waving a fiaker down and climbing into the carriage.

Werthen followed, barely having time to take a seat as Gross spit out the address of the *Arbeiter Zeitung* office.

'Did you ask him?' Werthen said as the carriage bounced along the cobbles.

'Ask him what?' It was as if a black cloud were over Gross's head like some comical caricature in the magazine *Kikeriki.*

Werthen sighed. 'Herr Sonnenthal is an excellent journalist, but how was he to know you were investigating matters at Schönbrunn?'

'I damn well pay him to do so.'

'I assume he sent on news of this outrage along with other news that might be censored.'

Gross folded his arms over his bulky chest and puffed his lips out.

'Am I right?'

'Yes, yes.' Gross waved the question away.

'So he earned his money. It was up to you to seek further information once we were summoned for this case. You can't blame Sonnenthal for your oversight.'

'Who says I am?'

Werthen made no reply to this.

After a moment, Gross said, 'You are correct, Werthen, as usual. My oversight. I do not like making errors. Let us just hope that it is not too late to retrieve the casings. They are our only lead thus far.'

Werthen tried unsuccessfully to hide the shock on his face. That magisterial Doktor Hanns Gross should admit a mistake! The world must surely be coming to an end.

'If I'd known . . .' Bernhard Sonnenthal appeared quite abashed at Gross's revelations, shrugging with his hands.

They had left the offices of the newspaper and were huddled over a table at a small café near the editorial offices on Mariahilferstrasse. Obviously Sonnenthal did not think it appropriate to discuss his moonlighting ventures in the confines of the newspaper office. It was, however, as Werthen well knew, common practice for journalists to find another outlet for their hard-won stories, articles the powers that be would never allow to be printed. Much better a block of white space in the page than to allow the Viennese to know someone had tried to assassinate their beloved emperor.

'Well, you didn't and that is my fault,' Gross admitted. 'Do you in fact have evidence from the groundsman Müller?'

He nodded and took a sip of his mocha. 'They are in my desk at the office. If you wait a moment, I'll dash back and get them.'

True to his word, it was but a moment before Sonnenthal returned and placed three brass casings in front of Gross and Werthen. No expert on arms, Werthen left the examination to Gross, who immediately pulled out his travel magnifying glass and closely inspected the bottom of the casing.

It took him only moments to set the brass down on the marble table with a clink.

'As I suspected. Serbians at work.'

'You can determine that simply from spent bullet casings?' Werthen said with a degree of skepticism.

Gross sighed, but then decided to be lenient with his pupil and explain the process.

'This is clearly from a Nagant M1891 revolver, made in Belgium and Serbia with a 7.5 millimeter bullet. It has been the standard sidearm for the Serbian military for a decade. It has a most distinctive mark on the case.'

He held the casing to Werthen's eye; even without the aid of a magnifying glass he could see the *Nagant* etched in the brass.

'It is highly unlikely that such a weapon would fall into the hands of civilians, and even less likely still that two such models would.'

For Gross had determined from further marks that the three casings Sonnenthal had produced were fired from two different weapons.

'What you are saying is that the Serbian military ordered the assassination of the emperor,' Sonnenthal said with passion.

'Yes,' Gross replied, 'and it might be wise to keep your voice down, Herr Sonnenthal.'

There was no need to ask why; it was a simple matter of geopolitics. Austria had for decades wanted a foothold in the Balkans; Serbia on the other hand had dreams of becoming the leader of a pan-Slavic empire in the region. Long dominated by the Ottoman Empire, Serbia went to war against the Turks and managed to win Bosnia. However, following these hostilities in 1876 at the Congress of Berlin, Austria–Hungary managed to maneuver the great powers into giving her a protective mandate over Bosnia-Herzegovina. When Serbia itself was declared an independent state two years later, the rivalry only increased, spurred on in part by Russia, defender of the Slavs and eager to checkmate Habsburg ambitions in the Balkans. There were those who said war between the two was inevitable, but Werthen was not so sure. With interlocking alliances, nobody would be so foolish as to set off the Balkan powder keg.

A simple act of assassination, however, was a different matter.

'They've had their go,' Werthen said. 'I doubt they will try again. Not on Austrian soil.'

'Thank the Lord, Werthen, that you chose the law and not foreign affairs,' Gross remarked at this comment. 'I have heard tales of a secret society of Serbian army officers, the Black Hand, who vow to bring down the monarchy. Either ours or theirs. Fellow by the dramatic *nom de guerre* of Apis is at the head of it. So, I respectfully disagree. I very much doubt that this will be their last attempt. We are not talking about wild-eyed anarchists here, but rather a concerted effort by one state to eliminate the head of another state.'

Werthen and Sonnenthal exchanged looks; there was little reassurance to be gained from each other, however.

Gross went on: 'There will be further attempts, though I doubt any quite so clumsy and incompetent as this one. They may even bring in an international.'

'How do you mean?' Werthen asked.

'A paid assassin. A real professional and not more amateurs such as the ones who staged the fiasco at Schönbrunn. There are plenty such killers about for the right price.'

'We need to show these casings to Montenuovo,' Werthen said. 'If this proves Serbian involvement, then . . .'

'It proves nothing – not in a court of law, at any rate. And Vienna can hardly issue an ultimatum to another sovereign state – even one so deserving of it – with such flimsy evidence.'

Seeing the consternation on Werthen's face, Gross pushed on: 'Though unable to prove it in a court of law, I am undeterred. I have a superior intelligence. I am willing to join lines, make connections where others see only a series of dots. *And* I am not held accountable by matters of state. We will, of course, share this evidence. But do not delude yourself, Werthen. It will be up to us to foil the next attempt on the emperor's life.'

# SEVENTEEN

The lights went down and a less than imposing figure suddenly appeared on stage, sharply illuminated by a spotlight. Fans in the audience began clapping and a few also started a rhythmic chant: 'Hou-di-ni! Hou-di-ni!'

Harry Houdini, the famous escape artist, *der Ausbrecherkönig*, as he was billed, bowed at this reception, his long, wavy hair fluttering like a conductor's at the opera. He looked rather out of place in his tuxedo, Klavan thought, as if he should actually be at the Court Opera and not about to entertain the throngs with his renowned feats escapology.

Klavan sat amid this crowd of working-class Viennese occupying the cheap upper balcony seats at the Ronacher theater, happy that he had arrived as soon as the box office opened at seven, for there were many turned away for lack of available seats. He was enjoying the anonymous proximity to the masses. Their smell of perspiration reminded him of nights gathered around the fire as a boy growing up by the Baltic Sea. His brothers and father would bear the same heavy scent after a long day of amber fishing.

His attention was brought back to the stage as an announcer, also dressed in a tuxedo, proclaimed that Herr Houdini – a son of the monarchy, having been born in Budapest – would present for the first time a death-defying new escape. He would free himself from an oversized milk can filled with water. Its lid was padlocked closed.

'Failure means drowning,' the announcer intoned impassionedly, and the audience gasped.

At this announcement, Houdini grabbed dramatically at the front of his tuxedo and it came away to reveal his well-muscled frame clothed in a tight-fitting bathing costume.

'Herr Houdini invites members of the audience to attempt to hold their breaths as long as he must to effect this escape,' the announcer said, eyeing the audience as if in challenge. Houdini merely smiled.

Two massive assistants wheeled the large milk can on stage,

demonstrated how the lid opened and closed, and then Houdini wriggled and contorted his way in. Klavan felt a chill at the mere tightness of the space. When the assistants began adding buckets of water to the can, he wondered if this were really the right amusement for him. He had never felt secure on the water, despite the family business. Soon the water spilled out the opening of the can, and Houdini, who had kept his nose above the water-line until now, made a brief nod at the audience and dipped under. The assistants quickly padlocked the sides of the lid to the neck of the can with hasps, and then wheeled it behind a screen so that Houdini's art would not be given away.

A young working man to Klavan's right suddenly exhaled and then sucked in a volume of air, having tried unsuccessfully to hold his breath along with Houdini. There were sounds from behind the screen but they clearly came from Houdini; anyone attempting to help him would be visible to the audience.

'Somebody let him out!' a woman with the bosom of an overfed turkey shouted.

The rest of the audience shushed her. More seconds ticked by; the silence in the house was profound. Klavan could feel the tension himself, similar to when he would be about to go into action.

Suddenly a metallic clanking sound rang through the theater and a dripping wet Houdini appeared around the corner of the screen. The audience exploded in applause and shouts of 'Bravo!' Klavan could not help himself; he joined in with the others.

The rest of the show was an anticlimax for Klavan: Houdini wriggling out of a straitjacket, escaping from locked handcuffs, foiling the padlocks binding a steamer trunk into which he had descended.

He slipped out at intermission – a strong man was going to show off his muscles in the second half and nothing could be more boring for Klavan than such impoverished animal displays of strength.

Outside, the night air was crisp, clean and, for the first time since he had arrived, relatively mild. The vernal equinox had come and gone without him even noticing; it brought with it a spring evening. It would not last, he knew. Soon, winter would return. But for now he, like the Viennese out on the sidewalks, would simply enjoy the balmy evening.

He decided to walk for a while through the Inner City before making his way back to the lodgings at the Pension Geldner. He was tired of fending off questions from the frau. As he remembered from his previous stay, she had not been so curious. He wondered if she suspected something, fearing that Klavan somehow could cause her problems. And Dimitrov! The man should just die and stop making his – Klavan's – life miserable. But then, of course, his perfect plan would be ruined.

He put all this out of his mind for the moment, blending into the crowds of Viennese out on the streets, tipping his hat at a comely young woman who blushed at his impudence. It felt good to be a common citizen for a time. Not that he would want to make a habit of it. Such a life would be stifling. The wife and kids waiting for you to return from the factory; the soul-destroying nature of it all. He squared his narrow shoulders as he made his way through the crowds, knowing that he could kill any of these without the slightest effort. Knowing he could do it without the slightest remorse. He lived on a different plane than these Viennese, so self-satisfied with their new spring outfits, their fat cigars, their ample waistlines.

He understood Houdini – his life lived on the edge. Every performance could be his last. A simple mistake could mean death by drowning. He felt a kindred spirit in the man and had been meaning to see his performance ever since reading of Houdini's escape from a Russian Siberian transport van. Hadn't he effected his own such escape?

It had been worth the wait, he thought as he came into the Stephansplatz with the cathedral looming overhead. An optimistic café on the square had put out tables but it was hardly that mild. Still, the area was busy with pedestrians and the low hum of voices. He felt a tug at his leg and was about to kick out, thinking that a dog had grabbed his cuff. However, looking down, he saw a young boy in a sailor suit staring up at him.

'Papa?' the child said, bewildered.

His parents caught up with the tyke, apologizing to Klavan about their child's mistake. But this sudden disturbance made him want to return to the solitude of the pension. Dimitrov was sure to be in an alcoholic stupor by now.

\*     \*     \*

He knew something was amiss as soon as he let himself into the pension. Frau Geldner was not at her designated place by the front desk. She had been when he left, interested to hear of his planned visit to the Ronacher. He approached his room stealthily; no other guests seemed to be about tonight. Too busy enjoying the mild evening, as he had. His door was partly ajar and he could hear the muffled sound of drawers being opened and closed from inside. He felt instantly on guard, filled with the same tension he'd experienced when Houdini was locked in the milk can.

He slowly opened the door, revealing a scene he had half expected. There was Frau Geldner calmly going through his and Dimitrov's things, picking up his notebook from the bureau and flipping through the pages, stopping to read an entry here and there. She would not understand the significance of these entries, he was sure, yet the fact she was snooping sealed her fate. And where was Dimitrov while all this was going on? In a drunken stupor?

But a quick glance at the man's cot let him know this was no stupor.

He entered the room like a cat, quietly closing the door behind him.

She spun around, the notebook still in her hand.

'Oh, Herr Wenno. I am so glad you came back. Your friend . . .'

She nodded helplessly toward the cot where Dimitrov lay, a spray of blood from hemorrhaged lungs covering the white coverlet. His face was as white as the unviolated part of the coverlet.

'I heard a terrible gasping noise and came to see if I could be of assistance. I did not know what to do.'

He smiled at her consolingly. 'He was a sick man. It was to be expected.'

He felt the ground slipping out from under him, his well-laid plan scuttled by this death and his privacy breeched by Frau Geldner.

But he kept the smile on his face as he approached her.

'I didn't know what to do,' she repeated, putting the notebook back on the bureau. 'I hoped to find some clue as to your where-abouts . . .' She caught herself, realizing her mistake.

'Ah, but then you knew where I was, Frau Geldner.'

'Yes. How silly of me. It must have been the shock.'

He nodded. 'Quite understandable.'

He was within arm's reach of her now; she realized it as well, taking a step back and knocking the back of her legs against his cot.

'The authorities,' she said. 'They'll have to be notified.'

'I'm sure they will,' he said.

The movement was swift, unexpected. He bent over for an instant and suddenly came back up with a knife in his hand retrieved from the sheath on his left calf. It was all one motion, really, and it was as if he were watching it from the outside, seeing the blade fly through the air with an underhand toss to land with a dull thud followed by a hiss of the frau's breath as she exhaled, looking in amazement at the blade sticking out of her chest, trying to make an audible sound but failing. Her eyes grew wide for a moment and then fluttered as she collapsed back onto his cot.

She was dead by the time he put a hand to her carotid artery.

And now what? he asked himself. What to do with this mess?

The first thing was to expunge any record of his presence at the pension. Assumed name or not, Klavan wanted no leads to him from the Pension Geldner. He went back to the front desk. Still there seemed to be no other guests about. He found the registration book and tore out the page with the name of Wenno on it.

He made no attempt to clean up the mess in his room nor to try and stage some dramatic contretemps between the frau and Dimitrov. Let the authorities make of it what they might. He retrieved his knife, cleaning it on the frau's skirt before returning it to the scabbard, and then packed his belongings quickly. He took the explosive device out of Dimitrov's suitcase: that would serve as his own insurance now if apprehended.

He spent another five minutes carefully searching the room for any trace of himself. Had other guests noticed him? That was something that he could not control.

He locked the door behind him and took the key with him as he left the pension. Two blocks away, he dropped the key in a rubbish bin.

He knew where he would have to go. It was his last trump card, but now was the time to play it.

The maid opened the door cautiously. After all, it was a bit late for visitors.

Klavan smiled reassuringly. The maid looked him up and down with disapproval.

'Perhaps you could tell your mistress that she has a guest. Herr Schmidt. I am sure she will remember me.'

The maid scowled at this, closing the door in his face. He waited another couple of minutes, unsure if the stupid woman was doing as he requested. He was about to knock again when the door swung open.

'What is the meaning of this—'

She stopped when she realized who it was.

'Nice to see you again too, Lisette,' Klavan said to the tall, elegantly appointed woman. 'Or should I say, Princess Dumbroski.'

# EIGHTEEN

Detective Inspector Bernhard Drechsler was at the canal waiting for him as he had said he would be on the phone, just below the Stephanie-Brücke. Very secretive he was, and Werthen couldn't help but conclude that this must be damned important to be called out on a sacred Sunday.

It had been some time since he'd last seen the inspector, and as Werthen stood momentarily at the top of the stairs leading down to the dock running beneath the bridge, he could discern little physical change in the lean, hawk-nosed policeman. Drechsler and two uniformed police officers stood over what appeared to be a body on the quay, draped in a canvas cover.

It had been a brief spring: last night's relative warmth was replaced today with a cold front out of Siberia. The sky was low and gray; ravens wheeled overhead, making their annoying gurgling croak of a call. A flutter of snowflakes was carried in the piercing breeze. Werthen took the steps slowly, fearful there might be icy patches.

'What have we got, Inspector?' Werthen asked as he approached the three men. He already had a suspicion but hoped he was wrong.

Drechsler tipped his derby at Werthen. 'Sorry to draw you away from your family on a Sunday, Advokat, but I need an identification.' He nodded to what was now very obviously a corpse at their feet.

'Why me?'

Drechsler took out a sodden bit of card from his coat pocket.

'It's badly damaged from the water, but you can still read the name on it.'

He held it out for Werthen to see. It was one of his business cards.

'I assume it's a client,' Drechsler said. 'There was no other identification on the body, no wallet. No telling how long it's been in the canal. Herr Doktor Starb can help with that later at the city morgue, but for now it would be nice if we had a name.'

Werthen breathed deeply. 'Let's see.'

Drechsler nodded at the policeman to his left, a young man who did not look old enough to even be out of school, his cheeks rosy like a cherub's in the brisk morning air.

The young policeman leaned over, grabbed a corner of the canvas drop cloth and drew it slowly back. He let out an audible gasp and began retching, moving away in horror.

Werthen felt the hair at the back of his head bristle as he watched a small eel squirm and writhe out of the corpse's left eye socket.

He showed no emotion, and nor did Drechsler, who had obviously seen worse.

He took in the corpse in a glance, noting the strange angle of the man's head, the sack of cobbles belted around his middle, the bloated stomach cavity.

Werthen nodded casually, but was feeling anything but. 'Yes. I know him. His name is Falk. A waiter at the Café Burg.'

The young officer's dry heaves had now turned liquid as he vomited into the canal. Drechsler nodded to the other policeman to cover the corpse again.

'Must have taken a fall,' Drechsler said, eyeing Werthen closely.

'I doubt it,' Werthen said.

Drechsler slightly cocked his head, questioning this assertion.

'I don't have to tell you your business, Drechsler. You saw the angle of his head. Somebody's broken the man's neck. And you don't get cobbles tied around your waist by a simple fall into the Danube Canal.'

'A jumper?' Drechsler offered. But it was clear he was just angling for information and Werthen wanted to forestall the next question.

Instead, he asked one himself. 'How was he found with all that weight to hold him down?'

Drechsler looked over his shoulder in the direction of a stone bench on the quay tucked right under the arches of the bridge. An old pensioner sat there, a small bottle of schnapps in hand. A thick cane fishing pole leaned against the bench.

'Going for carp, the old fellow was,' Drechsler said. 'Bottom feeders. Thought he had snagged the granddaddy of them all. It was quite a shock for him when he finally managed to tug up your client, but luckily he didn't just run off. He found a policeman on his rounds and they managed to fish the body out.'

Drechsler continued eyeing Werthen. 'He *was* a client?'

Werthen nodded.

The ravens swept low over the corpse as if they meant to spirit it off.

'Law firm or inquiries?'

Here it comes, Werthen thought. It didn't matter to Falk anymore, but for him there was the matter of not reporting a murder to the police. A serious matter, in fact, especially if Drechsler's superior, Chief Inspector Meindl, got wind of it. Meindl was no friend of private inquiry agents, and held a special animus for Werthen as the sometimes colleague of Doktor Hanns Gross. Like Werthen, Meindl had been mentored by Gross while in Graz. Meindl was now repaying Gross's infernal pomposity with his own as head of the Vienna Police Praesidium.

'A friend brought Falk to me a little over a week ago,' Werthen finally replied. 'He had witnessed the murder of his superior at the café—'

'Stop right there, Advokat. You mean to tell me this man witnessed a murder and did not go to the police?'

Another nod. 'He was afraid he might become a suspect.'

Werthen explained the situation to Drechsler and his promise to keep it a secret for the time being while he investigated the death of Herr Karl. 'Then came another investigation that could

not be refused and I had to put the waiter's murder on the back
burner—'

'You're losing me, Advokat. You seem to be a very busy man.
Why didn't you at least contact me once you had to put the
murder investigation on the "back burner," as you put it? And
why can't you tell me about this other investigation of yours?'

Werthen tried to redirect the conversation. 'Herr Falk went
missing last Wednesday. His wife has been frantic.'

'But I assume she did not go to the police, either.'

Werthen could merely shrug at this. His attempts at misdirection
were for naught.

Drechsler shook his head and sighed. 'And I thought you were
the sensible one of the pair.'

An obvious reference to Gross, but Werthen did not bother to
respond.

'Perhaps then, you will at least do me and the city of Vienna
the favor of sharing what you have learned thus far about the
first murder, this Herr Karl fellow.'

'Of course, Inspector. I'll bring my files to the Praesidium
tomorrow.'

'I think not,' Drechsler said with what was for him a degree
of emotion. 'I'll expect you this afternoon.'

'Well, you do seem to have entangled certain parts of your
anatomy in the mangle,' Gross said later that morning after
Werthen had explained his situation.

'You needn't appear so gleeful, Gross. If Meindl finds out—'

'That poison pigmy,' Gross spluttered. 'He's far too busy
playing the sycophant to the wealthy and powerful to take notice
of your misdeeds, Werthen.'

Werthen only wished that were so, but previous run-ins with
the chief inspector had proven otherwise.

'I shall accompany you, of course,' Gross said importantly.

'I don't need my hand held.'

'Oh, it's not for your sake, Werthen. But we must ensure our
investigations on behalf of the emperor are kept out of it.'

'And I cannot be trusted to keep my mouth shut, is that it?'

Gross shrugged in response.

'Not encouraging, Gross. Nor helpful.'

'It's all right, Karl,' Berthe said. She was seated on the leather couch next to him in the sitting room at their Josefstädterstrasse apartment. Gross sat opposite them in an armchair. 'Inspector Drechsler won't turn you in. I imagine he is merely feeling some pique at not being included in the initial investigation, especially so now that it seems to have grown to two murders.'

She was right, Werthen suddenly realized. Not about Drechsler necessarily, but about the murder of Herr Karl. There were two murders to investigate and clearly they were connected. He'd been so concerned about possible legal consequences of withholding vital information from the police that he had not given a thought to what the death of Herr Falk meant for the investigation of Herr Karl's murder. The head waiter's murderer must have felt threatened. Somehow he, or she, had discovered that the killing was witnessed. Falk, the lone witness, had to die. What the murderer had not known, however, was that Falk could not identify the perpetrator, not even the gender of the killer.

But how had this information gotten out? Only he and Herr Otto knew. Falk swore he had not told his wife. Had Herr Otto told *his* wife, Falk's aunt? Had hers been the loose tongue?

And then Werthen realized *he* had also told *his* wife.

'Yes,' Gross intoned. 'It does put a different slant on things, this second murder. This is beginning to catch my interest.'

'I am so pleased for you, Gross.'

'Sarcasm, my dear Werthen, does not become you. I merely wished to acknowledge the importance that this is taking on. It is unfortunate that both our talents are required by a higher authority.'

Neither spoke for a moment. Werthen still felt guilty that he had not shared the information about the bullet casings they had unearthed. He did not want Berthe worrying about him and knowing that an assassination attempt on the emperor was being arranged by Serbia, and that he and Gross were the ones duty bound to prevent it would do just that. *Verdammt*. It was worrying enough for him.

Berthe looked from Gross to her husband. 'Are you waiting for a volunteer? I should think Inspector Drechsler capable of handling the matter. After all,' she said directly to Werthen now, 'you only took it on because Falk was afraid of being implicated. You've done much of the early leg work. Drechsler can surely carry on with your notes in hand.'

Werthen nodded, but without much conviction.

'I feel somehow responsible for Falk's death,' he said. 'And I am sure Herr Otto blames me, but he is being too much of a gentleman to say so. However, if I had continued with the investigation, Herr Falk might still be alive today.'

'Turnips and pocket watches, Werthen. No good comes of traveling down the road of what-ifs.'

Then, to Berthe: 'And you, Frau Meisner, sorely underestimate your talents. Look at the Lipizzaner matter.'

Yes, she thought, and look at me the other day, humiliated by that frightful Dumbroski woman.

'What is it you would have me do, Gross?' she asked.

'Gross is right,' Werthen said. 'You do not give yourself enough credit for good work. And it would make me feel less of a shirker. Perhaps you could just monitor matters. See if Drechsler follows through with the threads of the investigation. Who knows what priority Meindl will give these murders? The victims are not wealthy industrialists or members of the aristocracy, after all.'

'Well,' Berthe said, 'if you put it like that . . .'

'Marvelous,' Gross boomed. 'That is settled then. Gather your papers, Werthen. We'll go to deal with matters at the Praesidium.'

# NINETEEN

'I do not care to listen to your lies, Herr Schmidt, or whatever your name is. I am finished with that business,' she said to him the next morning over coffee.

'As I am also, I assure you,' Klavan said. He paused a moment, then smiled as he addressed her, 'My dear Princess Dumbroski.'

'Don't ruin things for me here, I warn you. I have a new life.'

'You can never really leave the old life behind, Lisette.'

'Don't call me that. Never call me that again.'

'But we had some times, didn't we? Remember the French field marshal? The German war minister?'

It was as if she relented for moment, remembering those sweet victories, those powerful men brought to their rickety knees by a little tart from Trieste posing as a virginal prospect for the nunnery or a daughter of an impoverished duke willing to sell her tender flesh to save her poor father and his estates.

The stories had changed from man to man, but in each she had been the untouched, unsullied virgin sexually debased by an aged roué, who also happened to have access to sensitive information regarding his country's military formations, battle plans and mobilization schemes.

Klavan had been her handler in those escapades, unwillingly at first, for he felt like a pimp working such entrapments. However, he soon learned to share Lisette's malicious sense of pride in ruining the lives of these pitiful old men who had gladly ruined – as they supposed – the frail sweet flower offered them. How shocking and degrading for them it had been to discover their old man fantasies had been faithfully recorded in photographs secretly taken at their assignations.

Confronted with the images of their own perversity, each had blustered and spluttered at first. But threatened with scandal and social ruin, each had eventually capitulated, and served up the morsels of secret information St Petersburg required.

All but Count Bartczak in Warsaw. He had taken the 'honorable' way out, leaving his body hanging from the rafters of his mansion for wife and grown-up children to discover instead of providing information on the border defenses.

Lisette Orzov was her name, of unknown or at least unremarkable birth, picked out of a Trieste brothel by a local Russian agent for certain horizontal skills she exhibited. It helped that she appeared to have a preference for those of her own sex, for old man fantasies tended to be in that direction as well. Promised a way out of the brothel, Lisette was only too eager to take the chance, Klavan remembered.

There was something in Lisette's eagerness to blot out her personal history that reminded Klavan of his own journey, becoming an agent for the tsar. For her it was her parents selling her to a brothel-keeper at age fourteen. For Klavan it was a career as a concert violinist destroyed by the jealousy of other wealthy students at the music academy in St Petersburg. He was a scholarship student, sponsored by a wealthy patron from near his village by the Baltic who'd heard the youth playing at a local church. But the privileged sons of the upper class at the academy couldn't stand the idea of a poor little son of amber fishers outstripping them in their lessons. One day they had cornered him and broke both his little fingers, ruining his possibilities of playing anything but a gun or knife. He looked down at his ruined hands, at the little fingers which had healed wrong and still jutted out from his hands at an awkward angle. And it was a gun or knife that these hands had subsequently learned to master, as his patron had recommended him thereafter to a very different sort of academy: the tsar's training school of secret agents.

Klavan had jumped at the chance, just as Lisette had at her opportunity for escape.

Her voice brought him back from these evil thoughts. 'In future I am Princess Dumbroski if you desire to stay under this roof. And you perhaps are a long-lost cousin, a black sheep sort of cousin. Agreed?'

He nodded with a smile.

'That is settled, then,' she said. 'Now I shall take myself off to fencing practice. And I meant what I said about not spoiling this new life for me. I do not wish to know the nature of your mission in Vienna. I simply do not want it brought to my doorstep.'

'I shall be most discreet, rest assured, Princess Dumbroski.'

But he said this as an implicit threat; his discretion would come at the price of a place to stay and regroup.

She fixed him with a steely gaze, then turned on her heel like a martinet and was gone.

Good old Lisette, he thought after she had left him to the fresh rolls and pot of coffee. True to form, she had not even bothered to ask him how he was able to track her to Vienna, nor to attempt an explanation of her new-found wealth. He, however, had heard it all from Monsieur Philipot in Brussels, for it was a minor member of the royal house of Belgium who was Lisette's unwitting benefactor.

According to Philipot, after last working with Klavan – this was before his debacle in Vienna – Lisette had decided to cut out the middle man. She no longer waited for a target chosen by St Petersburg, but went hunting on her own, picking a minor, though not impoverished, member of the house of Saxe-Coburg and Gotha, third cousin to the Count of Flanders. Laurent II was younger than her other targets had been, yet he was still a man of certain appetites and fantasies.

'Laurent II is said to be a great admirer of the Austrian, Leopold von Sacher-Masoch,' Monsieur Philipot had told him with a sly smile. Philipot knew about the scheme because Lisette had come to him to hire a photographer who would not ask too many questions. The subsequent photo gallery she had produced for the astonished Laurent had obviously been scandalous enough that he had put up little resistance to Lisette's demands for money, selling off some of the family shares in the Congo Free State to finance this payoff.

'She's set up quite nicely, now,' Monsieur Philipot had gone on to tell Klavan. 'Calls herself Princess Dumbroski, from what I hear, and fancies herself a fashion setter in Vienna.'

Such gossip had meant little to Klavan at the time, but as with most information, he filed it away in his mind for possible future use.

The future had arrived more quickly than Klavan had planned.

As Klavan ate his breakfast, he took stock of his situation now that Dimitrov was no longer available. He suddenly realized it was Palm Sunday, just a week until Easter. Only four days from Maundy Thursday.

He had his work cut out for him. And suddenly, after recalling the painful incident at the music academy, after seeing once again the glee on the face of the wealthy bullies who had ruined his life, he was filled with a new urgency, even an eagerness for the job. It would be his own personal revenge on the world of wealth and privilege. After all, what did he have to look forward to but a life on the run, a life of servitude to people like Monsieur Philipot or Apis, men too greedy or cowardly to do their own dirty work? It was suddenly as if all this were preordained. The mission to Vienna, scene of his previous disgrace; the death of Dimitrov whom he must now replace.

Four days to go.

He would be ready.


Police Praesidium Inspector Meindl was in fine form today. It was their bad luck that Drechsler had felt compelled to telephone his superior; usually Meindl could be counted on to be at his favorite café on a Sunday afternoon, sharing a friendly game of Tarock with a group that included an assistant to the interior minister and two deputies to the parliament.

Instead, he sat behind his massive cherrywood desk at the
Police Praesidium, dressed neatly as ever in finely tailored
English tweeds, sporting the usual tortoiseshell pince-nez and
so diminutive looking that he seemed like a marionette rather
than a canny navigator of Vienna's corridors of power, which
in fact he was. Behind the pince-nez Meindl's brown eyes glared
at Werthen and Gross.

'Obstruction of justice, I call it,' Meindl said in his high,
nasal voice, strongly modulate with an acquired upper-class
Schönbrunn accent. 'Withholding vital evidence in a murder
investigation.'

'Strictly speaking,' Werthen was quick to point out, 'there was
no murder investigation. The death of Herr Karl was put down
as an accident by the police.'

Meindl's normally rosy cheeks grew brighter at this comment.
'And had you apprised us of this Herr Falk's confession, there
would surely have been such an investigation.'

'Information, not confession,' Werthen said. He could feel
Gross's eyes on him, for it was usually Gross who did the bear-
baiting of the preening Meindl. Werthen was beginning to enjoy
himself.

'No legal semantics today, Advokat. And you, Gross – with
your background in the law one would hope for more.'

'Actually,' Werthen replied, 'Doktor Gross had nothing to do
with the Falk matter. I took that on entirely on my own. I, of
course, had every intention of notifying the police once I ascertained the verity of his assertions.'

'I'm sure you did,' Meindl said with a degree of sarcasm.
'That is why it has taken almost two weeks for you to provide
us with your notes. Not to mention the death of another man.
Had you come to us in a timely fashion—'

'Quite,' Werthen interrupted Meindl. 'That is something I shall
have to live with. However, other events intervened.'

Meindl looked from Werthen to Gross with ill-concealed
contempt. 'And what other events are we talking about? More
obstruction of justice? And what are you doing in Vienna, Doktor
Gross, if not helping Advokat Werthen in one of his meddling
investigations? One would assume your students in Czernowitz
need your professorial attentions.'

'The University of Prague, as of this year,' Gross was happy to correct the inspector. 'And for your information, I am in Vienna at the request of a higher authority.'

Meindl clapped his hands in glee, fixing Werthen now in his glare. 'Hah. This would be the mysterious investigation you refused to share with Detective Inspector Drechsler, I suppose.'

'The very one,' Werthen allowed.

Meindl slapped his right hand down forcibly on the desktop. 'There will be no secrets from the Police Praesidium. Is that understood?'

Werthen and Gross merely looked back at the inspector calmly. They could hear Drechsler clearing his throat, seated in back of them.

Their ensuing silence made Meindl raise his voice another notch. 'If you two do not want to find yourself behind bars, I demand to know what diverted your attention from the murder of this waiter.'

'Head waiter, in point of fact.' Werthen could not help himself.

'Do not toy with me, gentlemen. You don't want me for an enemy.'

But we already have you as one, Werthen thought, though he decided silence was a better option at the moment.

'Meindl,' Gross said pleasingly, leaving off any titles in a collegial manner, 'we have no intention of angering you. It is simply that we have been sworn to secrecy in this matter. I can, however, share with you a missive that empowers us in said investigation.'

Gross brought the letter from Montenuovo out of his jacket pocket and laid it on the desk in front of Meindl. The inspector looked with suspicion from Gross to the letter then finally unfolded the paper, smoothing it carefully on the leather desk pad, and slowly read it, his thin lips moving with each word.

Finishing, Meindl held the letter up to the light from his window as if searching for signs of forgery.

'You can call the prince if you are unsure,' Gross said. 'Werthen here bears a similar letter of commission. We are at work on a case of the highest importance to the empire. That is, unfortunately, all that we are allowed to say of the matter.'

Meindl shoved the letter back across the desk at Gross as if it were a bad smell.

'Which still does not excuse your actions, Advokat. I assume you have brought all pertinent information so that we may initiate a systematic investigation into these deaths?'

'That is correct, Inspector,' Werthen said, though he was damned if he was going to turn over his notebook. 'Records of any witness I may have spoken to and any possible motives and suspects in the case. I am afraid I did not get very far, only to ascertain that Herr Karl, the first man killed, was running a bit of a fiddle on the side, extracting money from workers and vendors alike.'

'And this second death,' Meindl said. 'Another waiter.'

Drechsler spoke up now. 'The under waiter at the same establishment, sir.'

'Well there's motive for you,' Meindl said brightly. 'Hadn't thought of that, had you, Advokat? Kill the boss to get his job. Then contrition sets in, the man can't live with himself and commits suicide.'

Another clearing of the throat from Drechsler. 'Not a suicide, sir. Chap's neck was broken, according to the medical examiner.'

'He could have broken it diving into the canal. Hit a bridge brace.'

'No water in the lungs, sir,' Drechsler replied. 'Herr Falk had his neck broken before being thrown into the canal. It was murder.'

'Well,' Meindl said, trying to salvage some respect, 'I am glad we have cleared that up. And now, you two, remember what I said.'

Werthen and Gross exchanged glances. What *had* Meindl said? But neither uttered a word as they got up and left the Police Praesidium to its hit-and-miss investigation.

They were cutting it close: their appointment with Montenuovo was at one in the afternoon and they finished their business with Meindl at twelve-thirty. Gross did not bother consulting Werthen's wishes about walking or finding a fiaker. Instead, once out of the main door of the police headquarters, he set off at a furious pace toward the Ring, and Werthen was again left to catch up as best he could. Today was one of those days – with the renewal of raw, cold winter weather – when his left knee was acting up. Wounded in a duel in his first case as a private inquiries agent, his knee had a way of painfully reminding him of that earlier escapade. Every step was an agony and the wind whipped snow flurries in his face.

Finally he called out to the criminologist, 'Gross! For pity's sake, slow down.'

Gross turned abruptly, waiting for him. As Werthen approached, Gross smiled.

'Serves you right,' he said, 'for taking away my fun with Meindl. Now let's hop to it. Don't want to keep the prince waiting.'

Gross did not give him a chance to explain about his leg; any normal person with a sense of empathy would have noticed him limping. Not Gross, however. He was devoid of empathy – a characteristic as foreign to him as humility.

Gross plunged on into the darkening day, into the sheet of snow that had begun to cover the city.

And in the end it was all for naught. Montenuovo treated their discovery exactly as Gross had prophesied: too little evidence to proceed. How could Austria send an ultimatum to another sovereign country on the strength of three shell casings? Neither would his eminence, Franz Josef, agree to a curtailment of public appearances. Not at Easter time, to be sure.

'But it is not the sovereign state of Serbia,' Werthen protested. 'It is most likely a cabal of officers around this Apis fellow.'

'Do you hear yourself, Advokat?' Montenuovo said. '"Most likely." That is not good enough. Find me a perpetrator able to link this assassination attempt to Belgrade and we will do more than send an ultimatum, I can guarantee you. But for now there is nothing to be done but ensure the emperor's safety.'

'And how are we to do that,' Werthen complained, 'if the emperor insists on taking part in all manner of public appearances?'

'That, my friend, is what you have been hired to ascertain and to insure.'


'I appreciated your help back there,' Werthen said with heavy irony once they were back on the open square beneath Montenuovo's Hofburg office. The snow had intensified; there was already a good six inches coating the cobbles.

'I am sure you will not appreciate this, Werthen, but in fact—'

'I told you so,' Werthen finished for him. 'For God's sake, let us find a gasthaus and round of slivowitz before we suffer frostbite.'

# TWENTY

Werthen had transcribed his notes for Drechsler, keeping the original in his leather pocket notebook. Berthe was grateful for this; she had a starting point. Now going over those early notes the next morning, she was able to check off the unfortunate Herr Falk as a suspect.

Berthe was not so sure about her husband's theory of his death. It seemed a stretch that the murderer would somehow find out that there was a witness to his homicidal activity. And why strike nine days following the murder of Herr Karl? Surely the killer would assume that by that time Falk would have told the police everything he knew, if he were ever going to do so.

Berthe took a different tack: what if the murder of Herr Falk were not a matter of defense at all, but of offense? In this version of events, the deaths of Herr Karl and Herr Falk were related in motive and not a matter of the killer covering his or her tracks. But what could that motive be?

Examining her husband's list of suspects, she could easily check off those who might have killed because of Herr Karl's pay-off scheme and monetary kickbacks from vendors and staff. Herr Falk had himself been victim of this scheme. Likewise, the relatives of the previous head waiter at the Café Burg, Herr Siegfried, the traces of whom Herr Karl had thoroughly expunged when he'd become head waiter. Herr Falk had nothing to do with that, either.

Other ambitious waiters or jealous head waiters could also be put to the bottom of the list. From what Berthe's husband told her, Herr Falk was only temporarily serving as head waiter following Herr Karl's death. The management of the Café Burg was going to bring in another waiter from outside the staff. And the literary critic, Moritz Fender, could surely have no quarrel with Herr Falk, for it had been Herr Karl who had made his café the home of one of Vienna's many literary circles.

Also, if she were looking for common motive, then clearly

Herr Karl's Bosnian Serbian roots that Kraus had pointed to had nothing to do with these murders.

Which left her with only one avenue of investigation: Herr Karl's bosom friend, Oberstabelmeister Johann Czerny. Hardly a suspect, but her husband had been keen to talk with the man right up to the point where he was commissioned by Prince Montenuovo. Perhaps Czerny would have some information about his old friend that could help to explicate his and Falk's deaths.

But what to make of the mysterious stranger Falk saw talking with Herr Karl? Again, Berthe's husband seemed to find this incident of interest, mentioning twice in his notes that he should follow up on this possible lead. Yet such a possibility went against her new theory of shared motive for the deaths of Falk and Herr Karl. If the mysterious stranger – with an awkward way of holding his cup – were the murderer, that would take matters back to the original theory: Herr Falk's death was to keep him from talking.

She put a question mark next to this section of the notes.

And what to make of the name scrawled on a crumpled piece of paper and used as a bookmark?

'Hermann Postling.'

This could mean anything, but once again Berthe trusted her husband's instincts for keeping this scrap of paper found at Herr Karl's rooms. She wondered if he had included the name in his transcription of notes he'd handed over to Drechsler and somehow doubted it. The police would surely want the original for handwriting analysis.

With such a dearth of investigative leads, Berthe decided to keep her options open with Herr Hermann Postling. Perhaps there would be a *Meldezettl* listing for him, a way to track the man. Could Postling and the mysterious stranger at the café be one and the same? It was worth a bit of time in the city archives, she decided.

Her thoughts were interrupted as the double doors to the sitting room of their Josefstädterstrasse flat were thrown open and her daughter Frieda – dressed in a fur hat, long woolen coat and fur hand muff – came bursting in, her cheeks red and glowing with the cold from outside.

'*Mutti, Mutti,*' the excited toddler screamed as she raced to the leather couch where Berthe was ensconced with papers and pencil as she took notes. 'The snow was so white!' She jumped onto the couch, sending papers flying.

'Sorry,' came a voice from the doorway. 'She got away from us.'

It was her father, Herr Meisner, accompanied by his new friend, Frau Juliani, a small, energetic and outspoken woman for whom Berthe was developing a real liking.

Berthe held her daughter to her tightly, paying no attention to the disarray of papers. There would be too few opportunities for hugging in the near future, she feared. Children grow up so rapidly; she would take any opportunity for a nice, long hug. She felt even closer to her child – if that were possible – because of the events of last autumn, when they had almost lost her to scarlet fever.

'Snow generally is white,' she whispered in Frieda's ear.

The child drew back from her, shaking her head and looking quite serious. 'No. Not on the street. People step on it. Black like my bobo.' She lifted her coat and pointed to her stockinged shin. Underneath the layers of clothes was a black-and-blue bruise where she'd bumped her shin playing.

This made Berthe laugh with joy. 'A poet in the making. The bruised snow. Perhaps your daddy will use it in one of his stories.' And she hugged Frieda again.

Finally she looked over her daughter's shoulders. She had completely forgotten her father and Frau Juliani, who were still standing in the doorway like guilty children.

'I am sorry,' Berthe said. 'But you don't have to wait to be asked to come in, do you?'

Her father, who had his home in Linz, had lately taken a small apartment in Vienna to be near his friend. He was spending more time in Vienna now than in Linz, and they enjoyed spending time with Frieda, taking her on outings like the one this morning.

Her father shrugged, and she sensed there was something wrong. The two of them took off their heavy coats as Berthe helped Frieda out of hers. A bit of snow fell out of the fur muff and Frieda quickly gathered it up only to have it melt in her little hands.

Herr Meisner and Frau Juliani came into the room, sitting in the leather armchairs across from Berthe. Again, she felt the strain. A widower for many years, Herr Meisner was not a cloying, overly protective father. He had wide interests. In addition to his successful Linz shoe factory and to his reputation as one of the most noted Talmudic scholars in Austria, he was also an amateur musician of no little talent and a historian of prodigious knowledge. But suddenly something seemed not right with him.

'Sweetie,' she said to Frieda. 'Why don't you go find Baba? She's in the kitchen.'

Frieda's eyes grew wide with anticipation. 'Baba! Yes.'

She was off Berthe's lap and out of the room with no further adieu, in search of her beloved Baba – their cook, Frau Blatschky, with whom Frieda had developed a very special relationship.

Alone now, Berthe eyed her father. 'Is everything all right? You both look as though you've just broken a cookie jar.'

This made them smile, but did not ease the tension.

'Well,' Herr Meisner finally said, 'it's just that we have something to tell you.'

By the look on his face, she expected the worst.

'What is it?' she said with real concern. 'Are you ill? We'll see the best specialists.'

Herr Meisner waved his hands in front of him. 'No, nothing like that.' He looked sideways at Frau Juliani. She reddened as he said, 'In fact, I've never felt better physically in my life.'

Frau Juliani looked down at her cupped hands in her lap.

'Well, what is it, then?' Berthe said. 'Out with it.'

'We would like to get married,' Frau Juliani said, as it was obvious Herr Meisner was for once tongue-tied. 'And we would like your blessing.'

Berthe could not help herself; she began laughing, partly out of relief and partly at the absurdity of the situation of her father feeling he had to ask her permission to marry.

Seeing their shocked reaction, she put her hand to her mouth to still her laughter. Berthe jumped to her feet and went to them, kneeling in front of where they sat and attempting clumsily to embrace them both. They finally leaned in so that she could grab the outer shoulder of each.

'It's wonderful news,' she said. 'I am laughing only because I thought there was something wrong, not something right.'

Frau Juliani was the first to draw back, punching Herr Meisner's arm playfully. 'See, I told you that you'd raised a sensible daughter.'

'I just thought . . .' he began.

'You've been alone for almost two decades, Papa. You deserve some happiness.' And then to Frau Juliani: 'So long as I don't have to call you "Mama,"' Berthe said.

'Fredrika will suffice,' Frau Juliani said. 'Yes, I know, quite a mouthful. Close friends call me Freddi – I hope you do so, too.'

# PART FOUR

# TWENTY-ONE

K lavan walked along the street feeling invulnerable.
At any instant he could turn the sidewalk full of noon-time strollers into an abattoir. All it would take would be a little squeeze on the hollow India rubber ball he carried in his left trouser pocket. He had taken this trick from the British anarchists who vowed never to be taken alive by the police. The little ball was attached to a thin, surgical rubber hose that led up the inside of his vest and fed into a vial in the inside pocket of his suit coat. Squeezing the ball would create a puff of air, activating a shutter-like contraption which in turn would immediately spark the explosive material he carried in the coat pocket. Enough concentrated explosive material to flatten everything in a ten-yard radius.

It had been intended as his assassin's weapon for the unfortunate Dimitrov, though he did wonder if that man could have gone through with the deed when it had come down to it.

Now it served as his insurance that he would not live out his days in a moldy prison cell or dangle at the end of a rope.

He had a new idea now, for he could hardly expect old Hermann Postling to blow himself to kingdom come on his, Klavan's, say-so; neither could he see any way to deceive the old man into carrying and setting off such a bomb. So, Plan B.

He'd made his way by foot today from Lisette's spacious Ringstrasse apartment past the Hofburg, Parliament and Rathaus to the intersection with Währingerstrasse. This he followed north past the Votiv Kirche and he was now approaching his destination, the Military Academy for Medicine and Surgery, otherwise known as the Josefinium.

Klavan knew its history; knew that this was named after Emperor Joseph II, the reforming kaiser, built in 1785. For the last several decades it had served as medical library and museum of human anatomy. But Klavan had no interest in history other than in the secrets it might reveal for his personal use. That is why the Josefinium interested him in one major respect. During his last fateful mission in Vienna, Klavan had gathered a wayward bit of information from one informant. It seemed one section of the old academy was still being used for medical research, but of a type that needed to be kept secret from the Viennese. Office 3G it was innocently called, but within its small confines there was the potential to destroy Vienna.

Klavan had no real desire to destroy this city, though he did find it an intriguing possibility. To rid the earth of so many humdrum lives would be no crime.

He had a more limited goal. He wanted to destroy one small faction of the city; he would strike off the head of the snake. He tensed his hand in excitement at this thought, stopping just as it began to apply pressure on the rubber ball in his pocket. Klavan let out a barking laugh at his near accidental suicide. A young woman bundled in furs and wool scurried past at that moment and cast him a suspicious glance. He winked at her seductively and this sent her bustling along at increased speed.

He stopped outside the massive wrought-iron gates, looking at the rather pleasant classical facade – two wings jutting out from a central hall. The steep roofs were coated in snow; the bare trees of the first courtyard were still powdered white; the Habsburg eagle surmounted the third-story balustrade. Office 3G was in the rear of the third story of the left-hand wing.

He put his hand to the gate and pushed it open.

He had his story arranged, rehearsing it once more as he walked toward the main entrance past the statue of Hygieia, the goddess of health. At least he assumed that was who it was, with a snake wrapped around her arm and feeding from a bowl she held.

Symbols. Klavan hated symbols. Hygieia was the daughter of Aesculapius, god of medicine, whose own symbol was a snake curled around a rod. Snakes shed their skin, so the ancients took them as symbols of regeneration. Aesculapius's daughter kept the healing snake and added a bowl, the symbol of pharmacy. Another example of the useless information pumped into his brain during his all too brief stay at the music academy in St Petersburg.

That's why I hate symbols, Klavan told himself as he passed by the scantily clad statue. Too cerebral. Klavan much preferred action.

There would be plenty of that soon.

A sign at the main doors let visitors know that the Josefinium Collection of Anatomy and Pathology was open only on Saturday mornings and to men only. The 1200 wax figures, produced in Florence and painstakingly shipped from there, would not be allowed to corrupt the tender sensibilities of Viennese ladies.

It was the left wing that was Klavan's destination. Here was one of the finest medical libraries in Europe, taking up two floors of that wing.

He let himself in the main door and headed to the left. Today he was Professor Doktor Wilhelm Schieff of Hamburg come to do research otolaryngology, a Viennese specialty. The young man seated at the registration desk leading to the library took the identity papers Klavan offered him and which, together with several other false identities, he had stored in a rental locker at the central station in Brussels. Like the suicide bomb he wore, such papers were Klavan's insurance in an insecure world. In an emergency he could find other identities as well.

The young bureaucrat looked carefully at the papers. Klavan was unconcerned: they had been produced by the Office of Documents at his former employers, the Russian Military Intelligence. But the young man was hardly looking for forgeries; who would go to such lengths to be allowed in the medical library?

No. Klavan figured this was merely his way of appearing important, of making his shit work appear vital to the country.

Klavan made out the pulsing artery in his throat he would cut were this a true 'situation'.

That was what his trainer, Kolinsky, called a life-and-death confrontation. 'You have a situation, you need to know already where to strike your adversary. Determining that once the situation begins can mean defeat.'

Which meant death, of course, only Kolinsky liked to deal in polite evasions and euphemisms.

'Any person you see or meet, first thing is the examination for weak spots where you can strike. You don't care what he does for a living,' Kolinsky preached, 'you don't care if he is married or parts his hair on the right. You want to know his dominant hand, you want to judge his reach, look at his face for scars of other battles, see how he plants his feet. If you want to stay alive, you know these things before you ever shake his hand.'

The registrar handed back his identity papers and without speaking gestured Klavan to the door of the reading room. Klavan left his heavy coat at the cloakroom and then, entering the library, he found a large space, well lit with floor-to-ceiling windows. Several large tables were in the center of the parquet floor with chairs. He found free space at a more private table at the edge of the room by a window. He put down the brown pig leather briefcase on the tabletop to reserve his place and went to the card catalogue. He had bought the case today on the walk along the Ring especially for this visit. He had also purchased a number of pocket handkerchiefs and stored them in the back along with a notebook and pen. He opened the case and took out the pad and pen along with one of the handkerchiefs, which he'd shoved into his front pants pocket. He would need that later for padding.

Klavan checked the card catalogue industriously for several minutes, filled out five request cards and handed them to a white-coated attendant who would fetch the books from the shelves. He watched as the attendant went out of the room and headed for the stairs at the rear of this wing.

Klavan took up his place again at the table by the window, opening his empty notebook as if looking at notes. Five minutes later the attendant returned with four heavy tomes on the principles of otolaryngology and individual aspects of throat diseases.

'Sorry, sir, but *Treatise on Nasal Fungal Aspects* is currently at the bindery being repaired.'

Klavan made a great show of being annoyed by this inform-ation before waving the attendant away. He spread out the books on the table in front of him and began a careful inspection – not of their contents, but of the plan now hatching in his mind.

He knew now that the books were stored on the second floor and that white-coated attendants seemed to have easy access to that territory. He checked the clock on the wall next to the portrait of Joseph II. It was still twenty minutes until the sacred Viennese lunchtime. The library would close for ninety minutes, according to the listing on the front door. And that would give him his chance.

At ten minutes to noon, he packed his briefcase, placing it on one of the chairs, and left the books on the desk.

'I assume I can leave the books for later,' he said to another attendant, and the man nodded.

'They'll be here when you return from lunch sir. *Mahlzeit,*' he added in that annoying salutation the Viennese employed at times of eating, a much-diminished form of *bon appétit.*

Klavan gritted his teeth as he returned the greeting. 'And where might I find the washrooms?'

The attendant went out into the main rotunda and directed him to a set of doors just beyond those leading up to the stored books.

'But best to hurry, sir. Wouldn't want to get locked in and miss your lunch.'

'Most certainly,' Klavan agreed, but that was exactly what he *did* want.

There was no one in the washroom. He took up position in an empty stall in case one of the attendants was the overly conscientious sort. As the minutes ticked away, he discovered this had been a wise move, as someone called into the washroom at noon to announce the mealtime closing. He heard the door close slowly behind this herald, but was in no hurry to come down from his perch, sitting in a squat on the toilet seat so that his feet would not show under the stall door. He gave it another five minutes before getting down from the toilet and proceeding cautiously to the door of the washroom. He put his ear to the white enameled door but could near nothing from the outside. To be safe, he gave it another five minutes, then slowly opened the washroom door, peering out toward the entrance. The hallway was empty; no sign of assistants or the registrar by the library. He quickly made his way to the door across the hall leading up to the second floor, through which he had earlier seen one of the assistants disappear. He was in luck, for this door opened to a sort of landing before the stairs; on hooks next to the door hung several of the white coats the assistants wore. Perhaps this was where they divested themselves of their uniform before heading off to lunch.

He would borrow one and return it long before any of the assistants returned from their sausage and kraut. Klavan did not have a high impression of Viennese cuisine.

He quickly found one of the white coats that fit and slipped it on. He hoped this would provide him with double cover: for the book depository on the second floor and for Office 3G on the floor above.

He was working on old information there, but knowing the

glacial speed at which life in Vienna changed, he felt fairly sure Office 3G was still in operation.

He mounted the stairs, careful to do so as quietly as possible. He had no idea who might be about during the noontime closing. Surely there was a guard somewhere. Or were they all off to the gasthaus? How Viennese of them, he thought with venom. The land of *schlamperei*. Thoughts such as this only made him more disgusted with himself that his previous mission to Vienna should have been compromised. Yet it was not the Viennese that had tripped him up, but rather that meddlesome Advokat Werthen and his cohort, Doktor Gross, both originally from Graz if he were not mistaken.

He shoved such thoughts from his mind, concentrating now on each step he took upward. Finally he reached a door and discovered that on the other side of this was a hallway almost identical to the one on the floor below.

Where to now? One would think the stairs would continue into the floor above, but instead they ended at the second floor. Was there a separate outside entrance for the third floor? It would make sense, knowing the nature of the work that went on in Office 3G. But if so, such an entrance was most probably a recent addition, built since Office 3G had been moved in secrecy here from the General Hospital in early 1899. Surely the original plans built during the reign of Joseph II had included contiguous interior stairs to the third floor, and just as surely the existence of such stairs had been disguised.

He went back into the stairwell and examined the end of the steps at the second floor. Why hadn't he noticed it before? These steps led up to a wall; the door was to the right. Covering the wall was a large canvas sign demarking the second floor and book depository. 'Entrance restricted to library personnel only.'

He tapped lightly on the canvas-covered wall and heard a hollow sound. Then he ran his hands over the surface, feeling for any irregularities. As he suspected, at about waist high his right hand struck on such an irregularity. He ran a finger along the right corner of this wall and discovered the sign could be lifted out from the wall. Behind was a small door with a latch countersunk into the wood so as to be unnoticeable.

Whoever had renovated had left this access even after deciding to block the interior stairs. Makes sense, he thought. An emergency exit. There could well be need for such a means of rapid egress from Office 3G.

He turned the latch and the small door opened. He ducked his head as he entered, and then made sure that there was a corresponding operational latch on the inside before closing the door behind him. This led to a flight of stairs similar to that which took him to the second floor. He followed the stairs up and came to a full-sized door. He assumed that this one led to the third-floor hallway, but again took the time to listen for exterior noises before opening it. Hearing nothing, he slowly opened this door, peaked his head out and saw no one about.

Apparently noontime was as sacred for the researchers of Office 3G as it was for the library personnel below.

He proceeded down this long hallway, past one long room with a bank of interior windows giving onto the hallway like a nursery observation ward in a hospital. Instead of babies, however, there were dozens of cages holding an assortment of animals: white rats, rabbits, guinea pigs and some larger animal that Klavan was not sure of. A stoat?

He proceeded past this to another room which also had interior observation windows. Here were row upon row of test tube racks, each containing a glass tube stoppered with a ball of cotton. He nodded. This was what he was looking for.

He was just putting his hand to the door of this room when a voice sounded from behind him.

'Library personnel are not allowed on this floor.'

He wheeled around to confront a robust-looking young officer dressed in a blue military tunic with white buckskin pants tucked into high black books. He wore a sword at his side and looked like he might know how to use it.

Klavan made his usual immediate survey of the adversary. Sword worn on the left hip; the soldier would have to draw it right handed across his body.

'Sorry,' Klavan said in his most pleasant voice. 'I'm actually a visiting researcher. This was all they had to give me for the lab.' He pulled at the lapels of the white lab coat.

The officer looked at him more closely now. It was obviously better to be mistaken for an errant library assistant than caught in an obvious lie, which Klavan had the feeling he had been. He'd taken a chance with the visiting researcher story; it was not working with the officer, who was obviously familiar with every person in Office 3G.

Quickly now, he thought, as he continued smiling benignly at the officer. He was too far away from the man; nothing else he could do. He made the decision.

'Look,' the officer began, then stared at Klavan's hand as he brought out the hollow India rubber ball from his pants pocket, the length of tubing also showing.

'I squeeze this and we are both pieces of meat and whatever is stored in those glass tubes goes up with us,' Klavan said, still smiling. 'But it won't destroy that material. Merely spread it in the air for the entire city to breathe.'

The officer put his right hand on his sword.

Klavan shook his head. 'I wouldn't do that if I were you. Not unless you are prepared to have your name go down in infamy.'

'What do you want?'

Klavan nodded at this. 'Better. I am a simple journalist—'

'With a bomb?'

'An anarchist journalist,' he said, improvising and moving closer to the target. 'I have heard rumors of this secret laboratory. After the tragic events of October, 1898, this was supposed to have come to a halt. However . . .' Klavan swept his free right hand toward the observation windows.

The man gripped his sword again. 'How do I know you even have a bomb?'

Klavan smiled on the inside now. This was what he was waiting for.

'You see the tube here – it is threaded down my pants to an explosive charge taped to my calf. Here, I'll show you.' Keeping his eyes on the soldier, Klavan leaned over, reaching under his pant leg with his right hand to free his knife.

The subsequent movement was so smooth and rapid that the soldier was staring down at the handle of a knife blade sticking out of his chest before he realized what was happening. He took a stumbling step toward Klavan, then toppled to the parquet floor.

Klavan lost not a moment in deciding what to do. He took his knife out of the man's chest, wiped it on the tunic and quickly replaced it in its sheath. Then, grabbing the large soldier under the arms, he dragged him to the door to the stairs, manhandling him down the flights of steps to the small hidden interior door on the second floor. Still wearing the white lab coat, he raced back up the stairs to the third floor and the room full of test tubes about half an inch in width and six inches long. Each was stoppered with a hunk of cotton to let air in the tube. The liquid in each was brownish. Klavan searched the tubes until he found one with what looked like a tiny, light-colored thread coiling the length of the fluid.

He took this and carefully lodged it in a secure pocket in his vest meant for a thick writing pen or for a cigar, perhaps. The tube fit with room for more. On a sudden inspiration, he decided to find a second vial of the deadly fluid. It took him two more minutes, but he finally came upon another vial with what looked to be a string of developed bacilli in it. He placed this in the pen pocket next to the first. He then pulled the handkerchief out of his pants pocket and arranged it to cushion the two vials in his vest pocket.

Now he stripped the white coat off, scouring down any blood marks on the floor. He hoped to buy as much time as possible before the discovery of the officer's body.

Racing back down the stairs, he pulled the body as far into the corner of the landing as he could, draping the white coat over it. Then he exited the hidden door, making sure the canvas sign was in place and concealing its existence, and made his way down to the first floor again.

Now is where nerves come into play, he told himself. The obvious thing would be to try and get out of the building before anyone returned.

That was also the stupid, frightened animal thing to do. He would most likely set off an alarm doing so.

No, he would wait out the noontime closing once again in the first-floor washroom, he decided, and then when business was once again underway he would nonchalantly retrieve his checked coat and make his way out of the Josefinium, a respected doctor from Hamburg finished with his medical research.

Retreating once again to his toilet seat perch, Klavan counted the minutes until one-thirty. He could hear the hum of voices from outside and then someone entered the toilets to relieve himself after a heavy lunch. The man stood at a urinal and peed for at least two minutes while Klavan marveled at the elasticity of the fellow's bladder. Shortly after this man left, Klavan got down from the toilet perch and left the washroom as well. He returned to his books in the reading room, sat at the table for another ten minutes then told the assistant he was finished with them.

'You still have two hours until closing,' the assistant told him.

'Yes. Unfortunately, however, I just recalled another appointment I have this afternoon. Perhaps tomorrow.'

The library assistant actually looked put out at having to do his job sooner than expected. Klavan left the reading room, handed over the receipt coupon to the old woman ministering the cloakroom, nodded at the registrar and calmly made his way to the entrance.

Suddenly feet came running toward him. He twisted around in a defensive posture, his right hand curled in a fist, his teeth bared.

The library assistant stopped abruptly, his eyes growing wide in fright.

'You, you forgot this, sir,' he said, his voice breaking.

He held out the forgotten briefcase to Klavan, who quickly adjusted his body and unclenched his fist.

'How good of you,' he said pleasantly. 'And I thought I was too young to become an absent-minded professor.'

The assistant issued a small, nervous laugh at this comment, and Klavan was off into the cold afternoon, patting the vial of death in his vest pocket. It was that easy.


# TWENTY-TWO


Hermann Postling enjoyed the walk, plus it saved him transport money. They were paying for his travel. He could use that money however he damn well pleased, he thought. Nothing illegal in that.

He hoped they would have some food on hand. Usually they did: a bowl of fruit (not really his favorite food, but he'd eat a banana if it was free) or a plate of wurst and cheese (that was more like it – more like real food you could chew on). The frau was a funny one, though. You could never predict what there'd be with her. Some days there would be nothing for a snack. That's why Hermann had taken his lunch at the hostel before setting out for the Prater.

He couldn't walk very fast. A man at seventy-six like he was should be happy to be walking at all. Hermann had seen a lot in his nearly eight decades on Earth. When he was a baby, Francis I was still emperor; now his great-nephew, Franz Josef was running things, as he had been since the bad old year of 1848. Hermann remembered that time, too. It was the students who'd started it all. That's what comes from too much education, Hermann thought ruefully as he made his way across the Danube Canal and on toward the Prater. He'd already been working for ten years by that time, learning the cooperage trade, and here were all these pampered boys in their university hats out on the streets demanding a constitution and the right to vote. He'd wished he'd been in uniform then; he would have shown them their rights at the end of a sword.

This blustery day of March 1902 was much the same as that day in March in 1848 when he'd heard the thud of boots on cobbles as the throngs of students made their way along the Graben toward St Stephen's Cathedral.

'Watch where you're going, Grandpa,' a middle-aged lady yelled at him as he bumped into her just over the bridge.

He ignored her and shuffled along, a stiff wind off the canal buffeting him.

Hermann Postling wasn't the kind to demonstrate, to make demands, to blame others for his woes. And he'd had his share of woes. He'd built his own small cooperage firm by 1858 and married the daughter of his older partner. Had three children, though the boy thought he knew best and hightailed it out of Vienna when he was seventeen to immigrate to Canada, only to drown when his boat sank on the Atlantic crossing. One daughter had died in childbirth along with the baby; the other married an Italian and lived in Milan. She might as well be dead; he hadn't seen or heard from her in years. His wife had died of a broken heart, as far as he could figure, losing all the children that way and then the business going too with the panic of 1873.

Ever since then Hermann Postling had lived rough, finding work where he could, begging when he couldn't find work and finally not being good for much work altogether.

Still, he never complained.

But things were going to change now. Come Thursday he'd have something to boast about. On Thursday he'd be coming into a fair piece of change. And that slick little fellow wasn't going to cheat him out of it – he'd make sure of that. Herr Wenno, he called himself, but Hermann wasn't fooled. What kind of name was that, anyway? Couldn't be his real name. Thought he was being so clever, getting him chosen among the dozen men for the ceremony. Acting like he was just looking out for an old man. He was watching Herr Wenno. He wouldn't trick Hermann Postling; he wasn't going to take his twenty pieces of silver.

Maybe, just maybe he'd give one of those coins to the young boy. A nice boy, nicer than his own son had ever been to him.

Lost in these thoughts, Hermann approached the Rotunda in the Prater, entered the front door and was greeted by the frau.

'We were worried you weren't coming,' the painter, Tina Blau, said to him. 'You have some eager artists awaiting your arrival.'

Taking his coat, she led him to the dais where he would sit for the next several hours, modeling for a gaggle of women. But his eyes focused on the boy – he couldn't be much more than ten – who always sat close up and worked like a stevedore with his set of charcoals.

He winked at the boy, and the boy nodded back in greeting, a smile on his lips.

Franzl, the art teacher called him. He had that determined look about him that reminded Hermann of himself as a youngster.

They had spent most of this Monday attempting to track down leads to the two would-be assassins who had made such salami of the attempt on the emperor's life at the gates of Schönbrunn. If the Serbian lead was not enough for Montenuovo to send a broadside against Belgrade, perhaps it could at least aid in tracking the perpetrators. After all, they could very well still be in Vienna seeking another opportunity to strike.

On the other hand, it was equally possible that they had been called back to Belgrade for their incompetence and another team dispatched for a second attempt.

But one thing at a time. Werthen and Gross had personally visited over a dozen flophouses, hostels and run-down boarding houses where such guests might hope for a bit of anonymity. It was late in the afternoon when Gross suddenly recalled the Pension Geldner. Werthen well remembered it when Gross spoke the name. They had talked with the pipe-smoking hostess of the inn when trying to track a suspect in their very first case working together. It might very well be the sort of place where assassins from Belgrade would seek lodging. And if not, maybe the good Frau Geldner would have other suggestions for them.

When they reached the building on a bleak street in the Sixth District, they were surprised to find a constabulary sergeant stationed at the front desk. Werthen recognized him as a former witness for the prosecution in an art theft case that Werthen was defending. The officer had managed to make Gross, who was acting as an expert witness, look a bit of a fool. Werthen searched for the name: Friedman? Feltz? The officer gave him no time to wonder.

'Well, if it isn't Advokat Werthen,' the sergeant said. 'And his expert witness. I'm sure you remember me: Sergeant Feldman. What brings you two here?'

'I was about to ask you the same,' Werthen replied.

'Murder.' Sergeant Feldman said the word with relish.

'Who?'

'The old frau herself. Geldner. I always said it'd be the pipe-smoking that'd do her in or one of her anarchist guests.'

'Murder,' Gross intoned. 'Well, there goes a possible informant.' And then, as an afterthought: 'In that case, it *must* have been a guest.'

Feldman nodded.

'When did this happen?' Werthen asked.

'Saturday night, it appears. The body was discovered on Sunday by the woman's nephew. Pretty cut up about it, the boy was.'

'Murdered Saturday night and you still have the premises guarded?' This from Gross, who made such a proposition sound like a breach of good manners.

'That would be your doing, Doktor Gross,' Feldman said with a degree of irony.

'How so?' Werthen asked.

'I believe the good sergeant is making a small joke,' Gross said to Werthen. 'My dictum about protecting the crime scene from clumsy feet and fingers.' Then, to Feldman: 'Which means you folks have not yet had the time, more than twenty-four hours after discovery of the body, to visit the scene or to make more than a preliminary investigation. Which suggests,' Gross plunged on despite the efforts of Sergeant Feldman to reply, 'that the death of an anarchist innkeeper takes very low priority in the Police Praesidium.'

Sergeant Feldman shrugged. 'If you say so.'

'Oh, I do say so, sir. But for myself and my colleague, this death may assume very high priority indeed. I assume the body has been moved?'

'Bodies,' Sergeant Feldman said. 'Looks like the Serbian chap did the deed with a blade and then collapsed on his bed, dead from a hemorrhage or some such.'

'Or some such. Most scientific,' Gross said.

But the word 'Serbian' had caught their interest.

'How do you know the nationality of the other?' Werthen asked. 'I very much doubt the guests here oblige by registering with the correct information.'

'He was carrying a letter. Seems to be from his wife. The postmark is from Belgrade. They're still translating the Serbian, but it's pretty clear he was from there, too. Dimitrov's the name. But I shouldn't be telling you any of this. It's police business.'

'It's our business now,' said Gross, presenting Feldman with the letter from Montenuovo with a flourish.

Feldman glanced at the letter, then handed it back with a shrug. 'Means nothing to me. Like I said, this is police business. No one's allowed in the room.'

Werthen saw a phone on the desk and without asking permission he placed a call to a number at the Hofburg. It took fifteen more minutes, but a call came through for Sergeant Feldman that made his ears turn red. Werthen could hear the anger in the voice on the other end of the line.

'Yes, sir,' Feldman finally said. 'I understand, sir.' He hung up the receiver, looking like a well-chastised pupil.

'I assume we can examine the crime scene now,' Gross said with a satisfied smile on his face.

The sergeant nodded, not bothering to speak.

'The key?' Werthen said.

'For what?'

'The crime scene.'

Feldman sighed. 'It's unlocked. That's why I'm here.'

'Twenty-four hours a day?' Gross thundered. He looked at Werthen, exasperation replacing his former smile.

They both shook their heads.

# TWENTY-THREE

Down the hall, they soon came to a room which had a sign pasted on it: Entrance Forbidden.

Opening the door, Werthen was greeted with a smell from a butcher's shop. The stench of blood was strong; its visual presence was, as well – on the coverlet of one bed and on the floor beside another cot.

'Two beds,' Gross said.

Werthen nodded. It implied two occupants, not one.

They spent the next hour going over every nook and cranny in the room. In the first ten minutes Werthen found a length of metal pipe with stains at one end that looked like dried blood. The pipe had been ill concealed on top of the sole wardrobe in the room, as if cast aside and simply forgotten. There was no telling how long it had been there, but there was very little dust on it as opposed to the top of the wardrobe.

Not sure of the pipe's importance, he still handled it carefully, gripping it with a handkerchief from his breast pocket and setting it by the door to be taken away for further examination.

'What brought her in here?' Gross suddenly asked.

'Perhaps she was killed elsewhere and hidden in here.'

'Or maybe she was caught snooping,' Gross said. 'We need to inspect the bodies.'

Werthen was afraid he was going to suggest that. The morgue at the General Hospital was not his favorite place to visit.

There was a small valise in the wardrobe containing the meager belongings of the mysterious Herr Dimitrov. A shaving kit, grimy shirt with two celluloid collars, a change of underwear. At the very bottom was a ball of fur that unrolled into a very long and very real-looking gray beard.

'Stranger and stranger,' Gross mused, looking at the beard.

Feldman had decided to take a chair; he was seated behind the desk when they came back to the entrance.

'Who was sharing the room?' Gross asked.

Feldman looked up from the illustrated paper he was glancing at. 'What do you mean, sharing?'

'Two cots. Two occupants.'

'There was only one when we got here. Nothing in the registry.'

'May we see it?' Werthen asked. 'The registry.'

'Suit yourself,' Feldman said, getting out of the chair so that Werthen could sit in front of the large leather-bound registration book open on the desk.

He flipped the pages for recent dates and quickly saw that a page was missing. 'A page has been torn out,' he said.

Feldman didn't react.

'It could very well hold the name of the other lodger.'

'I'm not the investigating officer,' Feldman said. 'Talk to Drechsler. I'm just the watchdog.'

'This nephew that discovered Frau Geldner's body. Is he still around?' Gross asked.

Feldman made a slight laugh. 'He's about the only who is, I can tell you that. The rest of the lodgers had someplace else to go suddenly. Room twelve, down the other hall. He was in there last I knew.' He looked at Gross now, spying the length of pipe the criminologist was carrying. 'You can't be tampering with evidence.'

Gross stared at him for a moment. 'Sergeant Feldman, you may have a great mind for measurements but I have a feeling you would not know what evidence would look like if it came up and bit you. Now what is the name of this nephew?'

Feldman glared back at Gross. 'Kaufmann. August Kaufmann. And that's a bit of evidence, too. So there.'

As they walked down the hallway, Gross tucked the length of pipe into the deep evidence pockets he'd had sewn into the lining of his overcoat.

'Can't be frightening the witnesses now, can we, Werthen?'

Werthen realized something fundamental about Gross at that moment. Other people do their jobs; Gross reveled in his. He was enjoying this more than he would a plate of schnitzel or a fine wine from Gumpoldskirchen.

They knocked on the door of room twelve and it was opened

by a small man. His squinched face with eyes and nose too close together gave him a porcine appearance.

'May I help you?'

The man's voice was high and whiney; there was nothing very prepossessing about him.

'We are working with the police,' Gross said. 'My name is Doktor Gross and this is my colleague, Advokat Werthen.'

Kaufmann's eyes brightened at this announcement. 'Not *the* Doktor Hanns Gross? The eminent criminologist?'

Gross was rather taken aback by this at first, then smiled broadly. 'None other,' he said fulsomely.

'I live and breathe for publication of the *Archiv.* Fascinating reading.'

Werthen realized that Kaufmann meant Gross's semi-annual journal publication, *Archiv für Kriminal-Anthropolgie und Kriminalistik,* in which the maestro published accounts of his famous cases, among other articles by jurists, criminologists and chemists.

'And I've heard of you, too, Advokat,' he said, beaming at Werthen. 'Your cases with Doktor Gross.'

'You'll excuse me for saying so,' Gross said, 'but one hardly expects to find a reader of my little journal at the Pension Geldner. And may I extend my condolences for the loss of your aunt,' he quickly added, remembering common civility for once.

'Yes, *Tante* Emma will be missed,' Kaufmann said. 'But please, come in.'

His room was much better appointed than the others, with a large desk piled high in books and a pair of armchairs along with a real bed, not a cot, and a wardrobe of solid oak. On the walls were a collection of stories clipped from newspapers detailing crimes both petty and severe.

He followed their gaze to the cuttings. 'Not to worry, gentlemen. I am a student of law at the university, not a criminal manqué. Have a seat, please.'

They did so and Werthen offered, 'We actually met your aunt once. Several years ago, in another investigation.'

Kaufmann took the desk chair. 'One of her guests, I suppose. *Tante* Emma was rather emphatic about her political leanings.'

'As you are, sir?' Gross inquired.

Kaufmann shook his head, somewhat amused at the question.

'No. I stay here out of financial necessity. My aunt is . . . was good enough to allow me to stay gratis during my studies. I wouldn't be able to go to law school otherwise.'

'And what happens now?' Gross asked. 'I mean, now that she . . .'

Kaufmann pursed his lips. 'I'm not quite sure. I see what you might be getting at, though. *Qui bono*, no? Who stands to gain from her death? Not I, that I can assure you. She was most displeased with my bourgeois complacency. Perhaps she left the pension to the cause. It would be like her.'

'You discovered the body, we understand.' Werthen could find no gentler way to broach the subject.

'I did. She wasn't about for the morning coffee. I usually helped out with that, you see. My bourgeois way of paying back. Anyway, she was not in her room. I unlocked it after knocking. I was worried, you understand. *Tante* Emma was a woman of schedules despite her anarchist espousals. Well, I went looking for her, wondering if she were actually cleaning rooms on her own rather than waiting for Maria – that's the daily houseworker, you see.'

'Even on Sundays?' Gross said.

A nod from Kaufmann. 'Even on Sundays. There was no one about in the rooms – at least, no one answering their door.'

'So how did you finally find her?' Werthen asked.

'Well, not to put too fine a point on it but it was the smell, you see, coming from that room. I could distinctly sense it when knocking at the door. I had no idea what I might find inside. I only knew that someone had made a mess and it was only going to stink more as the day progressed. Not the blood, you know. But the other . . . When a person dies, there is no more control . . .'

'Quite,' Gross said. 'So you entered.'

'Yes, and I immediately saw my aunt laid out on one cot, blood around her chest. I ascertained she was dead before I saw the second victim.'

'Victim,' Gross repeated.

'Well, the other dead person.'

'Not the killer.'

'No. Hardly. That would be the other one. The man who was here first and then joined by the unfortunate second man. Herr

Wenno, I believe he called himself. Very private sort, suspicious looking. Most of our guests are the private type, but Herr Wenno made a profession of it. And his hands. There was something quite odd about the way he held his coffee cup. I noticed it just the once and then he no longer took coffee with us at the pension. He held the cup in both hands and his little fingers stuck straight out as if they would not bend. Quite odd. But the police must have already mentioned this. I tried to tell them on Sunday.'

'It seems to have been a professional kill.' Doktor Starb at the General Hospital morgue closed the drawer in the refrigerated unit and Werthen was grateful for his brevity. Frau Geldner's corpse was in fine condition; he had hardly been able to discern the incision above her drooping left breast, but it had been lethal.

'Almost surgical,' Starb said with a hint of admiration in his tone. 'No hesitation cuts, just a quick and decisive thrust. Perhaps even a thrown blade.'

'Is there a way to tell the difference?' Gross asked.

Starb shook his head. 'But either way, it's the work of a professional. Whoever killed Frau Geldner has experience. He's killed before. And it wasn't the unfortunate Herr Dimitrov, that I can assure you. My hunch is it was his dying gasps that brought her to the room in the first place.'

'Dying from what?' Werthen asked.

'Tuberculosis. Both lungs were riddled with lesions. Immediate cause of death was a hemorrhage. Poor fellow drowned in his own blood. I do not find him a likely candidate for murderer.'

And neither did Gross as they made their way from the hospital onto Alserstrasse. 'I vote for the mysterious Herr Wenno,' Gross said, tightening the collar of his coat against the chill late afternoon breeze. Winter was still maintaining a last round of fun in Vienna. 'The absence of the murder weapon at the scene would indicate a third party.'

He stopped and pulled his derby low over his forehead. 'Odd name that. One assumes it is a *nom de guerre*.'

'I thought so as well,' Werthen added. 'A warrior monk. Not a bad name for a professional killer.'

'You impress me, Werthen.'

'Why, because I have a smattering of history to remind me

that Wenno von Rohrbach was the first master of the Livonian Brothers of the Sword?'

'No. Because you did not faint when viewing the remains of Frau Geldner.'

'Sorry to have disappointed you.'

'Not me, Werthen. I believe Starb, however, was expecting more dramatics from you. His is a deadly dull job, you know.'

Werthen did not bother to respond to the pun. It was the sort of petty bantering Gross engaged in when contemplating a problem.

'So, Wenno as the main suspect,' Werthen said. 'I think Starb was right about Dimitrov's death-throws drawing the landlady into the room.'

Gross nodded, resuming his brisk walk. 'A likely scenario. And Wenno comes back to find her there. Perhaps she had become curious about her tenants. Maybe he caught her rifling his possessions. She learned something she should not have.' He paused for a moment, rubbing his chin. 'But what are we to make of this length of pipe?' He tapped the front of his overcoat where the pipe was secured in an interior pocket.

Werthen had been doing his own cogitating. 'It's a murder weapon.'

This made Gross again stop and stare at Werthen as if he were a circus freak.

'You saw the wound, Werthen. This could hardly—' A sudden smile crossed the criminologist's face.

'You mean your other murder?'

'Exactly,' Werthen said. 'Falk said the assailant struck Herr Karl with a length of pipe hidden in a coat sleeve. I am no scientist, but the stain on the end of the pipe surely looks like dried blood.'

'A large jump of intuition, Werthen. That could be the blood of a rat cudgeled to death in the pension.'

'The fingers,' Werthen said. 'Kaufmann mentioned the awkward way this Wenno held his coffee cup. I need to check my notes, but I swear Herr Falk mentioned something similar about the man Herr Karl had words with before he was killed. So, not so much intuition as deduction.' He smiled at Gross. 'And this begs a further connection: if it is the same man who killed Frau Geldner, Herr Karl and Herr Falk, then what is the connection between these deaths? Why would a professional killer bother with mere waiters or a landlady?'

'We'll know soon enough,' Gross said. 'We'll take this pipe to the crime lab at the Praesidium. They can use the Uhlenhuth precipitin test to at least determine if it is human or animal. We can search the pipe for fingerprints as well and then see if there are any matches in the pension room, but with so many people using the same room over time, I doubt that would provide anything conclusive.'

Gross looked suddenly downcast.

'No need to be glum about the fingerprints,' Werthen said. 'We're still making progress.'

'On which front? Our job is to keep the emperor alive, not solve the murders of two waiters and a landlady.'

'Perhaps they are all related. After all, there is the Serbian connection.'

'Tuition or deduction this time, dear Werthen?'

'All right, it seems a stretch, but if that pipe can be linked to Herr Karl's death then all this takes on a different complexion. We're dealing with a professional killer here. Drechsler said it about Falk's death. Starb said it about Frau Geldner. Someone expert at their job. Not simply some psychopath run amok, but somebody killing with intention, with a purpose.'

'A passionate courtroom performance, Werthen. You almost convince me.'

'And the letter Dimitrov had in his possession. We need to find out the exact contents of that,' Werthen added. 'There may be some inkling as to what a dying man was doing traveling from Belgrade to Vienna.'

'In search of medical treatment, perhaps,' Gross offered.

'Perhaps. But it would be good to know.'

Gross nodded, then fixed Werthen with an icy stare. 'You asked me a moment ago why I appeared so glum. There is another connection you're not making.'

Werthen shrugged. 'I am not the brilliant criminologist. Just a simple private inquiries agent.'

'The hands,' Gross said. 'We have encountered those before. The misshapen little fingers.'

A chill traveled along Werthen's spine as he remembered a bombing in his office that took the life of the building portier's brother. The man who'd cut off the little fingers of his victims as a prize. The spy for the Russians who ran a double agent in the very heart of Austrian military intelligence and who had almost cost Gross his life.

'But he's in Siberia. Archduke Franz Ferdinand told us so himself.'

'I find it difficult to believe that one so resourceful as Herr Schmidt, or whatever his real name is, would allow himself to be spirited off to the tsar's work camps. Perhaps we should have Franz Ferdinand check with his man in Petersburg.'

'It couldn't be him,' Werthen said again, but this time with little conviction.

# TWENTY-FOUR

Berthe's day had been spectacularly unproductive and she was not really in the mood to hear of her husband and Gross's discoveries. She had had to deal with the same fulsome bureaucrat who had kept Werthen from interviewing Herr Czerny, old friend of the murdered head waiter, Herr Karl. Neither had she been able to find any registration for the mysterious Hermann Postling.

But she hid these frustrations – or thought she did – and joined in with her husband and Gross as they discussed their revelations.

'It's only a pity we missed the archduke this afternoon,' Werthen said with real animation. 'We meet with him first thing in the morning.'

She liked to see Karl so full of life like this, so involved. But she couldn't help feeling a bit excluded at the same time. It was as if she had been given the leftovers in her investigations. Knowing it wasn't the case did not alter that feeling.

Now these two investigations seemed on the verge of coming together, and she was still obliged to hunt for the tail, leaving the dog for Karl and the ever-pompous Gross.

'Why so ruminative?' Gross suddenly asked her, as if sensing her displeasure. 'You are doing your part, you know. We really should talk with Oberstabelmeister Johann Czerny.'

'Don't worry, Gross. Berthe's not the type to sulk.' Then, to his wife: 'Are you, *Schatz*?'

To which question she had the irrepressible desire to tell him that sulking and frustration were two very different states. She loved Karl dearly, but sometimes his sunny optimism was as annoying as Gross's imperious manner.

'No, not at all,' she said. 'Actually, I was just hoping you two would ask Franz Ferdinand or Prince Montenuovo to intercede with Herr Plauder at the Hofburg about setting up an appointment.' The po-faced clerk at the Hofburg in his filthy white housecoat and muffler was obviously the same middling bureaucrat who had given Karl the run around about seeing Czerny. The man had actually had the effrontery to tell her that if she wished to apply for a position in the kitchen she was in the wrong office. She, Berthe Meisner, who had been commissioned by no less a personage than Archduke Franz Ferdinand himself last year to investigate a possible scandal at the famed Lipizzaner stud.

'I would like nothing better,' Werthen said. 'I'll see to it, my love. You should not have to put up with his obstructionism. I should have done so long ago.'

He reached across the littered dinner table where they were seated – Werthen's parents were still in town and entertaining Frieda in the sitting room – and squeezed her hand. And suddenly everything was all right once again.

Am I that simple a woman that a small kindness from my husband can erase hours of frustration? She decided to leave that question for another day and simply enjoy the moment.

'Another glass of wine, Gross?' she said, offering him the remains of the third bottle on the table. When Emile von Werthen was in town, the wine flowed freely.

'Don't mind if I do, Frau Meisner. Most kind of you.'

Later that night as they were preparing for bed, Berthe remembered what she had been meaning to tell her husband.

'Father brought some wonderful news yesterday,' she said. 'I completely forgot about it, being so wrapped up in murders and plots.'

'He's retiring,' Werthen guessed. 'And about time, too. He can move to Vienna full time now and be near his only daughter and granddaughter.'

'A big life change, but not that one. He's not quite ready yet to leave business and concentrate solely on Talmudic studies.'

'How many guesses do I have?'

'He's getting married.'

'Wonderful,' Werthen said. 'And who is the lucky woman?' he asked playfully.

'Don't be silly, Karl. Frau Juliani, of course.'

'Of course.' He pulled her to him in her chemise, holding her around the waist. 'And I hope she makes him as happy as his daughter has me.'

There was nothing playful about the kiss he gave her.

Time was running out and he still had not finalized the plan. He refused to allow himself to dwell on Dimitrov's demise. Look forward, not backward, he commanded himself.

He now had a powerful weapon in his arsenal, and must determine how best to deploy it. No longer a matter of Dimitrov serving as a living bomb in the disguise of an old man, one Hermann Postling.

No. And there was no time to organize another such human bomb from Belgrade.

Be logical, he told himself. Look at the options. It is either Postling himself for Thursday or I take his place in disguise. He had already drawn a line through that second alternative when he resolved to steal the vials from the Josefinium. If he was not prepared to blow himself up to complete his mission, he was surely not willing to kill himself in that manner, either.

So, Postling. But how?

He could put some of the material on the old man's clothes before going to the ceremony. Act as if he accidentally spilled a small glass or some such. But there it was again – he too would be sacrificed. Was there a way he could trick the old man into deploying this new weapon without him even knowing it?

As he paced the floor in the small servant's quarters the 'princess' had put at his disposal, he squeezed his hand in his pocket, once again almost setting off the charge with a blast of air from the hollow ball.

And then it came to him. The perfect plan. All of a piece.

\*     \*     \*

A fresh coating of snow had fallen in the night. Gross and Werthen took a fiaker to their meeting at the Lower Belvedere with the heir apparent to the Austrian crown, Archduke Franz Ferdinand. Werthen had formed a soft spot for the archduke in the course of their professional relations, for he had sympathy with the man held in waiting so long to take up rule. The archduke had established what some referred to as the Clandestine Cabinet at this former palace of Prince Eugene of Savoy, a Military Chancellery of his own which would be ready to move into positions of power once Franz Josef, his uncle, relinquished power or, more likely, simply died of old age.

A liveried servant awaited them at the columned entrance to the Lower Belvedere and led them through the Marble Room to an interior suite of offices where a number of officers were busy at desks, each with a telephone and some of which had typing machines upon them, seeming so out place among the gilded columns and tapestries on the walls. Finally they reached a far corner of the room where Franz Ferdinand greeted them heartily. It was clearly his day for reports and conferences, for he was at his more public desk and not his private one behind closed doors.

'How good to see you gentlemen once again,' the archduke said, bidding them to take seats across the desk from him. A picture of his wife, Sophie von Chotek, and their firstborn was in a silver frame on the desk. That was a marriage that had cost the archduke dearly, Werthen thought. And this was another reason for his fondness for a man who most found brusque and overweening. He'd married for love and had to live with a morganatic marriage as a result, his own offspring never to be in line for succession, his wife forced to sit at lower tables than he at formal receptions. It was the doing of Prince Montenuovo, who could be a spiteful creature at times.

'It's good to see you, as well, Your Highness,' Werthen said sincerely.

Gross added his good wishes and the archduke spread his hands apart as if asking the purpose of their visit.

As agreed, Gross took the lead, for the criminologist felt they had a delicate balance to maintain. Were the archduke to realize that Prince Montenuovo had commissioned them on their present case, he might very well be less likely to help them out with information from St Petersburg. Werthen had argued that surely Franz Ferdinand would not let animosity between him and Montenuovo come between him aiding his uncle, the emperor, in any manner possible.

'I would not be too sure of that, Werthen,' Gross had said on the fiaker ride to the palace. 'After all, the death of the emperor would be just the thing for Franz Ferdinand. No longer waiting like the bridesmaid who is never the bride.'

Werthen would not believe that of the man, yet agreed to let Gross find his own way in this matter.

'We have come about old business that may have new life,' Gross said importantly.

'Indeed?' The archduke's slightly bulging blue eyes sparkled at this rather mysterious introduction.

'There may well be the possibility of an old foe coming back to Vienna from the dead. Or rather, in this case, from Siberia.'

Franz Ferdinand nodded. 'Continue.'

'I assume you know of whom I am speaking?'

'The deadly Herr Schmidt, I believe he called himself. And what makes you think that he is once more a guest of our fair city?'

Gross carefully explained the deaths they were investigating, the description of the suspect's peculiar hands and the very professional manner of the killing.

Franz Ferdinand listened to all this closely and then said, 'This wouldn't have anything to do with the little job Prince Montenuovo enlisted you for, would it?'

'Well . . .' Gross looked flustered at this.

'Your eyes and ears at court are as thorough as always, Your Highness,' Werthen said, jumping into the conversation. 'And yes, I . . . we believe it could impact directly on your uncle. There are indications that this killer may have been dispatched from Belgrade.'

'Belgrade.' Franz Ferdinand repeated the word like a curse. 'Then we must determine what has happened to our Herr Schmidt.'

Werthen gave Gross a knowing look that did not go unnoticed by the archduke.

'Does my eagerness to help surprise you, Doktor Gross? Montenuovo and I are hardly on friendly terms. He has, after all, caused me and my family a great deal of discomfort, if not pain. But personal vendettas are put aside at such times.'

The archduke straightened in his chair. 'And though I do not know the particulars of the case, I assume that when you mention Belgrade, you imply that there may be an attempted assassination. I am well aware of the events of two weeks ago at Schönbrunn. If there was one attempt there may be more.' He eyed each of them in turn. 'My uncle and I may have our differences of opinion on international relations and yes, I am anxious to serve my country as its leader, but blood is blood, duty is duty. He is my uncle, but first of all he is my emperor!'

The small speech stirred large emotions in Werthen. Were he English, he might have shouted 'Here, here!' Instead he smiled broadly at Franz Ferdinand.

'Exactly what I told my colleague, Advokat Werthen,' Gross responded. 'Far too big a man to allow private grudges to impinge on matters of the state.'

Seeing that Werthen was about ready to explode in denial, Gross quickly blustered on.

'We were hoping that Your Highness might make use of that source of yours in St Petersburg. The one who informed you of Schmidt's fall from grace last summer upon returning from his previous mission in Vienna.'

'Yes. I think that would be a good starting point,' Franz Ferdinand said. 'I'll have my adjutant get in touch with him directly.'

Werthen was still fuming, but he decided to take a page out of the archduke's book and put personal animosities behind him.

'My wife sends her best,' Werthen added. 'She is once again aiding us in our inquiries.' He briefly told the archduke of their thwarted attempts to speak with the good friend of the murdered Herr Karl, and asked if it were possible for him to intercede.

'I will do what I can,' Franz Ferdinand said, 'but I have very little influence over affairs at the Hofburg. That one should really be directed to your employer, Prince Montenuovo. You actually think this Czerny fellow might know something useful?'

'We do not know,' Werthen confessed. 'But we have so few leads . . .'

'Understood. No stone left unturned. We appreciate your efforts. I have a small network of operatives at work on this matter as well, but they have been unable to turn up anything on the two gunmen at Schönbrunn. How did you come up with the Belgrade angle?'

Gross was only too happy to tell him of his discovery regarding the spent shell casings at the entrance to the palace and to the letter found in Dimitrov's pocket.

'We are on our way now to the Praesidium to see if there has been any new information to be gleaned from a full translation of that missive,' Gross said.

Franz Ferdinand rose and Werthen and Gross followed his lead.

'I wish you luck, gentlemen. I shall keep you apprised of whatever is discovered from our St Petersburg agent. And if it is our friend, Herr Schmidt, I remember that he may have a particular animus for you two. After all, you were the cause of his fall from grace with Russian military intelligence. Perhaps I should assign Duncan to watch your back.'

'I doubt that will be necessary—' Gross began.

But Werthen interrupted: 'By all means, Your Highness. If you can spare him, that is.'

Duncan was the tall, scar-faced Scotsman who had served as Franz Ferdinand's aid and bodyguard ever since he'd saved the archduke's life in a hunting mishap in the Scottish Highlands. Duncan had come to their aid twice before, one time directly saving Werthen's life. If it were Herr Schmidt who had come back from the dead, then they could use all the help they could get and to hell with Gross's sense of importance.

'Consider it done.' The archduke shook their hands.

Werthen had shaken hands with the man before when they had been faced with dangerous situations. This was the first time the archduke's palm was moist.

# TWENTY-FIVE

The man Werthen and Gross knew as Herr Schmidt, the Estonian, Pietr Klavan, formerly in the pay of Russian military intelligence, was shopping at this very moment. He took his time, knowing what he needed and not wanting to take second best. However, at the Parfumerie J.B. Filz at

Graben 13, there were, according to the well-attired clerk behind the counter, no second bests in this establishment. 'Filz is all first class,' she told Klavan. It was a tiny vault of a shop, nestled amid the other high-class emporiums of Graben in the very heart of Vienna's First District. The double-headed eagle was proudly displayed on the back wall, announcing that the firm had been Imperial and Royal Court Perfumers since 1872.

'But I need something fitting for an emperor,' he said. 'Price is no object.'

'Woman or man?' the clerk asked in her snotty Schönbrunner German.

'An emperor, not an empress.'

'I see. Not necessarily a figure of speech, then.'

She was the sort of self-satisfied cow he would love to have a few minutes with in private. She would not be smiling that supercilious superior smile of hers after he was finished.

But he controlled himself. 'Something quite elegant – regal, shall we say – for a man.'

'Ah, in that case, I should surely recommend Filz Feinste. They say it is used even in the Hofburg. A subtle blend of bergamot, coriander, myrtle and conifer resin, with just a trace of citrus.'

She pulled the top from of an elegantly packaged sample bottle and held the glass stopper under his nose. He almost retched. It was an automatic reaction with Klavan. Perfumes and colognes made him physically ill. But he pantomimed delight for the clerk.

'Just the thing,' he exclaimed. 'Do you have it in a small atomizer bottle?'

She looked again at his clothing – hardly the finest – and at his hands, which were badly in need of a manicure.

'It is quite expensive.'

He pulled out a wallet stuffed with bills. The perfumery clerks' eyes bulged at the sight of this wealth.

Earlier this morning he had made his way to an alleyway in the Second District, dislodged the third brick from the bottom on the right edge of the back wall and retrieved a key he had hidden there during his mission to Vienna the year before. He had similar hiding places in Warsaw and Berlin. Then he walked into the central office of the Rothschild bank, Credit-Anstalt, on Schottengasse, went to the safe deposit box section, handed the key to the clerk and after signing in as Herr Schmidt was shown to his box, number 2213, paired his key with the clerk's and opened the tiny door to it. He pulled out the long box, went to a private room and cleared out its contents: a thousand crowns in twenty- and fifty-crown notes, and identity papers in the name of Gregor Tollinger, a purveyor of fine cheeses from Bolzano in the Tyrol.

'Well, the good sir displays excellent taste,' the clerk gushed, still eyeing the money.

She sought out a small, handsome bottle of the prized cologne, a tiny rubber atomizer affixed to it.

'Should I have it wrapped?'

'No, I'll see to that. And make that two, please.'

A smile crossed her face. 'That will be eighty crowns then.'

He did not bother looking her way as he peeled two fifty-crown bills off the stack, all in blue ink with two toga-bedecked women seated and staring out like queens of the ball. What they were supposed to represent he was sure he did not know or care. But the money shut the clerk up as he traded it for the elegant little paper bag she settled the bottles of cologne into.

'Keep the change,' he said impulsively, merely to see her reaction. And it was worth it, for at first she seemed to be affronted that someone should dare to give her a tip, but then did the reckoning on the size of said tip, reddened and did a half curtsey instead.

'The good gentleman is too generous.'

'Not really,' he said, taking the package and leaving the tiny confines of the shop. Outside, he sucked in air like a drowning man.

First step concluded, he thought.

They stopped for lunch at Krawaler's near the Ring before going on to the Praesidium. Gross had a great need for *Bauernschmaus*, he averred, and there was none better served in Vienna than at Krawaler's. Werthen, who had noticed that his pants were fitting a little tightly around the waist of late, opted for a bowl of spicy *Bohnensuppe*, and felt very superior for his sacrifice as they later made their way to police headquarters.

After signing in at registry, they quickly headed for the new forensics laboratory built very much to Gross's own specifications in his writings. It seemed they were in favor today: their way was cleared for them as the Hofburg must have had a word with Chief Inspector Meindl following the misunderstanding at the Pension Geldner. That was as productive as it got, however, for they discovered that the lab had not even conducted the relatively simple precipitin test to determine if the stain on the pipe were human blood of from another animal – or even blood at all. The letter from Dimitrov's wife was still in the evidence box labeled 'G' for Frau Geldner.

'Jesus, Mary and Joseph,' Gross fumed at the lowly technician who brought the bad news. 'This is a murder investigation, not a picnic.'

He took the letter from the box, opened it and began making a rough transcription of his own.

'You speak Serbian?' Werthen asked. Though he was not surprised; Gross had a seemingly bottomless pit of scatter-shot knowledge that served him well as a criminologist.

'My *Amme* was from a Serbian family in Sarajevo.'

He said it with a sort of sweet lilt to his voice that Werthen had never heard come from the criminologist. Gross looked upward as if recalling a fond memory of this nursemaid.

'My parents were sticklers for proper German,' Gross said. 'They threatened to let my nursemaid Senka go if they found her speaking heathen Serbian to me.' He brought his gaze back from the ceiling, focusing on Werthen now. 'So it was our little secret.' He chuckled at the memory.

This was such uncharacteristic behavior on Gross's part that it gave Werthen a frisson of fear. Seeing Gross as a sentimentalist was truly frightening.

'But I finally told my parents about it,' Gross added offhandedly. 'Can't have the servants countermanding orders of the employers, can we, now? Didn't know her proper place, but she did provide me with a basic knowledge of the language.'

This pitiful news came as almost a relief to Werthen.

Gross peered at the scribble of missive on the cheap stationery. He pursed his lips, squinting at a difficult word here and there.

'The usual domestic drivel. She obviously did not expect this Dimitrov to return from Vienna. Nothing said in specifics, but she does thank him for his sacrifice for the family and,' he glanced again at the letter, 'yes, and notes here toward the end that little

Vaska – must be the son – will remember him always as a martyr for Serbia.' He looked up over the top edge of the letter at Werthen. 'I find that last line somewhat disturbing.'

Werthen agreed and at just that moment Inspector Drechsler entered the Forensics Laboratory.

'I thought I might find you here. Registry notified me you'd checked in.'

'Keeping an eye on us, are you, Inspector?' Gross said.

'There's been a development,' he said with a long face. 'Another murder similar to Frau Geldner's. Same professional style with the knife.' Drechsler looked at the lab technician Gross had verbally abused.

'We should talk in private, gentlemen.'

They followed Drechsler back to his small office, its wall cluttered with pictures of his family. There were straight-back chairs on offer across the old desk from the inspector.

'Have either of you heard of Office 3G?' Drechsler pronounced the name with dread in his voice; there was perspiration on his upper lip.

Werthen began shaking his head even as Gross responded: 'I have heard reports from sources about some peculiar medical research going on.'

Drechsler tilted his head at this. 'You have good sources, Doktor Gross. Medical research indeed. I am sure you both recall the events of late October, 1898.'

Werthen thought back. This was about the time of his first case as a private inquiries agent. He remembered that he was engaged in an investigation involving the tragic assassination of the Empress Elisabeth in September of that year. And in late October and for some time following that he had been involved in a desperate roll of the dice, preparing for the duel Franzl had asked him about not long ago.

So, no, Werthen had been so self-absorbed that he knew nothing of public events happening at the same time.

Gross, however, though also involved in the same case, had managed to keep a wider view of the world. 'The plague scare, if I am not mistaken,' the criminologist said evenly.

Drechsler nodded. 'They very one. Research doctors at the bacteriological institute of the General Hospital went to India and retrieved pneumonic plague bacilli during the epidemic there and brought it back to Vienna to study. And then somebody got careless. Two doctors and a nurse died when the plague was released in the institute. There was panic, I can tell you. The Viennese figured it was going to spread throughout the city.'

Werthen could only shake his head that he had not been aware of such a situation. But the prospect of a duel to the death rather reduces one's horizon of focus.

'It was, however, controlled,' Gross added. 'Quite fortunate.'

'Yes,' Drechsler said. 'And the public outcry was so great that the research was closed down.' He folded his hands on the desk in front of him.

'Except that it wasn't, was it?' Gross said. 'This mysterious Office 3G . . .'

Another nod from Drechsler. 'I just learned about it today when they called us in on a murder. Office 3G is located in an upper story of a wing of the Josefinium. Closed off and supposedly secure. But somebody knew of it and somebody was able to breach security.'

'This death,' Gross prompted.

'A guard. Killed with the same precision as Frau Geldner, according to Starb.'

'But we were just at the morgue,' Werthen said. 'Starb made no mention of such a similar killing.'

Drechsler raised his eyes at Werthen. 'It was thought a better idea that I apprise you of the situation.'

'What situation, Inspector?' Werthen asked, but it was clear what was coming.

'The researchers there say two vials of the bacillus have gone missing.'

Gross let out a long sigh. 'Enough to decimate a city like Vienna.'

'When did this happen?' Werthen asked.

'Yesterday afternoon. Well, during their lunch break, actually. The researchers discovered the missing vials when they came back from their meal. They found the body of the dead guard a bit later.'

'In the middle of the day!' Gross fumed. 'Are there any suspects? Did no one notice anything strange?'

'In fact, we do have one particular fellow of interest.' He consulted a paper on the top of his desk. 'A Professor Doktor

Wilhelm Schieff of Hamburg doing research on otolaryngology. Or so he said.'

'And what was so peculiar about this Doktor Schieff?' Gross demanded.

The library assistant there said the doctor was called away to another meeting but forgot his briefcase. He ran after the man and he said the fellow turned on him with – how did he say it?' He looked again at the paper on the desk. 'Right. "With death in his eyes and his fist clenched." Fanciful turn of phrase, I'd say.'

'He does work in a library,' Gross added.

'And that was the only strange visitor that day?' Werthen inquired.

'We're still taking statements,' Drechsler said. 'One other thing, though. This library assistant said he was startled not just by the man's eyes, but by the way he held his right fist. His little finger pointed out like a poking weapon. Now, why does that sound familiar?'

# TWENTY-SIX

'What are you doing with expensive cologne?' she asked, startling him.

Klavan was so intent on the procedure that he had not even heard Princess Dumbroski approach. He was sitting at the deal table in the maid's room he was occupying, and quickly covered the glass vials that lay near the two bottles of cologne.

'I am practicing being a gentleman,' he said. 'If you can transform yourself into a princess, surely I can become a lowly count.'

'Don't ridicule me,' she spat out, her tiny front teeth looking ferret-like and fearsome. 'And don't play me for a fool. I know you. I see all the signs. You're on a mission in Vienna, but you're washed up with the Russians. Just like me. So I ask myself, who are you working for? What poor bastard is going to suffer because of you? And then I hear from certain friends that there was an attempted assassination of the emperor not long ago.'

He smiled up at her. 'You have made inroads, haven't you, Princess? Quite the little spy yourself with informants at the very seat of power, it would seem.'

'Some suspect the Black Hand. They say there may even be another attempt.'

'I should say the house of Habsburg is cursed,' Klavan said dispassionately. 'First the death of the heir apparent, then of the empress, and now, if your sources are correct, the emperor himself is in danger. What a world we live in,' he sighed.

She drew a cut-throat razor from her scarf she wore around her waist, flicked it open and held it to his throat all in one swift movement.

'I told you before not to ridicule me,' she hissed, digging into his flesh with the edge.

He did not flinch.

'I should kill you,' she said. 'You're only going to bring me trouble.'

'Yes, I suppose you should,' he said calmly. 'But you won't. You fancy yourself that great mistress of the sword, but you're just like all women, aren't you, Lisette? Scared of things that go bump in the night.'

A low growl seem to come from her throat and he now moved swiftly, grabbing her wrist in an iron grip and twisting it until the razor fell to the floor with a clatter. He put his foot on it and simultaneously spun her around, pinning her arms with one hand and gripping her neck in a choke hold from behind. She coughed.

'Can't breathe,' she said in a hoarse voice.

'That is the idea,' he whispered in her ear. 'Now if I let you go, you promise to be a good little girl, right?'

She struggled against his arm crushing her windpipe, tried to kick him but missed.

He increased the pressure. 'Right?' he said again.

She stopped struggling and nodded.

He let go and she gasped for breath, putting her right hand to her bruised throat.

'And now you are going to leave me in peace, Lisette, or all of Vienna will learn of your most interesting past. I shall be gone in a matter of days and then you may return to your soirees and fiction of being a princess. But never forget, for me you are just a little slut I hired to make old and powerful men quiver and moan. Play the princess and the buccaneer after I am gone. For now, just leave me in peace.'

When she was gone, he carefully twisted the brass cap off the bottle of cologne. Looking inside, he had to laugh. It seemed the perfumery solved what he thought might be his first problem, for the bottle was far from full. The aristocracy, it seemed, was easily swindled.

Cloth handkerchief to his nose, he took one of the vials in hand and gently edged the cotton plug out.

Now comes the hard part, he thought.


They were sitting down to dinner when Archduke Franz Ferdinand's aide and bodyguard, Duncan, arrived, ushered in by a concerned-looking Frau Blatschky. He looked abashed at bothering them.

'The archduke indicated it was of the utmost importance.' He handed a large envelope to Werthen. 'He said I was to wait for a reply.'

Berthe's father and Frau Juliani were visiting for dinner tonight, and they waited with Frieda while Werthen, Berthe, Gross and Duncan gathered in the sitting room to read the message.

Werthen read it aloud to the others, and thus they discovered that the man they had known as Herr Schmidt was actually an Estonian named Pietr Klavan in the employ of Russian military intelligence, and that he had in fact escaped on his way to penal servitude in Siberia.

'Is it certain this Klavan and Herr Schmidt are one and the same?' Gross queried.

Werthen scanned the letter. 'The archduke says here that his agent in St Petersburg has access to the highest levels at the War Ministry. He is, as Franz Ferdinand writes, "my most trusted agent in place."' Werthen looked up from the letter, cocking his head at Gross.

'Klavan, it is,' the criminologist allowed.

Werthen continued reading the letter. 'He also reports that Klavan was traced to Brussels. There appears to be a sort of clearing house for commissions of a certain sort.'

'Monsieur Philipot,' Duncan interrupted. 'He is well known in certain quarters.' His Scottish brogue was still strong in German.

'Could we be less obscure?' Berthe said. 'What is it exactly this Monsieur Philipot does?'

Duncan nodded at her. 'Of course, madam. He operates a clearing house for those seeking freelance strong men and killers. He takes fees from both parties. Not a bad business opportunity from what I understand.'

'So Klavan went to Philipot for a job?' Berthe said.

Werthen nodded this time. 'It says here that when questioned, Philipot indicated Klavan's commission took him to Belgrade.'

'Then he is the one,' Gross said. 'He's our man. And I will wager hundred to one that his commission is to assassinate Franz Josef.'

Quiet came over the room like a pall. Though they had suspected this, to have their suspicions confirmed came as a shock.

And another thought from Werthen: why the waiters?

After a moment, Duncan spoke again. 'But that's not all. It appears that Monsieur Philipot wanted to make himself as helpful as possible to the agents who tracked him. He gave up another name connected with Klavan. It seems he once used a female for some of his operations intended to compromise various men. One Lisette Orzov.' He looked up meaningfully at the others.

'Is that name supposed to mean something to us?' Gross asked.

'It seems this Lisette Orzov decided to go out on her own, having learned various tricks of the trade from Klavan, and she used Philipot to help arrange various accomplices to entrap wealthy older gentlemen. She apparently made enough from a distant member of the Belgian royal house to retire in relative luxury to Vienna.'

'Orzov.' Gross pronounced the name again. 'But she must have changed her name by now.'

Duncan smiled at him. 'Indeed she has, Doktor Gross. Here she is known as Princess Dumbroski.'

It took them an hour to assemble the men. They did not bother with Prince Montenuovo after learning via telephone from an aide that the prince was attending a performance of *Manon* at the Court Opera. Instead they relied on men from Franz Ferdinand's personal staff on duty at the Lower Belvedere. Duncan was familiar with these men and a hurried call to Franz Ferdinand gained permission to mount such a raid.

They arrived at the Dumbroski residence on the Ringstrasse at just before nine o'clock in three separate carriages. There were twelve of them in all; Berthe had badly wanted to go along, but finally Werthen was able to convince her she needed to stay behind with Frieda. The nine officers Duncan picked were members of an elite team gathered by the archduke himself, and it was clear to Werthen they knew how to handle themselves.

The house door was still open; they left two of the officers to guard the entrance and made their way up the main staircase to the residence which occupied the top two floors of the building.

'If he's here, we'll get him,' Duncan said as Gross calmly rang the doorbell.

Klavan had just finished his preparations for tomorrow, with everything neatly stowed away in the pockets of his coat. His meager, nondescript belongings were also packed in readiness for his departure in the morning. His stay in Vienna was coming to an end. He would spend tomorrow night in a fine hotel with new clothing purchased with the money left from what he'd collected this morning from the safety deposit box.

He had earned some luxury.

When he heard the bell, he was instantly on guard. Though Lisette entertained regularly, she had nothing planned for tonight. He went to the window and eased back the curtain, glancing down at the Ringstrasse below. Two bulky military officers strolled up and down the street as if on guard duty.

Instinct took over. He threw on his coat, which also held the two doctored atomizers and the remaining plague bacillus vial in the pockets, and was out of the room on his way to the back stairs when the bell sounded again. The servants' stairs led down to the main floor of the apartment and now he saw Lisette coming out of her room, a startled expression on her face. He could hear male voices from the door now; the maid must have opened it.

'Who is it?' he hissed.

She shook her head. Then: 'Quick. Follow me.'

They moved quietly down the hall to a large ballroom. It was in darkness, but he could make out a book-lined wall opposite the floor-to-ceiling windows giving off to the Ring.

She went to the bookcase, put her hand over a volume and

suddenly a small door opened revealing a tiny room in back. 'My magic cabinet. Get in.'

He hesitated, but then could hear the voices coming closer.

'I must call my mistress,' the maid was saying.

'Quickly,' Lisette said.

He went in and the door closed behind him. It was dark; dark as a tomb.

Werthen saw Princess Dumbroski moving down the hallway toward them.

'And what, may I ask, are you gentlemen doing here at this time of night?'

'Good evening, Princess Dumbroski,' Werthen said. 'We have reason to believe that a most dangerous man might be in residence here.'

'I beg your pardon. Have you been drinking?'

'Klavan by name,' Gross thundered. 'A former colleague of yours.'

'Has the world gone mad? Get out of here this instant or I shall send for the police.'

'Madam, we are the police,' Gross said, stretching the truth for dramatic effect. 'Now take us to Herr Klavan, please.'

'This is an outrage! Leave at once.'

Gross ignored this. 'All right, men, search the place.'

Werthen had been closely watching as Gross confronted the woman, but she showed no sign of fear, only anger at the intrusion. He began to get a bad feeling about this visit.

Two hours later the small door opened again and Klavan was all but blinded by the candle Lisette held.

'They've gone. Now you disappear as well.'

'I'll get my things.'

She held a revolver in her hand. 'I don't think so. I told them they belonged to a long-lost cousin come for a visit and forgotten at departure. If they check again, I want them to still be in place.' She waved the gun. 'I won't be afraid to use it. Now leave. There's no one about – I checked.'

'Dear Lisette, thoughtful as ever. But I did enjoy my time in your little magic cabinet. Every apartment should have one.'

'Happy you approved. I had it installed myself. Now, I won't

say it again. Out of here. And do not come back. They know
who you are. They even seemed to know about us, but I denied
it all.'

'Who were they?'

'Military. And three others. I heard one of them being called
Doktor Gross and another was addressed as Advokat Werthen.'
She laughed. 'I know his wife.' Then her smile faded. 'The tall
one didn't have a name, just a scar on his face, and he stared at
me like I was meat hanging in a butcher shop.'

Klavan nodded and did as he was told, not because of the gun.
He could disarm her easily.

No, he needed the safety of the dark now. So close. And
Werthen and Gross were on his trail. Just like last time.

But he thought, as he slipped into the night, his pockets full
of money and death, they won't stop me this time. They are too
late.

# TWENTY-SEVEN

'And so you decided to take matters into your own hand,'
Prince Montenuovo said.

'You were not available, Prince,' Werthen said. 'And
we had it on the highest authority that Princess Dumbroski
and Klavan were connected.'

'The *highest* authority?'

'Well, from His Highness, Archduke Franz Ferdinand.'

'Yes, the archduke. His Majesty the emperor has heard of this
fiasco and he is none too pleased, I might add.'

'But Klavan means to kill the emperor,' Werthen insisted.

'Again on the very highest authority, I assume. No. It won't do,
gentlemen, it simply won't do. You cannot go about like Cossacks
storming into private residences—'

'Actually, we rang the bell,' Gross said.

Montenuovo shot him a withering look. 'This Klavan
appears to be a common criminal. A thug who murders waiters
and landladies.'

The remark, so closely echoing Gross's, would normally have

brought a smile to Werthen's face. But matters were too serious for that.

'He is a hired assassin,' Werthen pleaded. 'He was traced to Belgrade. The former attempt on the emperor's life surely came from that quarter . . .'

'So you say,' Prince Montenuovo replied. He sat back in his chair, sighing. 'Look, gentlemen, I am as concerned about the life of our emperor as you are, but you simply cannot go off willy-nilly like this, not when you are in my employ.'

'He was there,' Gross said with finality. 'There was a man staying in one of the servants' rooms.'

'A distant relation, the princess tells me, just as she explained to you last night,' Montenuovo said. 'Since gone back home to Czernowitz. Were you not once posted there, Doktor Gross?'

The implied threat of sending him back as penance to the university in Bukovina was clear. But Gross, happy with his current posting in Prague, still did not blanch at the remark.

'I have heard from very important people on behalf of Princess Dumbroski,' Montenuovo continued. 'And they are none too happy with this heavy-handed approach – treating her like a common criminal.'

'Which she is,' Gross said under his breath, but just loud enough for the prince to hear.

'Enough.' Montenuovo suddenly rose. 'Do not make me regret commissioning you two. Find this Klavan fellow if you must, and leave Princess Dumbroski alone.'

Werthen controlled his temper enough to remember to ask the prince to arrange an interview with the elusive Czerny. This seemed hardly important now. The hunt for Klavan was the primary focus, but after all, he had promised Berthe.

He arrived at the men's hostel a little after ten that morning. Hermann Postling was at his usual table and alone, as always. Klavan was exhausted, having spent the night in a small stable for fiaker horses not far from Lisette's. Easy enough to break in and then slip out again before first light. But the chill had kept him awake most of the night. No matter, he thought as he approached the old man. After this delivery I will find a fine men's clothier, buy new clothes and rent a suite of rooms. And he knew just the place.

They will never look for me there.

'Good morning, Hermann,' he said as he approached the old man's table.

Postling looked up, annoyed. 'It's about time. I've been waiting all morning. I have other appointments, you know. Now what is so important?'

'Just a final thought,' Klavan said. 'Something for the emperor tomorrow.'

Later, as he made his way from the men's hostel, Klavan felt the second bottle in his coat pocket.

Better safe than sorry, he told himself.


Professor Doktor Hermann Nothnagel was in his office at the bacteriological institute at Vienna's General Hospital. He wore a formal long black coat and his equally long white beard gave him the appearance of an Old Testament sage.

Gross thanked him heartily for seeing them on such short notice, then got right to the point. 'How can plague bacilli be used to kill?'

The doctor stared back at him with fierce blue eyes. 'Is this about Office 3G?'

Gross nodded.

Nothnagel squeezed the bridge of his nose between thumb and forefinger. 'Not again.'

He looked again at Gross. 'I warned them this could happen.'

'I have not come to apportion blame,' Gross said. 'I simply need to know how it can be used if in the wrong hands.'

'In the air. This is the pneumonic not bubonic plague. First is human transmission, human fluids or breathing the bacilli in. Contaminated or undercooked foods is also a possibility. But breathing it in is the most typical manner of transmission. Those infected cough and sneeze and spread the bacteria in that manner. Onset is relatively rapid: a couple of days, sometimes only hours. At first its symptoms are the same as any respiratory complaint: headache, weakness and coughing. Quite rapidly, however, the patient begins spitting or vomiting blood. Within a week, almost one hundred percent of sufferers succumb to the disease.' He shook his head. 'Was it an anarchist?'

Gross was taken aback by the question. 'What?'

'Who stole the vials. It sounds like the work of an anarchist.'

'We'll know that when we find our man. So breathing in the infection from those who have it, you say. Can it be atomized?'

The doctor clasped his hands together. 'I don't see why not. Somehow sprayed. Yes, that is a distinct possibility.'

Meanwhile, Werthen was meeting at Inspector Drechsler's office.

'We got word of it this morning. What were you thinking of?' Drechsler was enjoying this.

'He was there. Or he had been. There's no doubt of that.'

'And there was also no evidence of it, Advokat.'

'His suitcase.'

'Somebody's suitcase. A distant cousin, according to this Dumbroski.'

'Orzov is her real name. Lisette Orzov.'

'Says your archduke.'

'No.' Werthen felt his anger rising. 'Says *our* archduke and future emperor.'

But anger was unhelpful. 'Now what we need to be doing instead of trading barbs is getting this description out as widely as possible. Hotels, pensions, restaurants. Anywhere a man with no place to call his own might be found.'

Drechsler looked at the sheet of paper Werthen had handed him earlier, reading the description again.

He looked up at Werthen. 'The only thing distinctive is the little fingers. Otherwise, he could be anybody. It would help if there was a picture.'

Werthen shook his head. 'We don't have one.'

'I'm still not convinced that this Klavan is out to kill the emperor. Everything you tell me is circumstantial – or worse, assumptions.'

'Nothing circumstantial about him being a killer. You know that. You investigated the murder of that young woman when Klavan was last in Vienna.'

'You've got to be some kind of animal to snip off the finger like that. Like it's a memento.'

'A prize, more like,' Werthen said. 'So it doesn't really matter why we capture him, does it? For the murders he committed last time he was in Vienna, or for plans to assassinate the emperor. He's a mad dog. Mad dogs need to be put down.'

Drechsler looked at the description once again as if he could gain some insight to Klavan.

'Well, there's one good thing about that fiasco last night,' the detective finally said.

'What's that?'

'He knows you're coming for him. It's not just his game anymore. Somebody else is playing. Sometimes that makes a man nervous; forces him to make a mistake.'

The telephone rang three times before Berthe was able to dislodge herself from a Frieda hug and answer it.

'Werthen residence,' she answered, and wondered for the hundredth time why she did not include her name in that salutation.

'I am trying to reach a Frau Meisner. Is this the correct number?'

It was a man's voice, low and with the tone of authority to it.

'Yes, this is Frau Meisner. How may I help you?'

'Good afternoon. I hope I am not disturbing you, but Prince Montenuovo indicated you desired to speak with me. This is Oberstabelmeister Johann Czerny. May I inquire what this is in reference to?'

'Yes, of course. I would very much like to talk to you about your old friend, Herr Andric.'

There was silence on the other end of the line. Then: 'Andric? No, I can't say as I— Wait. You mean Herr Karl Andric. Sorry. Because of his work he always referred to himself as Herr Karl. Sorely missed. A good man.'

'So you do know of his passing?'

'Yes, yes. I was able to take time away from my duties at the Hofburg to attend his burial. How may I help you? I understand you are a private inquiries agent. But what is there to investigate? Poor Karl slipped on the ice and cracked his head.'

'It is not quite that simple, Herr Oberstabelmeister . . .'

'Herr Czerny will suffice. How is it not simple?'

'The police are now treating Herr Karl's death as a murder. One of a string of murders, in fact.'

An extended silence from his end this time.

Finally Berthe said, 'Herr Czerny?'

'Yes, I am still here. It's a bit of a shock though. Who would want to kill Karl?'

'That is what I am trying to find out, as well. May I come and talk with you?'

'Of course. Could you be here in half an hour? This is an extremely busy time for me what with the ceremony tomorrow, but I will make time. Though I doubt there is anything I can tell you.'

'Wonderful,' she said. 'I'll be there.'

Frau Blatschky was only too happy to sit with Frieda, and Berthe hailed the first fiaker she saw, even though she could easily walk to the Hofburg in under thirty minutes.

She was pleased to see the same officious clerk on duty at the Oberstabelmeister's Bureau; even more pleased when she told him she had an appointment with Herr Czerny. He reluctantly showed her into the man's office.

Berthe was surprised to meet Herr Czerny. From his voice on the phone, so commanding, she had pictured him as a large, florid man who might take his eating seriously. But now she discovered he was a man of medium height and slight build. He seated her in a comfortable leather chair across from him and then took his place in his own chair.

'As I said on the telephone, Frau Meisner, I am not sure how I can be of help to you. This is rather a shock. Poor, dear Karl. It is as if I must mourn him all over again.'

'You saw one another regularly?'

'Oh, yes. We met for a weekly game of chess at one café or the other, but never the Café Burg. On his day off, Karl said he deserved a respite from the Burg.'

'And did he seem different of late?'

'Different?'

'Out of sorts. Or as if something was troubling him.'

'Not really. Though I did receive an urgent telephone message from him just before he died. He told me that he needed to talk with me. We set a time for him to come here the next day.' Czerny sniffed a tear back. 'I am sorry, Frau Meisner.'

'That's quite all right. He was your life-long friend, after all.'

'Yes.' He applied a silk handkerchief to his eyes. 'Well, he never showed up for the appointment. He died . . . was murdered you now tell me . . . the night before. How terrible to think of him with the back of his head smashed in.'

Berthe paused a moment at this comment, then asked, 'Did he have any enemies?'

'Enemies? Karl? Everyone loved Herr Karl. He was an institution as head waiter.'

'Did he mention a man named Klavan? Or perhaps Wenno?'

Czerny twisted his mouth as if tasting the names. 'Can't say I ever heard of either. Were they customers?'

'Perhaps. Herr Czerny, I need to mention something about your friend, something that does not put him in the best light. I am not trying to be offensive nor to slander his name, but this may be germane to the investigation of his killing.'

'I can't imagine anything that Karl might have done to put him in a bad light. He was as honest as the day is long.'

She took a moment to explain Herr Karl's little system of bribery and kickbacks, not making eye contact with Czerny as she spoke.

When she finished, Czerny chuckled. 'The old devil. How Viennese of him. How very Viennese. But you can hardly imagine somebody would murder him for such paltry sums, can you?'

'I thought I should mention it in case you knew more about it.'

'No, nothing. Funny, you think you know a fellow . . .'

They spoke for several more minutes about the friendship between the two men, their rise from humble origins, the fact that they had both remained bachelors, their deep enjoyment of the weekly chess match. But there was nothing to be discovered.

Czerny glanced at the clock on the wall meaningfully.

'Yes, I should be leaving. I thank you very much for your time.'

'Not at all. Glad to be of assistance.'

Berthe was about to leave, but thought of one more thing. 'On the phone you mentioned a ceremony tomorrow. What would that be?'

'Why, Maundy Thursday, of course. On Holy Thursday the emperor washes the feet of a dozen old men at the Hofburg and launches the four days of Court celebration of Easter. And I tell you it has been a headache this year.'

'How so?'

'The selection of the old men, as usual. I mean to say, there is usually competition for this, jockeying for position. It seems everyone in Vienna has a near-indigent great uncle at this time of the year.'

'Well, it must be a huge honor.'

'The twenty silver coins each receives following the ceremony is also an incentive,' he replied with a sardonic smile. 'Anybody with a little *Beziehung* – pull, was plumping for their favorite old man. Herr Karl even got in the game this year. Quite a surprise.'

'You didn't mention this.'

'No, sorry. It slipped my mind. But yes, he did come up with his own name. Said it was a poor old fellow used to beg by his café. Just the type, he said. And you know, he was right. We interviewed the chap, and with that long beard of his, he looks almost biblical. It should make for a fine photograph for the newspapers.'

'So you accepted his nominee?'

Czerny nodded so briskly that his jowls jiggled. 'Very much so. Chap named Hermann . . . Wait, let me see.' He checked a sheaf of papers on his desk. 'Right. Hermann Postling. Resides at the Kubit Men's Hostel on Neulerchenfelderstrasse. We are due to pick him up there in a royal coach at ten tomorrow morning.'

The name sounded familiar. Where had she heard that before? Perhaps she had not heard it but read it. Berthe had brought along Karl's leather notebook with his notes regarding the Herr Karl investigation. She pulled it out of her handbag, shuffled through the pages, and then, turning one leaf, she discovered the little slip of paper her husband had retrieved at the dead man's flat. She handed the paper to Czerny.

'Yes, that's the name,' he said. 'Where did you find this?'

'In Herr Karl's belongings.'

'Hmm.' Czerny held the paper up to the light. 'Odd that.'

'What?'

'Why carry around a slip of paper with the old man's name on it? It's as if he had to remind himself of the name. I thought he knew the old fellow.'

# TWENTY-EIGHT

'**B**ravo, Berthe,' Werthen said when she shared her information with them. They had gathered at Werthen's office in the afternoon as arranged to discuss their next move. 'This Postling fellow could be very important.'

'He is scheduled to come into direct contact with the emperor tomorrow,' Gross said. 'I suggest a visit to the gentleman.'

'But what could he do to the emperor?' Berthe said. 'Is he infected with the plague? Is that the plan?'

'That, my dear, is why I believe you should remain home,' Werthen said.

'Not this time. I missed all the fun last night with Princess Dumbroski. I'm not staying home again.'

'A beard of biblical proportions, you say,' Gross said suddenly.

'Yes. That is how Herr Czerny described it to me.'

'And Werthen, you remember the false beard we found in Dimitrov's things at the Pension Geldner?'

'Yes, of course, Gross. You've struck on it. Dimitrov was going to take the old man's place at the ceremony. He was dying anyway. He would give his life to kill the emperor. Shoot him, stab him . . .'

'Blow him up,' Gross offered.

'And with Dimitrov dead, Klavan needed to figure out a new plan,' Berthe said. 'Hence the theft of the plague bacilli.'

'There is no time to lose,' Gross said.

On their way out they saw Franzl proudly displaying a charcoal portrait he had just completed to the secretary, Erika Metzinger.

She held it up for the others to see. 'Not bad, is it?'

Franzl's face reddened as she said this.

Indeed, it was not bad at all.

'Reminds me of a charcoal I saw by Michelangelo once in Florence,' Berthe said.

'You're only saying that.' But Franzl threw his shoulders back at the compliment.

'Saying it and meaning it,' she said as she ruffled his hair.

'Where are you three off to?' Erika asked as they hurried out of the office.

'To see a beggar,' Berthe said gaily.

It took almost an hour to travel to the men's hostel from the Inner City. There was work on one of the streetcar lines that halted them several times. They could have walked there faster. At the entrance Gross stopped and gave both Werthen and Berthe a fierce look.

'I am going to go in there on my own,' he said, 'and I want no arguments from either of you. This is not a lark, this could be deadly if the old man is somehow contaminated.'

'Now, Gross—' Werthen began, but the criminologist was adamant.

'You did not hear Professor Doktor Nothnagel this morning describing how deadly this form of plague is. If you had, you would know better than to argue with me. You have a young child. Now do as I say and wait here!'

A workingman passing by shot them a worried look, hearing the tone of voice, and hurried on his way.

'This is a one-person job anyway.'

He turned from them abruptly and made for the door of the hostel.

'Be careful, Gross,' Berthe called after him.

Gross went to the registration desk in the foyer where an attendant sat on a high stool, busy with the illustrated sports newspaper. The page was full of pugilists in tights.

'I would like to see Herr Hermann Postling, if you don't mind,' Gross said.

The man – about forty and not going anywhere fast in his career – looked up from his newspaper. 'My condolences.'

Gross scowled at him but the man had obviously deflected worse in his life.

'If he's in, he'll be at his usual table upstairs. Third on the right from the window. He's the one that'll be by himself. Sign in here.' He tapped a spatulate finger on a ledger book and returned to his paper.

Gross inscribed his name and then took the stairs to the second floor. He easily found the table in question, but it was unoccupied.

He glanced around the room, looking for another elderly man with a long gray beard. He was again without luck.

Gross stumped back down the stairs to the front desk.

'He was not there,' Gross said.

Up came the eyes again from the paper. The attendant had moved on to the cycling news.

'Lucky us. Hermann is a busy fellow. Got his begging to do. Lord knows all he gets up to. He's usually here for the food, though. Doesn't like to miss his meals, our Hermann.'

'And when is meal time?'

'Hungry, are you?'

'Look now, I have about lost my patience with you. Keep a civil tongue in that mouth of yours or I'll let your superiors know.'

'Six o'clock,' the man said without emotion. 'You've got over an hour to wait.'

Gross sighed mightily, turned on his heels and went back outside where Berthe and Werthen were carrying on an animated conversation with a beggar who seemed somehow familiar. Gross was about to send the old fellow on his way when he had a sudden inspiration.

'Herr Postling?' he said, coming up to the trio.

'Who wants to know?' The old man now turned on him suspiciously.

'This is the colleague we mentioned,' Werthen quickly informed the man.

'Pah,' Postling muttered. 'Looks like another resident of the hostel to me.'

Gross felt his temper rising. 'Now, see here . . .'

But Berthe now quickly cut in. 'Herr Postling was just telling us about Herr Wenno.'

'Indeed?' Gross said.

'You're not here to tell me it was all a hoax, are you? I've got my heart set on the twenty pieces of silver.'

'No, no,' Werthen assured him. 'Nothing of the kind.'

'You're to be the star of the show,' Berthe added.

This brought a smile to the old man's face, but it was quickly replaced by a suspicious scowl.

'Then what's this all about?'

'We were just curious if Herr Wenno has visited you lately. Say, since Monday.' Berthe smiled reassuringly at him.

'And what if he has?'

'Well,' Werthen began.

'You're not taking it back. Not on your life.'

'Slowly, Herr Postling,' Berthe said in the calmest of voices. 'What is it we can't take back?'

He warmed to her. 'The good smelling stuff. A bottle of cologne. One of those nice little bottles with the little rubber ball for spraying. He meant for me to make a present of it to the emperor tomorrow. After he washes my feet. Well, I figure an emperor can afford his own cologne. So—'

'Where is the bottle now?' Berthe asked. 'We may need to give you a replacement. That one might not be good anymore. Did you use any of it?'

'Not a drop.' Then Postling's face crumpled. 'That's not right. Not fair.'

'We'll get you another bottle,' Werthen reassured him. 'Don't worry. A bigger one even. Now maybe you could show us that bottle.'

The old man shook his head. 'Can't.'

'Why not?' Berthe asked.

'Because I don't have it anymore. I already made a present of it. To that nice little boy who drew my picture.'

Werthen, Gross, and Berthe made the connection at almost the same instant, suddenly understanding why the old man looked familiar to them. He was the man from Franzl's sketch.

'A young boy named Franzl?' Werthen said.

'Well, that's the very one. I sit for the folks to draw at this studio out in the Prater. Sweet young boy. Reminds me of my own before he ran off for Canada and got himself drowned. Gave it to him this afternoon.'

Werthen's mind raced. Then Franzl must have already had the cologne with him when he was showing off his sketch at the office. Had he sprayed it? Werthen could not remember any scent in the office.

'We've got to get to the boy, Herr Postling,' Berthe told him.

'Tell him I didn't know it had gone bad,' the old man said mournfully as they rushed off to a fiaker rank on the corner.

Gross told the driver they would double the fare if he could get them to Habsburgergasse 4 in half the time. The man's eyes bulged and he had the whip to the horse even as they were settling into their seats.

Later, Werthen could remember nothing of the ride. He was going over every possible scenario. It was obvious that Klavan had put the plague bacilli in the cologne bottle, hoping the emperor would use it, charmed by the gift from the old man. But what if Franzl decided to try it, sprayed it on in the office with Erika next to him? My God, they would both die horrible deaths. If Franzl sprayed it in an open area it could spread to all those around him. His heart was pounding in rhythm to the horse's hooves.

Finally the carriage came to a stop at the office and as Gross paid the driver, Werthen and Berthe leaped to the sidewalk and raced up the flights of stairs to the law offices, bounding in out of breath. Erika was at the typing machine, alone in the outer office.

'Franzl,' Werthen said, between breaths. 'Where is Franzl?'

'What is it?'

'Where is he?' Berthe asked. 'He may be in danger.'

Before she could answer, Werthen said, 'Did he have a bottle of cologne? A spray bottle?'

'Why, yes. He showed it to me, proud as anything. Said it was like payment for his art.'

'Did you smell it? Did he spray it in here?'

'Advokat. What is it? This is frightening me.'

'Did he spray it?' Werthen asked again.

She shook her head. 'No. Said it was going to be a special gift. He left early to give it to her. I said it would be all right just this once to leave early.'

'Her?' Berthe said. 'Who?'

'The friend he made when he was at Frau Schratt's.'

'Oh, Lord,' Berthe said. 'We've got to get there.'

Werthen went immediately to his phone, looked into his address book, found Schratt's number and had the operator place the call.

The phone rang five times before finally it was answered.

'Schratt residence.' It was Netty's voice, steely and efficient.

'Hello, this is Advokat Werthen. My colleague Doktor Gross and I conferred with your mistress about a missing letter.'

'Yes.' There was the hint of animosity in her voice. After all, they had incriminated her beloved mistress in their investigations.

'There was a young boy in service with you at the time.'

'Young Franzl. Yes.' Her voice softened.

'Have you seen him today?'

'He's at the kitchen table as we speak. Enjoying a cup of hot cocoa. Such a thoughtful gift for Anna.'

'Has she opened it? I mean, sprayed it?'

'I beg your pardon.'

Werthen did not know how to get through to her. Finally he opted for fear.

'It's poisoned. Understand. Do not spray the cologne.'

'*Gott in Himmel.*'

'Exactly,' Werthen said. 'Has she sprayed it?'

'No!' came a scream down the line, as if Netty were yelling at those in the kitchen. 'Don't touch it! It's poison.'

And then the line went dead.

# TWENTY-NINE

He stretched out in the comfortable chair in his hotel room. It had been a busy day, but it was all coming to fruition now, he thought, looking at himself in the full-length mirror of the wardrobe. He was amazed at the transformation a suit of clothes and a pair of glasses could make. The spectacles, purchased at an optical shop this afternoon, had glass for lenses as they had been the model for the window display. The optician had been only too happy to sell them, however, when he got a look at Klavan's money.

He smiled at the reflection, almost unrecognizable even to himself. With his hair combed back off his forehead as it now was and the new and very special clothes, his own mother might not recognize him.

All was in readiness. And he would be there himself to witness his great coup.

Berthe held him to her bosom, squeezing so hard Franzl had to finally plead for air.

'I didn't mean any harm,' he said again, and looking abashed at Fräulein Anna. 'I thought it would make a nice present for you, like saying thank you for being so good to me.'

Her face reddened as he said this. 'It's all right, little poppet. You couldn't know.' Then to Werthen, who was standing next to his wife and Franzl: 'Why would anybody put poison in perfume?'

'That's a good question, Fräulein Anna,' he answered. 'Some people are just bad.'

If only it were that simple, he thought.

'We really should be going,' Gross prompted. 'Business to attend to.'

Werthen nodded at him. Now that they had ascertained that Franzl was safe and that the cologne had not been used, they did have other matters to see to this evening.

Frau Schratt did not deign to make an appearance, even as they prepared to leave. They let Franzl and Fräulein Anna take leave of each other, each promising the see the other soon.

'And I mean soon, poppet,' Fräulein Anna urged. 'But no presents next time, all right?'

Berthe offered to take Franzl home in a separate carriage while Werthen and Gross went to an emergency meeting with Prince Montenuovo at the Hofburg. The prince was in a vile mood, obviously brought on by having to miss his dinner. It was as if he blamed them for the deadly bottle of cologne, which Werthen had passed on to laboratory workers from the General Hospital, who were specially dispatched.

'Lord knows what the boy was thinking of. He could have killed Frau Schratt and her entire household.'

'No,' Werthen interrupted, anger gripping. '*Klavan* could have killed them all. It was he that turned the cologne into a deadly weapon.'

'Well, yes,' the prince allowed. 'But it was damned cheeky passing on the cologne like that.'

Gross intervened before Werthen had a chance to well and truly outrage Montenuovo.

'It was a close one,' he said, 'but I feel this also presents us with a golden opportunity.'

'How do you come to such a bizarre conclusion, Doktor Gross? You may have tripped the man up, but you have not knocked him down for good.'

Now it was Gross's turn to take umbrage at the prince's testiness.

'There is no reason to let Klavan think he has been tripped up. He may show his hand if he thinks he's succeeded in his damnable scheme.'

'But he hasn't succeeded. We've stopped the old man.'

Gross exchanged a glance with Werthen at his use of 'we'.

'But I am proposing that we leave Herr Postling in place. Police are guarding the men's hostel. There is no way for Klavan to discover that the cologne has been taken. So, I say we go ahead with the ceremony as planned. I am sure we can secure another bottle of the actual cologne for Postling to give to the emperor.'

'But what if the old man was in on it?'

'I assure you, Prince Montenuovo,' Gross said, 'Herr Postling's only incentive in this manner is the twenty silver coins to be awarded by the emperor. He was taken in by Klavan. I think we can use him now. It might make Klavan lower his guard.'

Montenuovo shook his head. 'Too dangerous. Why, the man might already be infected with the plague. My God, we should have him isolated.'

'The cologne was still sealed when we took it into possession,' Werthen said.

'Still . . .'

'Prince Montenuovo, I firmly believe this would work,' Gross said.

But Montenuovo was adamant. 'Now to find a replacement for the old man.'

He gave Gross an appraising look, then shook his head. 'I need to contact Czerny immediately. I am sure you will excuse me, gentlemen. I have work to do now.'

'The pompous ass,' Gross railed later as they were seated around the table and enjoying Frau Blatschky's liver-dumpling soup. 'Passing up a golden opportunity. Klavan would surely want to check with Postling later to make sure the gift had been passed on. Idiot.'

His ire did not affect Gross's appetite, however. Once the soup was taken away, he indulged in a healthy helping of *Esterhazyrostbraten* – roast beef with root vegetables in a cream sauce of bacon, capers, tarragon, white wine, sour cream, and lemon peel.

There were just the three of them, as Berthe had put Frieda
to bed before dinner.

'How will he even know if Postling isn't among the twelve
tomorrow?' she asked.

'You're right,' Werthen said, setting down his fork. 'We should
keep a guard on the hostel in case Klavan shows up. Plain clothes.'

Gross considered this. 'I feel that our Herr Klavan will
somehow know if Postling is among the old men tomorrow. But
yes, I concur. It would do no harm. Duncan, I should think.
Perhaps he could arrange a small group from the Belvedere to
establish a casual surveillance following the ceremony. The police
are hopeless undercover, regardless of what clothing they don.
They might as well wear a sign around their necks declaring
their profession.'

Werthen eyed the criminologist. 'You say you think that Klavan
will somehow know if Postling is there, which means you suspect
he may be at the Hofburg tomorrow.'

Gross took time to finish masticating the mound of beef he
had wedged into his mouth before bothering to nod. Then a final
bite and swallow. 'Yes. Astute of you, Werthen.'

'Are we planning to have a watch at the Hofburg then?'

'It had crossed my mind.' Gross pointed a greedy finger at the
bottle of Bordeaux lazing about on the table and put it to work
once Berthe had passed it to him. 'Duncan is once again arranging
things.'

'I am going to be there, as well,' Werthen said with determin-
ation. 'I am sick of this Klavan attempting to bring death to the
office. First the bomb from last year, now the bottle of plague
bacilli.'

Berthe was contemplative. 'You know, things begin to make
more sense now. I mean, all the deaths are connected, aren't
they?'

'Ah,' Gross said, helping himself to another slice of beef and
sauce. 'I was waiting for someone to broach that. Yes, my good
woman, connected, indeed.'

Werthen had been working on this, as well. 'It all started when
Klavan had the idea to place a living bomb at the Maundy
Thursday ceremony.'

The others nodded.

Werthen went on: 'We cannot know what came first, the

idea or the candidate for foot washing, Hermann Postling. But whichever, Klavan then needed to get the ear of the Hofburg.'

'Czerny,' Berthe said.

'Right.' Werthen poured some wine for himself; Berthe put her hand over her glass.

'One assumes he scrutinized Herr Czerny,' Gross said, picking up the thread. 'Looking for a weak point, perhaps some way to blackmail the man into accepting Hermann Postling. But better yet, he uncovered the man's lifelong friendship with the head waiter, Herr Karl. And it would take a man of Klavan's skill no time at all to discover the head waiter's dirty little secret of bribery and graft. Much better to blackmail the friend than Czerny directly.'

'But then Herr Karl must have thought better of it,' Berthe added. 'The urgent meeting he made with Herr Czerny.'

'Yes. That would appear to be the reason for Herr Karl's death. Was the waiter naive enough to inform Klavan of his intentions to speak to Czerny about the old man? If so, that sealed his fate. Klavan killed him before he could get to Czerny and spoil his wonderful plan.'

'And Falk's murder would be a matter of insurance for a man like Klavan,' Werthen said, 'in case the under waiter remembered seeing him at the Café Burg. The irony is that Falk did remember and had already told me. So Falk died for nothing.'

'Not for nothing,' Berthe interjected. 'His death brought our attention back to Herr Karl and the whole sordid affair. It led us to Czerny.'

'What an evil bastard,' Werthen said. 'I hope I see him there tomorrow.'

Berthe said nothing, but she fervently hoped that her husband would not do so.

# PART FIVE

# THIRTY

The day dawned, sunny and fine. Sun poured in through the open curtains on Werthen's face, waking him from a dream of passing through endless doors in an old house and discovering room after room, unexpected and unexplored. One door beckoned and he felt a sudden fear as he opened it. Waiting for him on the other side was a small man with massive hands, the little fingers jutting out from both like daggers. He thrust these at Werthen's eyes.

His heart was racing as he woke to the sunshine. Berthe was already up. He could smell freshly brewed coffee.

And then he remembered what day it was. He glanced at the alarm clock on the bedside table. Past nine in the morning. He never slept in. And today of all days.

He got up and hurriedly washed and dressed in his finest wool suit. He needed to look presentable.

He was going to the Hofburg.

The ceremony began promptly at eleven in the magnificent Ceremonial Hall at the Hofburg, site of weddings and balls. Today it would be the site of the ceremonial foot-washing in celebration of Maundy Thursday, an event the Habsburgs had sponsored for generations, a holdover from Christ's ritual cleansing of the feet of his disciples at the Last Supper. The very name of the holiday came from the Latin *mandatum*, or Jesus' commandment at that final meal – after Judas had departed – to love one another. The priests in attendance today seemed very intent on that principle as they readied the emperor for his task. Franz Josef was looking rather frail, Werthen thought, even though he was decked out in the full regalia of his office, his left chest bedecked by medals. Gathered in the great hall were the mighty and powerful of the empire and from abroad as well.

Werthen stood a little apart from the dignitaries, near Prince Montenuovo, but not too near. Gross was on the other side of the hall. Duncan and his men were situated in the Schweizerhof

below, where the carriages were kept, and some fewer church
dignitaries and clergy milled about in hopes of catching a glimpse
of the emperor.

Suddenly the great doors of the Ceremonial Hall opened and
a line of old men was led in, taking chairs at the front of the
hall, opposite the emperor. There were twelve of them; Hermann
Postling was not among them.

But what of the other chairs? Werthen wondered. For there
seemed to be another dozen in a line next to those the old men
occupied.

Again the doors swung open, and now a line of old women
was marched in, some so feeble that they had to be supported
by court servants. They took their places alongside the men.

Of course. How many times had he read of the ceremony in
the papers at Easter? The emperor bathed the feet of twelve men
and twelve women.

But it still confused him, for he had not thought ahead to this.
None of them had.

Now the emperor, flanked by the cardinal archbishop of Vienna
and the papal nuncio, approached the two dozen elderly people.
At this point, the cardinal archbishop was in charge, and the
emperor had left his earthly realm behind. The cardinal read from
the Gospel of St John in a bellowing voice that rang throughout the
hall: '*Posuit vestimenta sua.*'

Werthen's gymnasium Latin was still good enough for the
translation: 'He laid aside his garments.'

At this, the emperor handed an attendant his hat and his
sword. Werthen felt a sense of menace, just as he had in
his dream. The emperor was truly now at the mercy of these
elderly people.

'*Et coepit lavare pedes disciploruum.*' Werthen further translated: 'And he began to wash the feet of his disciples.'

A servant handed Franz Josef a silver ewer filled with perfumed
water and the emperor kneeled in front of each elderly person
in turn, so vulnerable, so frail.

Werthen sought out Gross's eyes, and it was evident by his
intent and fixed gaze that his colleague, too, had overlooked the
fact of the women involved in the ceremony.

But what could it matter? He watched as the emperor carefully
washed and then dried the feet of each, handed the person a fresh

pair of stockings and stout new shoes, then moved on slowly to the next.

What could there be to fear from these old people? Werthen asked himself. We found the one that Klavan had planted.

Yet he was worried.

Outside in the courtyard, Klavan kept a watch on the balcony to see when the ceremony would finish. He tried to still his anger, for Hermann Postling was not among those arriving in the royal carriages at the Schweizerhof. He had been betrayed, but he would see to that pompous bureaucrat later. He consoled himself that all was not lost. He was pleased now for his diligence. At the time it had seemed an unnecessary nuisance; now it was his last hope.

He kept his eyes on the balcony. When would it end?

The emperor was making his way down the line of elderly to where Werthen stood. The advokat eyed the last of the elderly to have their feet washed. Thus far, the ceremony had gone without incident. Only three women were left. He examined each in turn, and as with those before, on two of these he saw nothing in their faces but a sort of joyful expectancy. To have the emperor himself bathe their feet! Such an honor.

But on the face of the last lady he thought he discerned something different. More than expectancy. Her left eye twitched. Her hands were so tightly clenched in her lap that they were white at the knuckles.

He slowly made his way forward toward the seated women. Montenuovo shot him a nasty look, but he ignored the prince. He did not know why, but he moved inexorably toward the last of the women just as in his dream this morning he had moved toward the last of the doors.

The emperor slowly rose, shuffling to this final parishioner, then kneeled in front of her, taking her gnarled white feet in hand and beginning to wash them.

She slowly unclasped her hands, moving the right one casually toward a small reticule in her lap. The age-freckled hand dug its way into the reticule and bit by bit began to withdraw again.

When Werthen saw a small rubber bulb he could no longer restrain himself. He shouted out, 'No! Stop!'

Startled, the woman who had by now pulled the bottle of cologne out of the bag suddenly dropped it.

Werthen did not think. He took one galloping step forward and then leaped through the air, his hands held out. Time stood still as he felt himself floating in the air, and then his hands encountered the hard enamel of the bottle and folded around it as he crashed, belly first, to the parquet.

There was pandemonium as guards rushed to the side of the emperor and rough hands were put on Werthen, who managed to hang on to the deadly bottle.

'Let him be!' Franz Josef cried out at the guards. 'The man has saved my life.' The emperor, who had been appraised of the earlier threat, gazed at the cologne bottle cupped in Werthen's hands, identical to the one Postling had been given by Klavan. 'I believe he has saved us all.'

Klavan, like all the others gathered in the courtyard, heard the commotion from above and smiled. It is done, he thought. The old woman has achieved it. Still, he would have to kill the granddaughter. Loose ends needed to be tidied. He looked upward to the balcony hoping for some announcement, some strangled cry of doom and dismay.

Werthen lost not a moment. Once the cologne bottle was secured, he, along with Gross, questioned the old woman, Ursula Huber.

'He's a demon,' she kept saying. 'He told me he would kill my darling Gitty if I did not do as he told me.'

'Calm yourself, please,' Werthen said. 'We know you were coerced into this. Tell us about this man. Did he call himself Wenno?' God help us if he has an accomplice, Werthen thought.

'He was no simple man,' she spluttered. 'He was a priest.'

'Jesus, Mary and Joseph,' Gross muttered, and immediately they turned around to examine the religious congregation gathered in the hall.

Impossible, Werthen thought. There was no way an imposter could gain access to the Ceremonial Hall. Then a sudden thought.

'Gross, the courtyard. He must be down there monitoring his deadly scheme.'

They raced to the tall windows giving off to the balcony over the Schweizerhof, threw open the doors and peered down below at the gathered priests and the drivers by their carriages ready to take the men and women back to their homes.

'There he is,' Werthen all but shouted, looking down at a priest who was staring back up at him with hatred showing on his face like a scar. 'Duncan,' he shouted out. 'There, the priest in front.'

This shook Klavan out of his rage-induced lethargy. He knew that once again Werthen and the infernal Doktor Gross had put paid to his carefully wrought plans. He would get his revenge, but for now he needed to make his way out of the courtyard, avoiding this Duncan, whoever he was. He pulled his revolver out of its holster and shot off two quick rounds into the air, causing those in the courtyard to panic and begin running in every direction for cover. He joined in, running in the chaos, but in the direction of the arched entryway to the courtyard.

'Stop or I'll shoot,' commanded a burly looking man in a suit and brandishing a Colt.

Klavan did not miss a step as he pulled off two more rounds, the second taking the top of the man's head off.

Military or police, he thought as he leaped over the man's body. Had to be one or the other to be so stupid not to shoot first, command later.

A tall, hawk-nosed man with a scar on his face was not so stupid, as he dropped Klavan with a shot to the left bicep. The bullet burned, but he could still take a shot with his right hand, down on one knee. And then the soldiers arrived, running in between him and the tall man. They saw the gun in the tall man's hand first and quickly demanded he drop his weapon. Klavan wisely holstered his own and stood up, attempting once again to blend into the crowd. His upper arm was bleeding, but it was not immediately noticeable on the black serge of his priest's coat.

By now the military men had surrounded the tall man and taken his gun even as their prisoner pleaded, 'He's getting away, damn you. The priest. In disguise.'

Klavan forced himself to walk unhurriedly past the clump of military men, with more rushing into the courtyard as he passed out under the stone archway. He said to one of these oncoming soldiers, 'The tall one. He attempted to kill our beloved emperor.'

'Bastard,' the man cried out as his boots clattered on the cobbles.

\* \* \*

By the time Werthen and Gross had raced down the wide, curving flight of marble stairs to the courtyard below, all they could see was a crowd of soldiers surrounding a man near the entrance. They hurried over and as they approached, Werthen caught sight of Duncan's head above the others, his hands raised high.

'Try to kill the emperor, you son of a bitch,' one of the soldiers was saying as Gross and Werthen waded into their midst.

'This is not the one, you fools,' Gross said in a fury. 'He was disguised as a priest.'

'Mother of God,' the soldier who had taken Klavan's lie to heart said.

'I tried to tell them, Doktor Gross,' Duncan said, feeling safe now to lower his hands. 'He shot Hartmann.' Duncan nodded his head to a body lying in a pool of blood ten feet away.

Werthen did not bother to listen to more but dashed out under the archway to the courtyard into the Hofburg grounds. But he could not see Klavan and there were numerous directions of escape from here.

Back in the courtyard the focus was now on the body of Hartmann, a lieutenant in Franz Ferdinand's bodyguard detail.

'He was just a kid,' Duncan said, kneeling down by the body. 'Engaged last month.'

He looked up at Gross and Werthen as he spoke next. 'But I wounded him. Left arm. He'll need a doctor.'

'This is inexcusable,' Prince Montenuovo declared. 'How could you let this happen?'

'If you will remember rightly,' Gross said, 'it didn't happen. Advokat Werthen here saved the day.'

'There should have been nothing to save. Why did you not know of Frau Huber beforehand?'

They sat in his office quarreling when all Werthen wished to do was track down Klavan and kill him. That would be justice.

'I admit to failure there,' Gross said with a voice that sounded for once genuinely penitent. 'I should have inquired personally at the perfumery. Had I done so, I would have ascertained that two bottles of cologne had been purchased.'

'But if it had not been for your own Herr Plauder none of this would have happened,' Werthen said, coming to the defense of his colleague. For it had quickly been determined that the officious Plauder – the assistant at Herr Czerny's office who had delayed his and Berthe's interview with his boss – had been the one to allow the list of elderly participants to be assayed yesterday.

'But he said he was a priest,' was the unfortunate Plauder's excuse. 'He was dressed like one.' Klavan had told Plauder a tale of needing to confirm the names for the archbishop in order to get a look at the list of participants.

'Do not be concerned with Herr Plauder. I am sure he shall find his new posting in Galicia more in tune with his capabilities.'

'None of this is getting us closer to Klavan,' Werthen finally said in exasperation.

'By now he has skulked off into the underground world of Vienna,' Gross said.

'Dumbroski?' Werthen was sure of a connection there, despite their embarrassment. But would he dare to return to her place?

'Stay away from the princess,' Montenuovo ordered.

'She's no more a princess than . . .' But Werthen stopped himself before making the obvious comparison with Montenuovo, whose pedigree was the result of a tryst between the dashing Adam Albert, Count von Neipperg, and the Empress Marie Louise, wife of Napoleon, which produced his father, born illegitimately. Hardly a princely background.

'As I was saying, Klavan has skulked off to the shadows for now, but what of the poor granddaughter of Frau Huber?'

For they had learned that Klavan had kidnapped the girl, threatening to kill her if the old lady did not follow his orders and spray the emperor with the cologne. A 'new baptism' he had called it, according to Frau Huber. The old lady had no idea of the contents but was so frantic she would do anything to save her beloved Gitty – Brigitte – who had just turned thirteen.

'That is a police matter,' Montenuovo said, as if the life of a young girl were neither here nor there. 'Your mission now is to track down this mad man before he finally succeeds in killing the emperor.' He shot an evil look at both of them. 'And let me tell you that your duplicity is not appreciated.'

'I beg your pardon,' Gross spluttered, and for a moment Werthen thought he might actually take a swing at the pompous little ass.

'You know exactly what I mean. Bringing that riff-raff from

the Lower Belvedere here as your assistants. Tell the archduke
that the Hofburg has no use for his dubious gestures.'

Werthen was about to argue and then thought better of it. It
would be a waste of time. The feud between Montenuovo and
Franz Ferdinand would only end with the death of one of them.

'Gross, we should get word to hospitals and clinics about a
priest with a gunshot wound.'

But the criminologist was too busy glaring at Prince
Montenuovo to hear him.

Werthen tapped his arm. 'Gross. We need to get underway.
We cannot let Klavan get an advantage again. Now is our time
to press on, to ferret him out.'

Finally Gross turned his attention to his friend. 'Very well,
Werthen. You are right. Our business is elsewhere.'

# THIRTY-ONE

He cleaned the wound back in his hotel room. No one had
seen him come in. He had waited across the street for
the doorman to leave the entrance for a moment before
he made his way up to his room.

Klavan was lucky in one regard: it was only a flesh wound.
He washed it with carbolic soap, wincing at the pain and watching
as the blood turned the basin of water rose pink.

Lucky. That was worth a laugh, but he did not have the
energy even to so much as smile at his reflection in the bathroom mirror.

He tore one of his new shirts into strips and wound several of
them tightly around his arm one-handed, using his cheek to help
get the knot tight. The bleeding would soon stop, but not the
pain. He would not have to risk a doctor, and the pain would
keep him on edge.

He took stock of the situation. He could not stay here. Too
risky for obvious reasons. Neither could he go to Lisette; they
would surely look for him there.

Klavan gave no thought to simply leaving Vienna and saving
himself. Not a hesitation. No. He had another plan now. Perhaps

it was always there in the back of his mind. It would take some planning, but not much, and it would be a fitting end to Werthen and Gross.

He would need to change his appearance one more time. He had not yet used the identity papers of Herr Gregor Tollinger of Bolzano that he had collected from the safe deposit box. His priest's collar had been sufficient identification to check into the hotel; that and he had paid in advance. And he still had plenty of cash left from that same box.

Now he managed a smile at his reflection in the mirror. He was still wearing the fake glasses. He took them off quickly. He would leave them with the rest of the priest clothes in the room. The other new suit he'd purchased yesterday would help him look the part of a man from the Tyrol.

As he was finishing dressing he suddenly remembered the young girl he was holding as hostage to make the old frau do his bidding.

Leave her there to rot, he thought. He did not want to waste energy on killing her nor risk being seen going to the cellar. Neither did he have time now for revenge on the bureaucrat who had betrayed him with Postling.

He had time for something else, though: a gift for Doktor Gross.

As he was leaving his room dressed in his new clothes and freshly cleaned, his hair pomaded and parted in the middle, he passed an elderly couple in the hallway making their way to their room. They nodded at one another as they passed. The old man reminded him of someone, but Klavan could not make the connection.

At twelve thirty-two that night the night clerk at the Hotel zur Josefstadt made his way down to the wine cellar, using the special key kept behind the desk and marked 'X'. The porter, Wilhelm Kraiczek, heard the day clerk one time comment on the X-factor knowingly with Frau Steiner, their bookkeeper. It took him another month to learn what that meant: it was their secret way of referring to the special wine cellar below stairs. Since that time, he had used it judiciously when all the clients were safely tucked in their beds.

Herr Kraiczek could not afford good wine on his salary, and

so he occasionally treated himself to a bottle of Bordeaux. The hotel would never miss it.

He was just inserting the key when he heard what sounded like sobs coming from the gloom deeper in the cellar. He held the candle above his head to try and illuminate the darkness.

The sobbing grew louder, as if in response to the light. He wanted to turn around and flee back to the safety of the front desk, but something about the sobs drew him into the darkness. He was startled with a skittering in the shadows and saw a rat darting along the wall. He pushed on and then he saw a bundle of clothes crumpled on the floor. He almost dropped the candle when the lump of clothes suddenly stirred.

Then he could see the long hair and frightened eyes blinking out of the darkness at him.

Gross was just buttering his semmel the next morning in the breakfast room at his hotel when he saw Inspector Drechsler stumping down the stairs in the company of the desk man and another police officer. Drechsler noticed Gross at the same moment and looked startled at first, then shook his head, a grin on his face.

'Fancy finding you here, Doktor Gross,' the inspector said as he approached Gross's table.

'It is my usual residence when visiting Vienna,' Gross said. 'The surprise is to find *you* here.'

Drechsler rubbed his long chin. 'Not much surprise in that. I go where crime has been committed.'

This piqued Gross's curiosity. 'And what crime has been committed at the staid Hotel zur Josefstadt? Perhaps someone has made off with the shoes of a guest left out in the corridor for polishing?'

A shake of Drechsler's head. 'Real crime, Gross. Crime that you should be interested in. A kidnapping.' He eyed Gross closely. 'And by a priest, no less. Or someone dressed like a priest.'

'*Mein Gott*,' Gross bellowed, disturbing the other guests. He could not help himself. 'You don't meant to say he hid the girl here?'

'Not only that – he was staying here himself.' Drechsler, despite the seriousness of the matter, seemed to be enjoying himself.

'Imagine he wanted to be close to the great criminologist to find out your next move.'

'How do you know this?'

'Well, the night clerk apparently heard sobs coming from the cellar. The girl had badly damaged her mouth managing to partially remove the tape.'

'I don't mean that,' Gross said irritably. 'I mean how can you know Klavan was staying here?'

'The girl's description of the man who abducted her matched that of one of the guests, a Father Hoffmann, he called himself. A clerk called the police Praesidium and we investigated this morning. Gone, of course. But he left behind his calling card. A dark jacket with blood on the left sleeve. He'd been here a couple of days, as it turns out. In room 206.'

'Well, that is the most dastardly thing I have heard of,' Gross sputtered. 'Room 206 is just above my own.'

At that moment, Werthen's parents entered the breakfast room. The father, Emile von Werthen, had an eager look on his face. He was a man who enjoyed his breakfast. Seeing Gross, his face lost a bit of glow, for he also liked eating his first meal of the day in the privacy of his wife's company.

Frau von Werthen, on the other hand, was only too glad for some company at breakfast, and took the opportunity to approach.

'What is so dastardly, Doktor Gross?'

Gross and Drechsler both glanced around the breakfast room. This was not the sort of conversation to be having in public. The attempted assassination at the Hofburg yesterday was, like the earlier one at Schönbrunn, being kept out of the press. No mention was made to those involved of what was actually in the atomizer.

Gross decided to redirect the conversation. 'Might I present Inspector Drechsler?' he said. And then to Drechsler, 'These are Advokat Werthen's parents.'

They made small talk for a time, discussing the advantages of proximity of this hotel to Werthen's flat and the coming Easter holiday.

But Emile von Werthen was not to be put off. He might want privacy in the morning, but given the opportunity to reflect on the situation, he decided he enjoyed receiving insider knowledge on the workings of the criminal justice system in Vienna even more.

'And what brings you to our hotel?' he asked Drechsler. 'It can't be solely for the possibility of socializing with Doktor Gross.'

'Emile!' his wife said, touching his arm in reproof.

'It's quite all right,' Gross said to her.

'You mentioned room 206,' von Werthen plunged on. 'That is quite near our own.'

Drechsler and Gross again exchanged glances.

'Perfectly nice chap staying there,' von Werthen added. 'We saw him last evening just as we were coming back to our rooms.'

'Interesting,' Gross said, controlling his excitement. 'Can you describe him? A priest, was it?'

To which von Werthen laughed lowly. 'Hardly. By the looks of him the man was from the west. Tyrol, perhaps.'

'You'll pardon me for asking, sir,' Drechsler said, 'but how could you tell that?'

'The *trachten*, of course. Fellow wore a green loden jacket, leather britches and cardinal red vest. He was either from Tyrol or the Burgtheater.'

He laughed at his little joke, but neither Gross nor Drechsler joined in. Klavan had opted for a new disguise, a new persona. At least they knew he was still in Vienna, which meant that he planned to go on with his mission.

Where would he strike next?

# THIRTY-TWO

H e almost missed the note.

They left the von Werthens in the breakfast room without an explanation. Gross wanted badly to examine room 206 to see if he could find any clue overlooked by Drechsler and his men.

In the event, they reached the room just in front of two cleaning ladies who were intent on preparing it for new guests.

Drechsler looked embarrassed that there was no policeman on duty to keep out intruders. Then he protested: 'They've been thorough. Noting to be found here but a bloody coat.'

Gross made no reply, waiting for the inspector to unlock the door. There was a close and stuffy odor to the room once the door was open. Gross immediately went to the curtained windows and drew back the heavy drapes. Light flooded into the room. He began methodically going through every drawer of the night stand and dressing table, examining the interior of the wardrobe, digging through the medicine chest of the bathroom. The killing business must pay well, Gross ruefully thought; he himself could only afford a room with a bath in the hall on a professor's pay.

Drechsler dogged each step. Finally he said, 'If you told me what it is you're looking for, I could be of some help.'

Gross turned to face him. 'If I knew what I was looking for, I would.'

This shut the detective up for a few more minutes as Gross went back into the combined bedroom and sitting room. He surveyed the walls now.

'Really, Gross. My men may not have read your books on crime scene inspection, but—'

'Ah,' Gross said with deep satisfaction.

On the wall hung a reproduction of Brueghel's *Hunters in the Snow*, one of Gross's personal favorites. And lodged in the lower left-hand corner of the frame was a playing card. He picked it out of the frame; it was from a Tarock deck. He nodded his head excitedly.

'A playing card,' Drechsler said. 'So what?'

'He's talking to me,' Gross said. 'He stayed at my hotel. He puts a card in a reproduction of a painting I love, that I have written about. Klavan knows me. He wants me to understand that.'

'It's still just a playing card,' the inspector said.

'No. Not just any playing card. Do you know Tarock, Inspector?'

'Don't have much time for card games.'

'No. I thought not. You see this is the Pagat, and this little beauty is one of twenty-two trump cards.'

'It's got a number one on it.'

'Very good, Inspector. Yes. It is the lowest of the trump cards, but together with the twenty-one and the joker it has the highest point value.'

'This is precisely why I do not play cards,' Drechsler said, losing interest.

'Patience, my good man. All shall be revealed. You see, this little card has a particular move. If you play it last and win the trick, or even better, tell the others you are going to play it last and do so and win – then there are extra points. But even more so, there is a certain elegance to such a play, a confidence, even a cockiness. It is called Pagat Ultimo. The ultimate move.'

'Like checkmate in chess,' Drechsler said.

'Yes, Inspector. Very much like it. An apt analogy.'

'And you're saying this is a message from Klavan to you personally.'

Another excited nod of the head from Gross.

'His final move,' Drechsler said. 'But what is it?'

Gross shook a forefinger at him. 'That is what I need to discover. But now I know it is in this room. He has left me a message. And as I know it is directed at me specifically, I ask myself, what connection do Klavan and I have?'

His eye went back to the wardrobe, for at their last confrontation, Klavan had humiliated Gross by locking him in a wardrobe dressed rather unceremoniously.

Drechsler had been on the scene at that time as well, and knew what Gross was thinking.

'You may be on to something, Doktor Gross.' He tried to keep a smile off his face, remembering the scene of the eminent criminologist attired in a green silk evening gown that Klavan – going by the name of Schmidt at that time – had forced Gross to put on.

Gross wasted no time in returning to an inspection of the wardrobe. There must be something, he told himself. Something I missed the first time examining the wardrobe.

It took ten minutes, but finally he saw the corner of a piece of white paper barely peeking out of a seam in the cedar lining. Gross gingerly drew it out and unfolded it to see it was written on hotel stationery.

'Jesus, Mary, and Joseph,' he sighed as he read the hastily scrawled message.

Readers of the afternoon edition of the *Neue Freie Presse* may have been curious at the small notice placed in the bottom right of the front page, cutting into the space for the daily feuilleton.

'Researchers in Vienna agree that communicable diseases may be on the rise due to increased population mobility. More on this story in later editions.'

It was hardly the sort of article or notice that a paper such as the *Neue Freie Presse* would print voluntarily.

Klavan, seated at a window table of the Café Burg, read the notice with evident glee. His teeth showed when he smiled. It was not a usual occurrence, this smile.

So Gross found my message, he thought. I declare Pagat Ultimo.

Prince Montenuovo threw the newspaper to the floor. 'Outrageous,' he fumed. He glared at Gross. 'How dare you take it upon yourself to play the game of this lunatic?'

'There was hardly time to consult the Hofburg,' the criminologist said, exerting great effort to control his own temper. 'The deadline for the afternoon edition was upon us. We were simply buying time . . .'

'Negotiating with the enemy, more like. You've given him the upper hand in this ludicrous threat.'

Drechsler spoke up now. 'It's too early to determine how ludicrous or realistic his threat is, Prince. The researchers at the lab tell me there are two vials missing. But there is no way to know the quantity of bacilli used for each of the atomizers. Klavan may well have another vial in reserve, as his note implies.'

Montenuovo glanced down at the note on his desk, the very one Klavan had left for Gross. He read the salient part out loud once again: 'If I do not receive the sum of one million Krone by Easter Sunday, I will turn Vienna into a charnel house. The plague shall once again stalk the House of Habsburg and its minions.'

The prince stabbed the note with an angry forefinger. 'The man is living in cloud cuckooland.'

Werthen, who was also in attendance at this emergency conference, hoped the prince was right. However, the rhetoric rather than the monetary demand bothered him. It was the sort of inflated writing that someone very sure of himself would employ. The 'minions' stood out in this regard, as did the verb 'stalk.'

'And why go to all the bother of hiding the note?' Montenuovo asked.

'It was a test,' Gross said. 'I passed.'

'And if you hadn't?'

'One assumes he would continue with his plan, whatever it is.'

'So this is about you now?' Montenuovo said. 'Not the emperor?'

'We do have a history,' Gross allowed. 'There is obviously a touch of personal animus in all of this.'

'In that case,' Prince Montenuovo pronounced in a very un-princely manner, 'perhaps we should use you as bait.'

'We're getting ahead of ourselves here,' Drechsler interrupted. 'One assumes there will be a further communication from Klavan after he reads the notice in the newspaper. On one level, this should be handled as a straightforward case of extortion.'

'Yes, but with all of Vienna held hostage,' Montenuovo added. Finally he appeared to realize that his behavior was unseemly. More sensibly, he asked, 'If he is serious about spreading the plague, how would he go about it?'

'I've been over that with Professor Doktor Nothnagel of the bacteriological institute at Vienna's General Hospital,' Gross replied. 'He told me that airborne transmission is the most effective for this form of pneumonic plague. A sick person coughs or sneezes and releases the bacilli from their own infection.'

'Thus the atomizers,' Montenuovo said.

Gross nodded. 'But there are any number of other ways of spreading the infection, from contaminated or undercooked food to spraying the bacilli in a crowded area. Open-air markets, theaters, churches, public transportation – anywhere people gather en masse could be the staging ground for this perverse menace.'

'In other words, our Herr Klavan could carry out his deadly threat with impunity. Who's to stop him? The same as with these infernal anarchists and their bombs.'

The large baroque room was silent at this statement.

'Perhaps we should take the precaution of closing public entertainments for the time being,' Drechsler said.

Montenuovo shook his head. 'We can close a theater down, but an entire city?'

It was a statement that resonated with Werthen. He needed to get Berthe and Frieda out of Vienna until this was sorted out. Klavan was crazy enough to follow through with such a threat, he knew.

Gross spoke again, picking up the conversation from several statements before. 'Not without impunity.'

'I beg your pardon?' Prince Montenuovo looked at him as if he were wearing his hair backwards.

'You said Klavan could carry out his threat with impunity. But that is not the case. *We* will stop him.'

Or die trying, Werthen thought.

'I'm not going without you, and that's final.'

'Think of our daughter then.'

'We don't even know if he has the bacilli.'

'Do you really want to wager against Klavan's perfidy?' Werthen asked.

She sighed at this, for she was witness to it herself when they were last confronted with the man.

'And there is your father and his bride-to-be, as well as my parents.'

'They should go back to Hohelände,' Berthe said before she could stop herself. 'I mean, it would be safer for them there.'

'Yes, but who is going to tell them to go? They would only get suspicious and ask questions. The fewer people who know about this affair the better, or else panic will set in. There could be riots.'

She still kept her arms crossed stubbornly in front of her, the muscle in her jaw twitching.

'Invite everyone for a nice house party in the country to celebrate Easter.'

'My father, the Talmud scholar, celebrating Easter? None of us are Christians except for your parents, and that's only on paper.'

'Spring, then. Make it a vernal celebration. No one need be the wiser.'

'I don't like putting my tail between my legs.'

'I am not asking for acrobatics, *schatz*, just a simple sojourn in the Vienna Woods.'

'And don't be so humorous. I'll worry myself sick over you.'

The Emperor Franz Josef finished his solitary meal later that evening and went back to his Spartan quarters to continue work. So many petitioners, but he needed to read each request individually.

He wished he had the ear of his dear Katharina, but she was

still upset about the matter of the missing letter. He'd never accused her, but she obviously felt guilty and so took out her feelings on him. There was no word from her about the little mix up the day before at the ceremonial washing of the feet. He was sure her spies let Katharina know about the attempt on his life. But not even that would break her silence. And he could use his silence broken now; just to hear the pleasant melody of her laughter.

Such a long life it has been, he thought. He felt indestructible in a certain way. After all, how can you kill someone half dead already? The tragedies of the last years had taken their toll: the death of his son and wife. That is how he always thought of those two tragedies: bound together as one death.

A knock at his door and he turned to face it as he said, 'Enter.'

He was surprised to see Prince Montenuovo at his door, one of the emperor's guard behind him.

'Isn't it rather late for you to be in attendance, Prince? There must be some theatrical performance, some dinner party which you would rather be attending.'

Then Franz Josef saw the solemn expression on the prince's face. 'There is something you need to know, Your Majesty.'

Montenuovo told Franz Josef all the details of this dire new threat to Vienna, and the emperor remained still throughout, as if listening to a bedtime story, a fantasy.

When Montenuovo finished, the emperor said, with almost a frisson of pride, 'And all this just because the swine could not kill me? What a petty man he must be. Were I younger I would challenge him to a duel.'

The casual remark in the face of such grave danger would remain with Montenuovo for the rest of his life.

# THIRTY-THREE

Saturday morning and still no word from Klavan.

Werthen and Gross, however, were not merely sitting and waiting for that psychopath to determine the rules of the game. After sending Berthe, Frieda and the in-laws off to the country (Frau Blatschky was due to visit her sister in Linz this weekend and so did not have to be convinced to leave Vienna), Werthen joined Gross at the Lower Belvedere for a war council.

The archduke had a grim look on his face. 'The fool Montenuovo is fearful of causing concern in the populace. He refuses to put the army out in the streets to hunt for this animal. Well, I'm damned if I'll be timid about this threat. I have a battalion of dragoons in my service and they will be scouring the city for Klavan.'

Werthen partly agreed with Montenuovo on this one, but said nothing. Troops questioning the public with a description as vague as the one they would have of Klavan were sure to raise suspicion and anxiety. But what else was there to do? Police had already notified all legitimate hotels, pensions and lodging houses in the capital. Klavan's last known description – dressed in Trachten – was used with the caveat that he may have changed attire by now. And the only distinctive feature of the nondescript Klavan – his stiff little fingers – was being emphasized.

'Do your men have a likely story?' Gross asked Franz Ferdinand. 'They are sure to arouse curiosity with their questioning.'

A flicker of smile crossed the archduke's face. 'As a matter of fact, they do. I instructed them to tell any curious citizen that the man was being sought in connection with selling our military secrets. Hardly far from the truth in light of Klavan's activities the last time he visited Vienna.'

'And sure to work up a patriotic fervor in the populace,' Gross said. 'Make them eager to help out. But not so eager that they might attack Klavan were they to see him, one hopes. Force him to actually use the vial of bacilli.'

Franz Ferdinand looked stunned. 'I hadn't thought of that.' He shook his head. 'But then one had to do something. It's the infernal waiting that wears one down.'

Contingency plans were being arranged by Doktor Nothnagel and his colleagues at the General Hospital in the event that Klavan was not bluffing. Quarantine huts were being constructed in the grounds around the hospital, as they had been in the 1898 plague scare. This time, however, it was not a matter of a few huts, but of hundreds. Lord knows how they were going to explain those away when the public became aware of them, thought Werthen.

\*   \*   \*

They all traveled together in one carriage. Berthe made it sound like a happy family get-together. They could all help out preparing the house in Laab im Walde for summer residency. She deeply loved the old farmstead they had purchased a few years earlier. From the seventeenth century, the farm was what was called a four-square: a house that was more like a fort built in a rectangle around a central courtyard. They had opened it up somewhat, putting in a series of high windows on the outer walls that gave onto the fields beyond and the grass tennis court Werthen's father had arranged for.

Today, however, she approached the place with foreboding. Her family was not complete; Werthen's absence was keenly felt. She tried to keep a gay facade so as not to make the others suspicious.

She had also felt like a coward abandoning Vienna and the Viennese in this time of danger. She felt as she imagined a captain might who abandons his ship, leaving the passengers to fend for themselves in cold Atlantic waters. She had contacted Erika, their legal secretary and friend, and told her cryptically that this might be a good weekend for a trip with her fiancé, Herr Sonnenthal. But Erika said he was too busy trying to verify a rumor of another attempt on the emperor's life. She had been about to tell Erika of the plague threat, but remembered her husband's warning about not spreading the news and causing a panic that might be deadlier than even the bacilli. She had also placed a call to Frau Rosa Mayreder, and was happy to discover from her maid that Rosa and her husband had gone to an architectural conference in Paris. Should she tell the maid to leave town? Where would it ever stop? And what of young Franzl and his aunt and Frau Blau, the painter. Klimt, and a hundred more? There was no end to it; she could not warn her entire circle of friends and acquaintances, yet she still felt a coward for slipping away.

And then Frieda whispered in her ear that Opa had a whisker in his ear, and she remembered all over again why she had to leave Vienna, and she hugged her young daughter to her tightly as the carriage bumped along the macadamized road.

'I say we have lunch first at the gasthaus across the road from the house,' Herr Meisner said. 'I'll bet they have some of their famous venison stew today.'

His thought was seconded by the von Werthens and Frau Juliani.

Berthe joined in the chorus of approval, buoyed up momentarily by the good cheer. They will capture him, she told herself. They're bound to. It will be fine. You'll see.

They left the Lower Belvedere later that morning, taking a fiaker to the hospital where young Brigitte Huber was still being held for observation, as she was near hysteria from her ordeal. The doctor allowed them to speak with her for only a few minutes, but it was all they needed to ascertain that the girl knew nothing of her captor; he had not even spoken as he abducted her and took her in unseen in the back entrance to the Hotel zur Josefstadt. She had no idea even why she had been abducted.

They wasted no more time there but instead took another fiaker to Neulerchenfelderstrasse and the Kubit Men's Hostel. Postling was their only other human link to Klavan.

The same insolent attendant was on duty at the front desk.

'You again?' The illustrated sports newspaper was again spread out in front of him.

'The ledger, if you please,' Gross said, not wanting to engage the man.

'Be my guest,' he said, shoving the large book toward Gross. 'But he's not here.'

'Herr Postling?' Werthen said.

'Right. Out on his rounds.'

'Rounds?'

'Begging,' the attendant said as if it were the most obvious thing in the world.

Gross turned and stumped out of the building.

'Your friend's got a serious problem with anger,' the attendant said.

'Yes,' Werthen said. 'He does have a short fuse. I don't suppose you know where Herr Postling might be found?' Beggars often had their own pitch they returned to, Werthen knew.

The man eyed Werthen, scratched his cheek then nodded slowly.

'Old Hermann, he's got his sacred ground, all right. Take a bottle to anybody who tries to crowd him out.'

'And where might that be?' Werthen asked pleasantly, but all

the while wanted to grab the man around and choke the information out of him. Time was dear; with no further word from
Klavan the situation seemed even more desperate, as if he
expected them to figure out how to get in touch with him. Just
as with the hidden note to Gross. Like a challenge, a puzzle for
the great criminologist to solve.

'It's on the Wienerberg in Favoriten, near the park. That's
where you'll find Hermann.'

Reaching the street, he saw Gross striding toward the fiaker
rank. He had to run to catch up with him. 'I know where he is,'
he said.

'Well, bravo for you,' Gross said, and then thought better of
his ill temper.

'I apologize, Werthen. This matter has well and truly got my
dander up.'

Thirty minutes later a fiaker delivered them near the gates to
the park on the Wienerberg. The weather was fair this Saturday
and the park was filed with families; the sports fields were also
in full use with kite flyers and some amateur teams were busy
on the football pitch. It did not take them long to spot Hermann:
he was squatting with his back against the park gates, a tin dish
on the pavement in front of him.

He spotted them as they approached. 'Stay away from me,
you two. You've already cost me my twenty pieces of silver.'

'That's what we've come about,' Werthen said, improvising.
'We have spoken with the emperor and he does not think it
fair that you should lose your reward simply because of your
association with Herr Klavan.'

Postling's face screwed up in a question. 'Who's that?'

'Sorry. The man you knew as Wenno,' Werthen explained.

'Man's got a curious taste in names. Wenno, Klavan. Not
Austrian, that's for sure. Not German.'

'No,' Werthen agreed, eager to steer the conversation back
on track. 'How did you meet Herr Wenno, if I might ask?'

'Well, take a coin out of your pocket, tip it into my plate and
you'll know.'

Werthen began digging into his coin purse, but Gross stopped
him.

'I believe Herr Postling means that Wenno put a coin into
this very plate. Is that correct, sir?'

The last word made Postling thrust his shoulders back and sit up straight. 'That I do. Dropped a half crown into my plate with a rattle that woke me right up. Told him that was all well and good but not to expect any thanks.'

'How did you come to make the arrangement for Maundy Thursday?' Werthen asked.

'So maybe now you might practice some of that coin tossing.'

'Go ahead, Werthen,' Gross urged, as usual playing free with the money of others.

Werthen put in a ten-heller piece, but Postling just glared up at him.

'Really, Werthen,' Gross grumbled.

He added a twenty-heller piece, and when Postling continued to glare, he dropped in a second twenty-heller piece. 'That should satisfy,' Werthen said. 'After all, it's the same that Wenno gave you that day, by your own admission.'

He knew better than to antagonize witnesses, but the old man could get under one's skin.

Postling scooped up the coins and shoved them into his coat pocket. Then he stood with some effort, stretching his legs and arching his back.

'It was me that gave him the idea, wasn't it? Told him when I got my bag with twenty pieces of silver from the emperor there'd be no more begging for me. He was curious about that. And so I told him. Why, the man had never even heard of the foot-washing ceremony. That should have been my first clue he was a bad one. Any man calls himself an Austrian knows about that. Well, he gets all excited, buys me lunch, takes me back to the hostel in a fiaker. Treated me like a lord.'

Another rueful laugh. 'Another clue. I should have known. I mean I figured he was out to get something too, but I wasn't going to let him get his hands on my twenty pieces of silver.'

'Did he ever speak about himself?' Gross asked. 'Tell you what his business was.'

The old man shook his head.

'Nothing?' Werthen said.

'I wasn't interested. What would it matter, anyway? Most men are liars. Actions don't lie, though. He had time on his hands.'

'How do know that?' Gross asked.

Postling looked again into his empty plate.

'Werthen,' Gross said.

'I don't suppose you bother with such mundane details as carrying change with you,' Werthen said.

Gross scowled at this comment, and once again Werthen dropped a half crown worth of change in the dish.

'Lovely sound, that is,' Postling said.

'You were saying that Wenno was a man with time on his hands,' Gross reminded him. 'And what makes you think that?'

'I saw him out here often enough, didn't I? Wandering about, gazing out over the hillside like he was some kind of lord himself. Took a particular interest in that water tower, he did.'

Postling pointed a dirty finger to the massive water tower sitting atop the Wienerberg.

'Used to come up here quite a bit. Just sit and gaze out over the city. I'm sure he never knew I was watching him. Always by that water tower.'

'My God, that's it, Werthen. The water tower. That's where he means to dump it.'

'Dump what?' the old man squawked as Werthen and Gross ran toward the tower.

# THIRTY-FOUR

They were contented after a filling lunch at the gasthaus. As Herr Meisner had predicted, the proprietor had prepared venison stew for the menu. Now they walked down the country lane toward the house; the carriage, after depositing them at the gasthaus, was to leave their luggage at the front door. A slight breeze played through early wild flowers to each side of the dirt track leading to the house.

Berthe felt a sigh of contentment as they drew near.

'I hope somebody remembered to bring cards,' Emile von Werthen said. 'A bit of Tarock might be in order this evening.'

'Or we could play charades,' Frau Juliani suggested.

'Yes, poetry charades,' Frau von Werthen said as they marched along. 'My first is a letter, my second I mix, my whole points direction no compass can fix.'

'Cunning,' Herr Meisner uttered.

Berthe focused on the problem. The first syllable made the sound of a letter. Not much help there. The second syllable formed a word that meant to mix. The whole word was a direction.

'I've got it!' Frau Juliani said. 'Easter.'

'Excellent,' Frau von Werthen said.

'I do hope someone brought cards,' Herr von Werthen muttered, which made the others laugh.

'What?' he said. 'Cards are convivial.'

Reaching he farmhouse, they saw the luggage piled on the step as arranged. Berthe unlocked the door and threw it open for light and fresh air. They had not been here since Christmas, and there was the usual musty smell of a closed house.

Herr Meisner and Herr von Werthen brought the luggage in while the three women took sheets off the furniture and opened curtains and windows on both sides of the long sitting room. In the meantime, Frieda was running about shrieking for joy. Several minutes later they were about to prepare the various rooms when there came a knock at the door. Berthe went to answer it as Herr von Werthen peered out the window.

'Now what's he doing here?'

Berthe had just begun to open the door when Herr von Werthen added, 'That Tyrolean chap from the hotel.'

She immediately tried to close it, but Klavan burst in, a revolver leveled at her chest.

'That's no way to welcome a guest, Frau Meisner.'


They were both winded by the time they reached the water tower with its ornamental roof that made it look as if a muezzin should appear at any moment and call the Musulman to prayer. Built only a few years earlier, it already looked part of the environment, its brownish-orange brick exterior seeming to grow out of the landscape.

They stood sucking in air while Gross surveyed the place.

'There are a thousand cubic meters of water inside there,' the criminologist said.

More of his vast store knowledge, much of it useless. Useless, that is, Werthen thought, until a time like this.

'He's planning on poisoning the water supply,' Werthen said.

Gross did not bother with a reply, but opened the gate surrounding the tower. The massive front doors were secured with a padlock of gargantuan proportions. Undeterred, he began walking around the unguarded, untended building. Of course, there would be no one in attendance: this was Easter weekend. Even the trams were idle.

The building was banded with a series of latticed windows ten feet high each. One of these in the back of the building had been shattered.

'He's been here already,' Werthen said. 'He never gave us a chance to pay his ransom.'

'I don't like this, Werthen.' Gross stepped first through the window, which led to a walkway around what appeared to be a huge indoor swimming pool.

Gross looked into its depths. 'The water supply for a quarter of the citizens of Vienna, Werthen.'

'No.' Werthen was not listening to Gross. Instead, his eyes focused on the rim of the tank not four feet from where they were standing.

A glass vial lay there next to a paper plug. The vial was empty.

Gross looked at these for a moment, neither he nor Werthen speaking. Gross suddenly took out a pocket handkerchief and, holding it with both hands, began unfolding the crumpled stopper.

'What are you doing, Gross? There could still be bacilli on it.'

But the criminologist did not stop until he had it laid out flat and could see the words scrawled on it:

*This has been fun, Doktor Gross. I hope you too are enjoying my little puzzle game. Feel free to keep the money yourself. But do carry on! Carry on to the third place!*

'This is a disaster,' Montenuovo said. 'What is to be done?'

'Quarantine the districts the tower supplies,' Gross said. 'Immediately. This is no time for half measures.'

'How can we be sure he dumped the contents of that vial into the water?' Inspector Drechsler said. 'Perhaps it was one he had already used for the atomizer – just a bluff.'

'You don't really believe that, do you, Inspector?' Werthen asked. 'Not after seeing what Klavan is capable of last time we went up against him.'

The tall inspector let out a sigh long enough to empty his frame.

'A disaster,' Montenuovo repeated. He looked incapable of action, stunned by the news.

'Prince,' Gross said, trying to get through to the man. 'We have no time to waste. Delay will cost lives.'

The telephone on Montenuovo's desk jingled to life. The prince could only stare at it as if it were a bomb about to explode.

'Prince Montenuovo,' Werthen said. 'Should I answer it?'

Montenuovo sank back in his chair, waving a listless hand at the phone in assent.

Picking up the receiver, Werthen announced himself and then listened to the man on the other end.

'Just a moment,' he said into the speaker, then handed it to Gross. 'It is Professor Doktor Nothnagel.'

Gross took the telephone. 'Gross here.'

He listened for a time. Werthen could hear the excited tones of Nothnagel on the other end. Gross nodded once. 'You are sure of this?' More loud speaking from Nothnagel, loud enough to make Gross move the earpiece more distant from his ear. Another nod.

'Very well, Professor. And many thanks.'

He put down the phone, looking grave.

'What is it, Gross?' Werthen asked.

He seemed to come out of a momentary reverie, blinking his eyes as he spoke.

'It was Nothnagel at the General Hospital.'

'We know that Gross. What did he say? Have there already been cases of the plague?'

'No, not at all. Quite the contrary. In fact, the researchers inspected the two cologne atomizers and found no living bacilli. That made them curious, and after re-examining the entire batch of plague bacilli from which Klavan stole his vials, they conclude that the bacteria was no longer viable.'

'What are you saying?' Drechsler asked.

'It is dead. It is harmless.'

'So even if he dumped it . . .'

Gross shook his head. 'No. It could do nothing.'

'Well, that is tremendous news,' Drechsler said with more volubility than he usually showed. 'Why so glum, Gross?'

'This is wrong. We have been playing Klavan's game all along. He led me to the note in the hotel. Then he expected us to track

Postling and discover his connection to the water tower. The note he left there proves that. This is not over.'

'But where next?' Werthen asked.

'It's in his note. The "third place."'

They wasted the next hour scouring first the Café Burg and then Werthen's café, the Frauenhuber. No sign of Klavan.

And then Gross did a very uncharacteristic thing. He took off his derby and swatted his thigh with it in disgust. 'I've been a fool. It's not about cafés. It's another type of third place. Home, office and country home.'

Gross gave him a look filled with fear and pity.

'God, no,' Werthen cried out. 'It can't be.'

'I fear it is so, Werthen. Call them quickly. Tell them to lock the doors.'

'There is no phone,' Werthen said. This had been a solace, that their country home would be a sanctuary from the outside world.

'The gasthaus across the road, then.'

Another shake of the head from Werthen.

'Then call Franz Ferdinand and tell him. We will need his automobile. And we could use a contingent of his men. Quickly, man. There is no time to lose.'

'I am afraid you lose once again, gentlemen,' Klavan said, picking up the final trick with the Pagat. This was truly his day. The women were safely tied up by their hands and feet. and gagged, the child locked away in a back bedroom. She had given up long ago with her useless screaming. The two men sitting at the table with him were also tied up, hands in back and feet bound, but he had not gagged them. They needed to talk to give him instructions what to do with their cards, which he held up for them to look at. He did not peek into their hands; he played fair. This slowed the game no end, but then life was filled with all sorts of obstacles.

He was enjoying himself. He would enjoy it even more when Werthen and Gross arrived.

'You are a despicable person,' Herr von Werthen said. There was a strip of torn sheet wrapped around his head from where Klavan had hit him with the butt of the pistol upon his entrance.

'I do appreciate the recognition,' he replied. 'Now, shall I deal another hand?'

'He will expect us to come storming in,' Gross said as the rode in the open car. 'He is feeling very good about himself at this moment, I am sure. He is winning, as far as he reckons. He does not know about the inactive bacilli, however. It is our one weapon.'

'I don't care about any of that,' Werthen said. 'All I want is for my family to be safe.'

'Oh, they'll be safe until we get there. Klavan wants a Götterdämmerung, not a simple homicide here and there.'

Duncan, who was accompanying them, nodded in agreement.

Werthen seemed to come out his shock, Gross's last words finally reaching him.

'If that is the case, I think I might have a plan.'

'Why so glum, ladies?' Klavan said as he finished another winning hand.

The three women were lined up against the wall near the door. Berthe glared at the creature. She was also quietly working at the knots binding her wrists behind her. When her father-in-law was forced at gunpoint to tie her, Berthe did not let her arms go back as far as they could. Thus, now she could work the slack on the rope, and had managed to wriggle a fingernail into the knot. For the last several minutes she had been loosening it slowly and painfully.

'Such a pity to have it all end this way.' He shuffled the cards with a cascading, ratcheting sound, shoved the two blocks of cards into one deck, knocked the edges in line on the table, divided the deck again and shuffled once more.

'And such a waste, too.' He looked straight into the faces of each woman in turn, ignoring the men, who were now gagged. 'Advokat Werthen and Doktor Gross let you all down, did you know that? Oh, yes. They had me in their grips and were not clever enough to tighten their fingers. Thanks go to Princess Dumbroski with her hiding compartment behind the bookcase, but credit is also due to the stupidity of those two men. Only a matter of inches from me and they let me go.' He shook his head.

Berthe would not be baited; she continued to work on the knots. She also filed away the information about Princess Dumbroski for later.

There would be a later, she reassured herself.

They parked the automobile a quarter mile from the farm, not wanting to risk Klavan hearing them approach. The driver remained in the machine while Gross and Duncan took up position as planned and Werthen made his way on foot to the house.

He was not going to wait for the rest of the archduke's men. What good could they do? This battle would not be about numbers but strategy.

Werthen was sure that Klavan was in the house and holding the others captive, waiting. Waiting for him and Gross to figure out the last of his puzzles and to come in a rush to save the day.

He was unarmed and defenseless as he walked down the long drive to his home.

A lone man in the flat landscape trudging to what fate held in store for him.

Klavan heard the footsteps in the courtyard and took up position behind the door, next to Berthe. She heard the footsteps as well and desperately wanted to shout out a warning. She dug her fingertip now into the knot, but could not open it. She began wriggling and Klavan put the gun to her temple.

'Move once more and you die,' he hissed.

Feet sounded on the steps, a key fitted in the lock and the door opened.

Werthen's voice came from the other side. 'I'm unarmed, Herr Klavan. I've come for my family.'

Berthe could see Klavan flinch at the use of his real name, like an insect exposed to the sunlight by a lifted rock.

He slammed the door into Werthen with sudden force. There was a groan and Klavan dragged him quickly inside, shutting and bolting the door behind him.

Blood streamed down Werthen's face from where the door had struck him.

Klavan held the gun on him. 'How nice of you to join my little party, Advokat.'

Berthe's eyes grew wide; she wanted to somehow communicate to her husband with them.

Werthen quickly surveyed the scene: men and women tied up. He forced a smile at Berthe.

'My daughter? Where is she?' He tried to move closer into the room toward the windows on the exterior wall, but Klavan waved at him with his gun to stay where he was.

'She's safe enough, the little brat. Cried her eyes out in a back bedroom. Now where is your faithful colleague? Didn't have the heart for the final chase?'

'He left once we discovered the bacilli you stole were useless.'

Klavan said nothing, but the gun wavered in his hand minutely.

'Professor Doktor Nothnagel at the General Hospital let us know himself. The whole batch had already died off by the time you stole the vials. There's no need for a quarantine on the water from the Favoriten water tower. Gross thought it more important to get in touch with your employers in Belgrade than waste time with your juvenile games.'

'The silver-throated Advokat. Telling lies like all of you do. Gross was too cowardly to come face-to-face with me. No matter. I'll see to him later. For now, I guess I'll just have to settle for you.'

He pulled out a hollow rubber ball from his pocket; Werthen could see a tube attached to it.

'I assume you know what this is?' Klavan said.

Werthen had read about such explosive devices; anarchists used them to self-detonate rather than be taken alive by the police. He nodded, and then grabbed his wounded head, seeming to stumble deeper into the room to his left, forcing Klavan to alter his position as well.

'You say you want your family. Well, here they are. You can watch one of them die. Who shall it be? Try to stop me and I squeeze my magic ball. Then we all go to hell together.'

Berthe's finger nudged deeper into the knot; it began to loosen now as Klavan approached the line of men and women.

'Who shall I start with?'

'Lie still, Doktor Gross,' Duncan ordered. 'I can't get a clean shot if you wiggle.'

Gross was supine on the grass, hands over his ears, and a bug had decided to trek across his cheek – hence the twitch. Duncan was using him as a makeshift tripod, the rifle barrel propped over his back, perpendicular to his body so that the blast of the shot would not burst his eardrums. With his ears cupped by his hands, he could barely hear Duncan's command.

'There was a moment there,' Duncan murmured. 'I can see Advokat Werthen but not the others. I think it was Klavan, but just for an instant.'

'Take your shot, man,' Gross insisted.

'But what if it *is* one of the others?'

'They'll be tied up,' Gross said. Or dead, he thought.

Klavan hovered menacingly over Berthe, the pistol pointed straight at her head.

'You don't have to do this, Klavan,' Werthen pleaded. 'There is still time for you to get away before the archduke's men arrive.'

'You don't understand, Advokat.' He looked from his intended victim to Werthen with an expression approaching sexual ecstasy. 'Your kind never would. This is what it is all about. This moment. This supreme moment.'

Keep talking, you bastard, Berthe thought, loosening the knot further.

'You've won,' Werthen said. 'Isn't that enough?'

Klavan let out a howl of laughter. 'You call this winning? I failed to kill that decrepit old man you call emperor, and now you tell me that the plague bacilli was also a failure. *This* is my victory.'

He nudged the gun closer to Berthe's head. The others lined up against the wall made grunting protests through their gags.

Werthen knew it was a lie, that Klavan would kill them all. But part of him also doubted. If he jumped him, Klavan would squeeze his damned ball. But what if that was a bluff?

What if? What if?

His mind reeled. It was time for action, not thought. He would not let Klavan kill his wife. That was all there was to it. No more balancing of one life against another. This was Berthe's life and obviously Duncan was unable to get a clear shot.

It was up to him now. He braced himself as he watched Klavan's finger tighten on the pistol.

\*    \*    \*

Berthe slipped her right hand out of the rope and brought it up suddenly with the middle knuckle foremost between Klavan's spread legs, digging it into his scrotum with satisfying fury. He let out a strangled cry, stumbling backward, and suddenly dark liquid matted the front of his loden jacket followed immediately by a cracking sound from outside as if a whip were snapping. Werthen was immediately by his side, kicking the pistol clear and pulling the rubber tube out of the ball just as Klavan squeezed it in a death grip.

He looked up at Werthen with eyes already growing glassy and transfixed. A smile crossed his face, and he was dead.

# THIRTY-FIVE

They were all gathered in Prince Montenuovo's office at the Hofburg two days later as arranged. It had been Franz Ferdinand who had talked his uncle, the emperor, into this final act. The old man owed Werthen and Gross, and by extension, Werthen's wife, Berthe. She had remembered something, a small comment, an unguarded utterance that changed everything.

Besides Berthe, Werthen, Gross, Franz Ferdinand and Prince Montenuovo – looking angry and annoyed – and Inspector Drechsler, there were others present who were also involved in the case. There was Herr Karl's hausfrau, Frau Polnay; his old friend, Czerny; the failed lawyer, Bachman, who was once a suspect in the death of Herr Karl; Herr Otto, who had initiated the investigation by bringing Falk to Werthen; and there was also the nephew of the murdered Frau Geldner, August Kaufmann.

These guests had no idea why they had been summoned to the Hofburg, but an imperial summons was not to be ignored.

Berthe waited until they were all seated in chairs added to the office for this very purpose. She would be the master of ceremonies. 'Your discovery, your unveiling,' her husband had insisted.

She took a deep breath.

'This all started with the death of a head waiter,' she said. 'An insignificant sort of man, except to his loyal customers for whom he provided a comfortable, gemütlich third place. His murder would have escaped attention, listed as accidental, were it not for an eye witness, Herr Falk, who also subsequently was murdered. One assumes the ruthless Herr Klavan – who apparently talked with the unfortunate Herr Karl on the very day he was murdered – was fearful lest Falk might remember him, might somehow identify him if ever Karl's death were suspected to be a homicide. So Falk had to die, too. Or was there another reason for Falk's death? But we will get to that presently.'

As she spoke, Berthe eyed each of the guests in turn, searching their faces for a reaction, any change of expression. And she thought she saw one, then plunged on with her description.

'Herr Falk subsequently came to my husband with the information of what he had witnessed. He feared going to the police, thinking they would suspect him. My husband looked into the matter, searching for people who might want Herr Karl out of the way. Motive seemed a problem, until it was discovered that Herr Karl was not all he seemed. Indeed, he was involved in a series of kickback schemes with his fellow workers and café suppliers. But would that be something kill for? Then, other events impinged. The investigation of Herr Karl's death took second place to a more pressing matter. Someone was trying to kill the emperor.'

Another dramatic pause.

'It must have been during that conversation with Herr Karl that Klavan produced this little slip of paper.' She held up the paper with 'Postling' scrawled on it. 'It is clear that he demanded of Herr Karl that he convince his old friend, Oberstabelmeister Czerny,' she nodded at him, 'to add Herr Postling to the list of pensioners for the Maundy Thursday ceremony. Herr Czerny himself confirmed that this was the case.'

She smiled in his direction, and Czerny solemnly nodded his head at her.

'Yes,' she said evenly, 'that all makes perfect sense. One assumes that the dogged Klavan was able not only to learn of the close friends the Oberstabelmeister might have, but also to dredge up any dirt he could on them. And as we know, Herr Karl could be compromised in this respect with his numerous kickback schemes—'

'I really do not know where this is going, Frau Meisner,' Prince Montenuovo complained. 'It would suffice to include it in a written report. I am sure none of us can spare our valuable time—'

'Give the woman a moment,' Franz Ferdinand said in a voice that commanded respect.

Drechsler shot Werthen a nervous glance, but the lawyer merely smiled in return.

'As I was saying,' Berthe continued, 'Klavan likely blackmailed Herr Karl into talking his old friend into adding Herr Postling to the list for the foot-washing. Initially, Klavan planned to substitute Postling with a dying man sent from Serbia who would be in disguise and then detonate a small bomb just as the emperor was washing his feet, killing all those around him. Money was to be paid to the family of this man who was dying already of consumption. His death, however, came too soon, and Klavan had to change his plan to spreading the plague at the ceremony.'

She paused, again casting her eyes around the room, from the face of the prince, wearing an exasperated expression, to Gross smiling like a basilisk.

'We know how that all ended. It was part good luck and part bravado.' She smiled at Werthen.

'And we know what became of Klavan. But in all the storm and thunder, the death of Herr Karl has been neglected. We assumed it must have been Klavan who killed him, again covering his tracks or to stop him from an attack of conscience. But now we see that is not really possible. You see, Herr Karl was killed before he could even speak with his old friend. Before he could solicit the name of Hermann Postling.'

'What?' Prince Montenuovo said, irritation oozing from him.

'Ridiculous,' Czerny spluttered. 'He spoke with me on the phone about it the afternoon before he died.'

'That is true, but he did not mention Postling's name during that call.' Berthe lifted a file and held it for all to see. 'This is the testimony of one Ignatz Plauder, formerly the head clerk at the office of the Oberstabelmeister, as sent to the offices of Archduke Franz Ferdinand.'

'If he had something to share, he should have sent it to me,' Prince Montenuovo said.

Berthe ignored this interruption. 'Herr Plauder was blamed for giving the list of participants to Klavan, disguised as a priest, and for that misstep he was banished to Galicia. He is anxious to make amends.'

'I'll bet he is,' Czerny said.

'He reports that he sometimes listened in to telephone conversations his former boss might have. I do not see how such an admission furthers his cause for reinstatement, but there it is. He confirms that on the tenth of October, late in the afternoon, he listened in on a conversation between his boss and a friend who often called and who was always given special access to the Oberstabelmeister. It was in this conversation that an appointment was made for a meeting the next day. It was neither a friendly nor a cordial conversation, according to Herr Plauder. At one point he quotes his former boss, Herr Czerny, as saying, "Don't push me too far, Karl. I have my limits." Herr Plauder also informs us that the name of Hermann Postling was added to the ceremonial list on October 11, the day *after* Herr Karl's murder.'

'Lies!' Czerny spluttered.

Berthe shook her head at him. 'Is it a lie that you are near bankruptcy? That is further information provided from Herr Plauder from overheard telephone conversations. And your creditors confirm it. One wonders what a bachelor who makes a very handsome salary could do with all that money. And then Inspector Drechsler, at my suggestion, made inquiries into the financial affairs of Herr Karl. This morning the Länderbank reported a safety deposit box in the name of Karl Andric.'

Berthe smiled at the inspector. 'Perhaps you could tell us what you found in that box, Inspector.'

Drechsler looked a bit embarrassed at having this assemblage learn that a woman had to tell him how to do his job, but he obliged. 'It contained fifty thousand crowns.'

She looked directly at Czerny now. 'Was he doing the same to you as he did to all the others? A little friendly blackmail? What did he have on you, Herr Czerny? What secret from your past was he using as his source for blackmail? But that is not important now. I am sure we shall find out in due course. What is important is that you had reached those limits you mentioned on the phone to Herr Karl.'

'You besmirch the name of a true friend,' Czerny replied.

'You make unfounded accusations. Why would I tell you of Herr Karl's request or give away the name of Hermann Postling if I had anything to hide?'

'Because you *had* something to hide. The murder of Herr Karl.'

The room became absolutely still at this accusation.

Berthe glared at him now – an enemy she would break; a coward who surely knew the placement of Herr Postling could endanger the emperor but allowed it to happen in order to save his own skin.

'How did you know it was the back of Herr Karl's head that was caved in? It was never mentioned in the newspapers. There was no record of it. Why not the front or the side? Or is it because you were there? You struck the fatal blow and then lifted his head to crush it on the cement pillar, crushing it like a pumpkin.'

'The woman is mad!' Czerny shouted.

'You were the one who mentioned the manner of death when we first spoke,' Berthe said calmly.

'This makes no sense,' Czerny said. 'If I supposedly killed my best friend before he could even make the request for Herr Postling to be included on the list, then how did his name get there?'

'Why, via Herr Klavan, of course,' she said, as if it were the most obvious thing in the world. 'That is the only explanation. He followed Herr Karl that night to make sure the man was going to do what he demanded. Or perhaps he followed you. He was an obsessively thorough man about such things. Whatever the case, he was near the Maria Theresa statue when you ambushed Herr Karl. You'd had enough of Herr Karl's extortion, of his controlling you and bleeding you of your wealth. A mere head waiter able to bring down the Oberstabelmeister if he so chose to do so. Thus, Herr Karl had to die. And Klavan witnessed it. He probably even saw Falk – another reason that man must die, too. Klavan followed you. You must have thrown the murder weapon away at some point, to be retrieved by Klavan. That is why my husband later found it in the room he had rented at Frau Geldner's. And then Klavan caught up with you and demanded Postling be added to the list or you would hang for murder.'

'Demented,' Czerny said. 'Supposition on supposition. "Must have" this, "must have" that.'

'Not all supposition,' Inspector Drechsler spoke up. 'We examined an overcoat at your apartment this afternoon, Herr Czerny. And there was a good deal of what our laboratory people tell us is blood on one sleeve and on the front as well, as could be expected with such a brutal attack.'

He moved quickly for a sedentary man, but a casually outstretched leg from Herr Bachman tripped Czerny to fall at the very feet of Drechsler, who was even then getting his handcuffs ready.

'That was enjoyable,' Bachman said. 'Makes me wish I'd never been drummed out of the legal profession.'

# EPILOGUE

She took up new residence on Prince Michael Street in Belgrade.

It was a far cry from her city palace in Vienna, but she had learned to adapt in her life. The Austrian archduke had made it impossible for her to live elsewhere; every capital in Europe had been poisoned against her by that bug-eyed creature.

How he had found out about her secret hiding place behind the books, she did not know. Certainly Klavan had not told him. But his men had stormed in early one day and examined the bookcases until discovering the secret door. His adjutant had given her the choice between jail and banishment.

She, of course, had taken the latter.

'There is no real space for a gymnasium,' Elise said with a touch of scorn as she surveyed the bare rooms of the apartment.

Princess Dumbroksi was beginning to regret bringing the maid with her, but she was privy to too many secrets to leave behind. Elise, it was turning out, was not quite so adaptable as she was herself. Prince Michael Street may be the finest in Belgrade, but it hardly compared with the Ringstrasse in opulence. And their accommodations did leave something to be desired.

However, Princess Dumbroski – for that is how she thought of herself now, not as simple little Lisette Orzov of Trieste – knew she could better her situation. She had an appointment this afternoon that would start such a campaign of improvement and rehabilitation.

Princess Dumbroski had not come to Belgrade by accident. True enough, it was one of the few half-civilized cities that might allow her residency. More importantly, it was where her rebirth would begin.

After leaving Vienna with barely the clothes on her back and the strongbox of her life savings, she had gone to Paris, not believing the threats of the archduke's officer. But gendarmes had sent her packing within two days of her arrival. The same happened in Berlin and Amsterdam. In Brussels she had gone straight to the watchmaker, to chubby Monsieur Philipot. She had no intentions of trying to stay in that city; it was already closed to her after her business dealings with a certain member of the royal family.

Instead, she was seeking vengeance. And when Philipot reluctantly told her the identity of Klavan's last employers, she knew how she would get that revenge.

'Let's not worry about a gymnasium at the moment, Elise,' she said. 'We have other plans to make.'

Apis, she thought, might very well like to know the identity of the man who was responsible for foiling his assassination plot. She was tempted to lay it at the door of those truly responsible, Advokat Werthen and Doktor Gross, or perhaps even Werthen's wife, whom she suspected of somehow knowing about the secret hiding place.

But she wanted deeper revenge. She did not want to divert Apis's rage. No, she would tell him later today who was truly responsible for the fiasco in Vienna: Archduke Franz Ferdinand.

That would make him a marked man with the Black Hand.